An Unusual Practice

D1521954

By Tom Jolly

ACKNOWLEDGMENTS

Thanks to Brent Harris, Shawn Klimek, Michelle Olinger-Jolly, Leslie Stapleton, Dan Andoetoe, my Mother, and numerous others who've reviewed and commented on this book as it grew. The book is better as a result, I think. I take the blame for anything really dumb in here, especially some of the medical stuff.

I really should learn to write names down when people help. Over a few years, one forgets.

And thanks to Irena Czusz for the wonderful cover art.

An Interview with a Golem

In the community of supernatural creatures, I am called a Historian: a neutral party recording the events occurring in this odd world, since these records will never appear in the annals of common humans. It gives me some protection from dangerous creatures I talk to, and extra leeway when I wish to ask a sensitive question. But it's still a hazardous occupation.

I stepped into the shadowed alley. Visiting a hidden clinic that caters to supernatural customers made me nervous, even though I'd been here before. I was only human, and most of the people or things I interviewed were aware of this. It didn't make them less scary. I was never certain whether or not my next interviewee would try to eat me. I've learned to be cautious.

Thirty paces in, I turned right to look at a blank brick wall, and said the word that would make a door appear. The brick wavered in my vision for a fraction of a second, and then a metal door materialized. There was an arcane symbol engraved on a plastic placard and bolted to the center of the door, and above it the name, "Backdoor Clinic." Normally hidden from casual human eyes by this strange magical glyph, but disabled for a moment with my spoken word.

I opened the door and stepped inside into a brightly lit reception area. Behind a small counter, Medjine greeted me. Her skin was as pale as ash. There was a slight odor of sandalwood in the air—incense—and a ventilation fan humming overhead. Backdoor Clinic had a reputation for hiring supernaturals, even the undead.

She smiled and said, "Good afternoon, Mr. Edgewood."

"Good afternoon," I replied, and glanced at my notebook. "I'm here to see a Mr. Bacallum, I think? I'm not sure I got his name right." Really, I wanted to speak to Dr. Hamilton. The history I was interested in was centered upon his activities, after all. But he had been missing for a month, and one of his assistants had been assigned to aid me in my research.

Medjine looked confused for a moment. "Bacallum? Oh, you must mean the Book Golem. He's expecting you."

I must have looked a little startled. "B-book Golem?" I stuttered.

"You won't be unsatisfied. The Book Golem knows more about Dr. Hamilton than he knows about himself."

My apprehension went up a notch. I hadn't met this creature on my prior visits. And golems, in general, weren't known to be friendly. But I tried to put my biases aside.

A bright hovering light appeared next to my ear, buzzing softly. "Mr. Edgewood, good to see you again. I can lead you to Dr. Hamilton's office. The Golem hungrily awaits."

"Hello, Sprite," I said to it. "Aren't you funny."
Sprite buzzed and brightened with what I took as

amusement. I followed it down the short hallway. It stopped at Hamilton's office door, dipping briefly to encourage me to step inside. I opened the door, and stepped into what was more of a library than an office.

Over the years, Dr. Hamilton had turned his clinic office into a small library, knocking out an inside wood-framed wall in the old brick building to expand the available shelf space. The library was small, but impressive; old dusty oak shelves that were stuffed with worn and ancient books lined the red brick walls, odd volumes filled with the habits, physiology, and peculiarities of the various members of the supernatural community. I'd visited his office a few times before, covering some of the minor events that seemed to attach themselves to Dr. Hamilton like sticky yellow notes, and was always tempted to pull down a volume or two from his library and browse.

Today, however, there was a Book Golem. It had already manifested and was waiting quietly for me.

Entering the room with the golem took a little willpower. Most of the supernatural world both scared and awed me. The golem was large, composed of hundreds of books, everything from paperbacks to worn out leather tomes. His broad fingers looked like cracked book spines. His shoulders were encyclopedic, his chest a ridge of leather plates with gilded patterns embossed upon them. His eyes were black as ink. He grunted, a sound I felt in my bones, and motioned for me to enter and sit with a flutter of pages in his hands. The bookshelves in the room were mostly empty, the books that normally filled them constituting the bulk of the golem's strange body.

I sat and cleared my throat. "I'm William

Edgewood, a Historian. Please excuse me if I seem a little nervous, but I've never met a Book Golem before."

The end boards and pages that made up his wide mouth curled and twisted to accommodate the sounds of human lips. His voice was deep, but also carried the rustling sound of a thousand sheets of paper blowing down a street. "I understand," he said, "I know some golems can be mindlessly aggressive, tearing limbs asunder and consuming people." He leaned forward, looming over me, leather creaking, and I leaned backward. "We make people nervous. But golems become what they absorb when they are created. Stone is hard and mindless, plants and wooden things live only to eat and grow, but books are a repository for knowledge. So unless you're concerned about being bombarded by trivia, you have little to worry about."

I tensely held my breath as he spoke, and quietly let it out to hide the fact. "I've been told…" my voice squeaked, and I cleared my throat to regain my composure, then started anew. "Medjine says that you know more about Doctor Matthew Hamilton than he knows himself."

The golem nodded. "It's true. Many of his personal notebooks have become part of my own body on occasion, when he leaves them here in the library. He was a little angry at first, but I often revert to my stagnant form…"

"Stagnant form? You mean shelves of books?" I asked. I dug a pad of paper and a pen out of my pack, along with my cell phone.

The golem chuckled, an odd sound from a paper throat. "They aren't really shelves of books anymore when I revert. More like piles scattered about the floor, but yes, just books, and Dr. Hamilton often adds new information to his notebooks as he treats new cases. Since I learn new things in this manner, it works out well for both of us. I don't think he minds picking up afterwards. Much." He dismissed the issue with a shrug.

"There are a lot of unbelievable stories about him," I said. "I suppose you're familiar with most of them."

He nodded again. "Since he started in this business, he began writing detailed case notes and kept a diary of events from his life. I can tell many stories about Dr. Hamilton and Backside Clinic that I doubt even he remembers. But they are a part of me."

"Can we start at the beginning?" I asked. "Before Backside Clinic was planned?" I fiddled with my cell phone and opened a recording app. Tapping the 'record' button, I placed the phone between us.

"Certainly. There was a time when Dr. Hamilton knew nothing of the supernatural community and the Backside Clinic was not yet conceived. Or planned, for that matter! It was not something he expected or desired. You might even say he fell into it accidentally. I will tell you that story."

Chapter 1 – An Unusual Case

Matthew Hamilton got out of his Corolla, stretched his legs, and examined the building where he'd be spending the next few years, if all went well. The plastic sign at the top of the front window read "Pembrook Clinic."

Red brick covered the front of the building, common among the structures in the older parts of Redondo Beach. Though clean and free of graffiti, the mortar had crumbled away in a few places and cracks fractured the sidewalk where a big ficus' roots reached out in search of water. To the right of the clinic, a thrift shop tried to be upscale by hanging an "Antiques" sign in the window, and to the left, painted white windows hid the inner secrets of a vacant building.

He opened the swinging door and a soft chime sounded. The receptionist looked up from her desk and Hamilton smiled at her. "Good morning, Dr. Hamilton. All ready for your first day?"

"I hope so. No major surgeries scheduled for me, I hope?"

She laughed and nodded toward Dr. Madesh Chopra as he approached the desk. "Dr. Chopra will give you the orientation tour."

Dr. Chopra shook his hand. "Dr. Hamilton. Welcome aboard. It's good to have you here." He led Hamilton through the clinic, showing him the supply cabinets, paperwork, and the general layout of the exam rooms. "There will eventually be more exam rooms, of course. We are expanding. In fact…" Chopra pulled back a tarp hanging near the rear of the building and they stepped into a construction area. "There's your assigned office, I'm afraid."

Bare two-by-four studs lined the walls of his office. Blue and brown plastic tarps simulated walls and white drop cloths carpeted the floor. An orange utility cord hung from a stud overhead like a noose, with a single bare light bulb casting stark shadows in the room. His desk was a gray metal surplus job, likely from a school. Sturdy, but ugly.

Once the brief orientation tour was complete, Hamilton brought in a box of desk supplies from his car, put his coffee cup on the desk, and tossed some pens and pencils in the drawer along with a few pads of paper. He searched the sparse room for a place to hang his California Medical License and settled on a small nail projecting from a stud. He stood back and stared at it, shaking his head. A couple of folded metal chairs leaned against the beams. He flipped one open and sat down, folded his hands together across his flat belly and leaned back. "Open for business," he muttered.

Two new exam rooms, as raw as his office, also occupied the construction area. There was no furniture except for a tiny portable fridge where the construction guys kept sodas and water. Two plastic-covered beds leaned vertically against one wall, along with a collapsible gurney and a few boxes of non-perishable medical supplies.

Hamilton spent the rest of the morning sitting in with Dr. Madesh Chopra as he cared for his patients, getting used to the process and paperwork they used at the clinic. During his lunch break, he purchased a couple of small succulents from a nearby nursery to brighten up his half-built office and put them on the firebreaks between the wall studs, hoping the construction crew wouldn't drywall them inside. They looked pathetic and lonely, but it was better than before.

During late afternoon, Dr. Chopra was giving him a rundown on the filing system in the event that the administrative assistant wasn't around to deal with it. Up front, they could hear one of the other clinic physicians, Dr. MacDonald, raising his voice. Hamilton glanced at Chopra and asked, "What's up with MacDonald?"

"Who knows?" Chopra said. "He's always shouting at someone."

Hamilton approached the front lobby where MacDonald was arguing with a man carrying a medium-sized dog. The dog's leg was bleeding through a rag that the man held tight against her leg.

"We don't deal with pets! There's a bloody vet a mile down the street," MacDonald snarled.

"Please," the man said, "she's been shot." Hamilton looked up from the dog to study the man. He had straight shoulder-length hair and abstract tattoos covered both arms. A closely trimmed dark beard framed his face, with thin bare lines cut in parallel patterns on the sides. Muscular and sharp-eyed. He didn't appear to be strung out like some of the patients he'd seen today. Torn blue jeans, an old Fixx tee-shirt, and tennis shoes. A heavy backpack suggested that he might be a student.

"It's a dog. Not a human. We deal with humans here, not animals, comprende?" MacDonald said.

Hamilton folded back the blood-soaked cloth and examined the wound. The dog looked at him suspiciously, but it didn't seem aggressive. It was a strange looking dog. More like a small wolf. When he was with Doctors Without Borders, dealing with animals was an inevitable part of the practice. Some of his patients figured if he could help deliver a baby boy, he could just as well help deliver a calf. Where he could help, he did, but he improvised a lot.

"Doesn't look too bad for a gunshot wound. Why don't you bring her in?"

MacDonald said, "*You* aren't going to contaminate one of our exam rooms with a dog," and moved to bar his way.

Hamilton glared. MacDonald sneered. "I'll take them in back," Hamilton said. "In the construction area, okay? If you have a problem with that, take it up with Gordon." He pushed past MacDonald.

MacDonald scowled at Hamilton. "Gordon *will* be hearing about this," he growled. He stormed out the front door and turned toward the stairs leading up to the administrator's office.

Chopra rubbed his forehead. "Well, that went fairly well, considering."

Hamilton opened the gate next to the front desk and motioned for the man to follow him. He led him back to one of the under-construction exam rooms and pulled out one of the plastic-wrapped gurneys, unwrapping it and extending the frame to make a temporary low bed. He locked the wheels. "Put her down there. I'll get some supplies and be right back."

"You'll be okay, girl. You hold on," the man said. Hamilton glanced over his shoulder as he left the room. A fluorescent light overhead cast shadows from the bare two-by-fours like prison bars. The wound wasn't bleeding that much, but the dog didn't really look that good, and the deep look of concern on the man's face made him wonder if something else was going on.

In the supply room, he scavenged some disposable towels, thread and needle for stitching the wound, Betadine solution, and forceps. Hands full, he returned to the back room.

"Quick," the man said, "You need to get the bullet out. It's killing her."

He examined the bearded man curiously. The bullet had already done its damage. The bleeding was light. Shaking his head, he sat down next to the dog. "We can't do general anesthesia here. Best I can offer your dog is a local, but you'd have to hold her down."

"No time. Get the bullet out, now. Please. I'll hold her." The man gritted his teeth and held the dog's chest and head tightly. The dog seemed unresponsive. *Just as well,* Hamilton thought.

He put on blue sterile gloves, cleaned the wound quickly with the Betadine, then started poking around in the leg looking for the bullet. The small bullet, a .22 from the looks of it, was lodged in the side of the tibia. It was amazing that the bone hadn't fractured. He placed a towel under the leg, grabbed the bullet with his forceps and wiggled it carefully until it came out, putting it on the edge of the towel. The man's eyes locked onto it, his face twisting into a grimace. "Please put that somewhere else, will you, Doc?"

His forceps hovered over the bullet for a moment while he thought about the request. There wasn't really any place else to put it. After looking around the room for a moment, he picked it up and put the bullet on one of the firebreaks between the studs in the wall frame on the far side of the room. The man sighed in relief.

Hamilton flushed the wound again with Betadine, patted it dry with gauze, and sewed the wound. He stood up and considered his work. It reminded him of an old man he'd treated in Kenya with almost as much hair on his leg as the dog. "I need bandages. Let me get some out of storage, and you'll be out of here in a jiff." He left the room, located the bandages, and returned. Inside the small room, the man was helping a petite woman get dressed. She didn't look well. Pale and shaking.

"Where's the dog?"

"What dog?"

"The dog you brought in here thirty minutes ago. The dog I pulled the bullet out of."

"Why would I bring a dog in here? The vet's down the street just a mile or so." The man's face was like stone. "You just pulled a bullet out of my lady's leg, here. Clinic's just for people, right?"

The man struggled to dress her as he talked, pulling clothes out of his backpack. The girl was out of it, in a daze, mumbling to the man. Hamilton could clearly see the stitches on her leg. The hair on the back of his neck stood up as he tried to process the situation. *What the hell*, he thought. *Mass delusion? I saw MacDonald shouting at this guy and his dog.*

He stared at the man, trying to make him twitch or give up some other clue. It was like staring at a brick. Hamilton took a deep breath, then let it out slowly. Trying to keep his voice from cracking, he said, "You'll still need a bandage on that. And she'll need antibiotics for ten days. I'll write you a prescription."

The man lifted her feet and slipped some cut-off jeans up her legs. She moaned and tried to grab his arm. He jerked his chin at Hamilton. "Go ahead and get that bandage on," he said, glancing anxiously toward the front of the building.

Hamilton bandaged her leg. By the time he finished, the girl was conscious and looking at him with bloodshot and bleary eyes, but was still a bit wobbly. "You know, this is a gunshot wound, and I'm supposed to report gunshot wounds when they come through." He scribbled out the prescription for the antibiotics and handed it to him.

"A gunshot wound in a *dog*? You don't need to report *that*."

He ran his hand backwards through his unruly hair. "But...no, I guess I don't. There are still some forms..."

"For a dog?"

Hamilton ground his teeth quietly for a moment, then said, "There's a back door here that leads into the alley. If you don't want to run into Dr. MacDonald again, maybe you want to go out that way."

"Thank you, doctor. Doctor..." he glanced over at Hamilton's desk, which he could see plainly through the studs in the wall. Hamilton had a name plaque leaning up against a dirty coffee cup. "...Hamilton." Grinning, the strange man pressed something cold into his palm. Hamilton looked down. It was a gold coin over an inch in diameter. When he looked back up, the back door of the building was swinging shut.

"What the hell," he muttered, shaking his head. He closed his fist on the coin, staring at the back door, then dropped the coin in his lab coat pocket.

He cleaned up the work area, dumping the soiled disposables into the hazmat bin. Picking up the bullet from the firebreak, he examined it closely. The edges were sharp. Curious, he took it to the sink and rinsed the blood off, then held it up to the light. It was shiny. He dug at it with his thumbnail but couldn't dent it. It wasn't lead at all.

A short while later, Dr. Chopra entered the construction area to find Hamilton sipping thoughtfully at a cup of coffee. staring at the little lump of shiny metal in the middle of his desk. "While you were back here with the dog, I could hear MacDonald shouting upstairs. I think Gordon talked him down, but he's still pissed off."

"Nothing I can do about that now," Hamilton replied.

"Try not to make it worse. He's a pain to work with even when he's in a good mood." Chopra shook his head. "I meant to come back sooner to see how the dog was doing," he said, "but I had another patient. Did you save it?"

"I think I did, but I'm not entirely sure."

"Some operations go that way." Chopra sat on the edge of his desk, folding his hands together. "I used to have a dog when I was a child. It disappeared one night. My parents told me it ran off to meet a girl dog, a little love story, but I'm fairly certain that it just got run over. Parents say things like that to take the pain away." He sighed. "I would like another dog someday." He leaned over closer to Hamilton to whisper conspiratorially, "MacDonald is a dick. He doesn't understand animals."

Hamilton laughed.

"So," Chopra continued, "why are you staring at this little piece of jewelry?"

"What?"

"This little piece of silver. My father was a jeweler for many years. But he never made a piece of jewelry as ugly as that."

"That's the bullet that was in the dog," Hamilton replied.

Chopra was quiet for a minute, staring at the bullet, then up at Hamilton, then back at the bullet. "Did it pay you?"

"Yeah, he gave me a gold coin. His idea of payment, I guess."

"A gold coin? Really? Can I see it?"

Hamilton handed him the coin. Chopra examined the coin closely, then handed it back. He seemed surprisingly casual about it. "It certainly looks like gold." Chopra said. "I don't recognize the letters, or the woman's face. That looks like a vine around a castle on the back. Definitely not a Krugerand."

"I wouldn't know. I've never held a gold coin before."

"I wonder how billing will handle it," Chopra said.

Hamilton flipped the coin in the air. It made a pleasant ringing sound as it came off his fingertip and slapped solidly into his hand. "I might give them cash for it. I've never owned a gold coin before."

Chopra smiled, but Hamilton sensed some sadness behind it. "So you said."

Chopra left the clinic before Hamilton, and it wasn't until he was gone that Chopra's words echoed in his mind, "Did it pay you?" It? Is that what he heard? That didn't make any sense. He shook his head, and by the time he got back to his apartment, he'd forgotten what Chopra had said.

Interview with a Golem

The golem unexpectedly did all the voices as he relayed the story. It took me back to when I was a child and my father altered his own voice for every character in The Hobbit as he read it to me. I had to smile. "That was his first supernatural case, then?"

The golem nodded. "But word got out quickly. Redondo Beach needed a doctor to treat its monsters, and Dr. Hamilton appeared to be ready, if not completely willing."

Chapter 2 – The Administrator

Carol Rafferty, the receptionist, came back to Hamilton's construction-zone office and told him, "Dr. Gordon would like to see you in his office at the end of your shift."

"Thanks, Carol." He nodded. This had to be about McDonald whining about the dog. Great first-day impression to make on the clinic's administrator.

As they were closing up for the day, he passed through the front office area and saw McDonald with a smug grin on his face. *What an asshole,* he thought.

Hamilton pushed the front door open and walked up the gravel-coated cement stairs. The railing looked like rusty wrought iron with ten coats of paint, but it seemed secure.

He knocked lightly on the door of the office and a gruff voice called out, "Come on in, it's open!" Hamilton opened the office door as a tall, portly man came around from behind his desk, extending his hand. "Dr. Hamilton. Thanks for dropping by."

Hamilton shook his hand, confused. It was a strong handshake, the beefy hand almost enveloping his own. Gordon was a few inches taller than Hamilton, over six feet. He was neatly dressed and wore a big, toothy grin above a closely-trimmed brown beard. He seemed friendly enough.

"Isn't this about the dog?" Hamilton asked.

"Well, technically, yes. McDonald did complain, and I have to respond to the complaint." He sat back behind his desk, and Hamilton took a seat across from him. "So," Gordon said, "you sewed up a dog today."

Hamilton nodded and said, "Yup," unapologetically.

"Was the customer satisfied?"

Hamilton raised an eyebrow and the corner of his mouth quirked upward, recalling the strange result and the gold coin. "I think so."

"Good, good. So, officially, I'm chewing you out for that. Unofficially, nice job, well done. You should understand that most of the funding for our clinic comes from the Western Baptist College, and we try to keep our noses clean to keep the money coming in. They like the way McDonald rolls, and generally, he's a pretty decent doctor, so he's going to be around awhile. It'd be nice if you two could tolerate each other."

"I'll certainly try," said Hamilton.

"Good, good." Gordon tapped a folder on his desk and continued. "The Board was pretty impressed with the breadth of your experience. In fact, I'm surprised you decided to come to a small clinic like Pembrook."

"As you might guess," Hamilton said, "working out in the field isn't exactly a stable environment. The places we travelled to were pretty rough. It was great experience, and I felt I was doing a lot of good, but I really wanted to find a place to settle down. I was raised in LA, so this is close to home."

Gordon flipped though the folder. "Pretty diverse background."

"Yeah, we never really knew what was going to be tossed at us. It was mostly family practice, but I assisted with a lot of surgery. We had a wide variety of tropical diseases to deal with. Some bullet or knife wounds on occasion. Our group didn't go into any combat areas, but we still had to deal with that sort of thing."

"You'll get some of that here, too," Gordon said. He closed the folder. "But mostly it's just a lot of Medicaid and Medicare patients. Pregnancies and the elderly are probably our two biggest income streams. You learn to filter out the junkies looking for prescription drugs. Serious surgeries get sent to West Coast Medical Center or Memorial Hospital, and we don't do abortions." He pointed to his PhD hanging on the wall. "Since WBC subsidizes the clinic heavily, they make the rules."

"But you still offer birth control?"

"Yes, we still offer that. Most of the Board of Regents recognize that it lowers abortion rates. Not all of them are happy about it." Gordon looked up at the clock on the wall. "Looks like I've been chewing you out for five minutes. That should make MacDonald happy. Or at least keep him quiet. So I assume you'll be staying with us?"

"I'm looking forward to it." Hamilton stood up and offered his hand again.

Gordon took his hand firmly. "I hope you enjoy working here."

Chapter 3 – The Unseen Patient

The next day at the clinic saw the usual number of colds, cuts, backaches, addicts, hangnails, food sickness, and hemorrhoids. A gunshot wound and a stroke were transferred to Memorial Hospital downtown, after Pembrook's small team did what they could to stabilize them.

Near the end of the day, Hamilton returned to his unfinished office, blew some dust off his backpack where some of the construction debris had found a home, hung his white smock on a nail sticking out of a two-by-four, and changed into a t-shirt. In front, Chopra and Mary Olgebright were taking care of the last two patients, then they were ready to close.

There was a light rapping at the rear door of the clinic, a doorway that opened to the alley.

Hamilton frowned. They weren't expecting a delivery, but with packages coming from the Postal Service, UPS, and FedEx, it was anyone's guess when packages would arrive, and where. Still, getting a delivery this late at the back door was unlikely, and it was probably just a junkie trying to get in to see what he could scrounge. Hamilton ignored it.

He slung his backpack over his shoulder and started

to walk out the front. He heard a soft voice at the back door. "Dr. Hamilton? Can you hear me?" Another light tapping on the door followed.

Hamilton hesitated. The guy knew his name and knew where his temporary office was. Was this the dog guy again? Or one of his friends? He walked over to the back door and said, "Come around the front like everyone else. But we're closing soon."

"I need your help. I can't let anyone see me." The man's voice was hoarse, like he was trying to whisper and shout at the same time.

Lodging his foot firmly in front of the steel door, Hamilton cracked it open to peer at the man. The guy's gloved hand was resting lightly on the door, but he wasn't shoving against it. He wore a hooded sweater and reflective glasses. Except for his face, there wasn't an inch of exposed flesh anywhere. His face was pale, reflecting the alley's few street lights, giving his skin a sickly yellow pallor.

"Dr. Hamilton? Can I come in? I…have this skin condition." He flexed his glove, staring at his own hand like it was a stranger's. "A friend of mine said you might be able to help. That you could be trusted."

"The guy with the wounded dog?"

"Raphael. Yeah. Wolfman." He gently pushed his way into the clinic, while Hamilton reluctantly stepped back out of the way.

"Wolfman," Hamilton repeated. "Why did he think I could be trusted? And with what?"

"You went all day without telling anyone about his girlfriend's transformation, right?"

Hamilton stared at him, still holding onto the

handle of the open door. "I wasn't sure it was real. And if I'm going nuts, I sure don't want anyone else at the clinic to know it. I need the job." He closed the door, scrutinizing the man, trying to see past the reflective lenses. You could tell a lot about a person by his eyes, and sometimes a bit from the brand name on the glasses. "You're telling me it was real."

"Yes. You helped a werewolf, who happens to be a friend of mine. He knew about my skin condition and told me I should drop by here. He said I should ask for you."

"Ah, good. References. Build up my client base." He spoke nervously, his voice tremulous. "A werewolf. Seriously?"

"I'd like to say that sarcasm doesn't suit you, but I've come to find that sarcasm suits everyone who has a bit of wit to them. Here," he said, pulling off one of his gloves, "this is my problem."

There was no hand in the glove, only a few floating brown spots wiggling in the air. Hamilton stepped backwards, tripping over a stud cutoff that the construction workers had left in the middle of the floor, but the stranger grasped his arm with an invisible hand, the brown spots demarking its position, and the indentation of his fingers on Hamilton's arm defining its shape.

"Sorry to startle you like that, but quite frankly, that never gets old. I have age spots. For some reason, they are visible when the rest of me is not. As you might imagine, this is highly inconvenient for someone of my type."

Hamilton glanced back and forth between the mostly-invisible hand and the man's face. "But your face…"

"It's just makeup. Over a lifetime, I've become quite skilled at applying a realistic skin tone." He helped Hamilton to his feet and took off his glasses. There were empty holes where his eyes should have been. Hamilton could see the backside of the man's hat through his eyeholes. "I could use full-eye contacts, but it's easier just to throw on some mirrored glasses. You can't imagine how tedious it is to put on makeup whenever you need to go get beer." He looked around the room, raising his eyebrows at the bare framed walls, tarps, and tools scattered around. "Not exactly what I expected. Don't you have an office?"

"Over there," he pointed. "It's not any better. They hired me before they really had a place to put me. It'll be finished in a couple of weeks." Hamilton grabbed an extra chair that one of the workers had been using as an OSHA-unapproved ladder and carried it into his small office. "Have a seat. How can you be invisible? That's not possible."

"And yet, here we are. Within my little community, since, as you might guess, I'm not the only person like this, we've speculated that the cells on one side of our body have some sort of neural connection that allows them to radiate images that are collected on the other side of the body. Like little cameras and projectors and cables built into each cell. We think there are extra communication paths in the cells that normal people don't have. Some of our people think that it's magic. Others think that our individual cells are just really transparent. But there are fools in every community. Still, we prize our independence and secrecy, so we aren't so curious as to approach the scientific community to delve into the dissectible wonders of our own peculiar bodies."

Stunned, Hamilton sat down at his desk and stared curiously at the empty sockets and floating age spots. The man sat down across from him. "When you want to be completely invisible," Hamilton asked, "do you go out nude?"

The man smiled. "Ah, yes, there's the dark side of being invisible. Naked, I can go anywhere and see anything."

"Like a locker room at the Y," Hamilton suggested.

The man lifted his hands noncommittally. "Hypothetically, sure. I can also steal things that fit inside my mouth or my clenched fist. And I can foil a bank robber by grabbing his gun out of his hand and kicking him in the nuts." He looked up at the bare-bones ceiling, reminiscing and frowning, "But of course, doing so might cause an invisible man hiding money in his fist to drop it. There's a downside for heroics. We try to stay out of the public eye."

Hamilton sighed. "So you're a thief, too?"

He shrugged. "One does what one must to survive. I can't exactly hold down a normal job. And now, I can't exactly do the invisibility gig, either. It's not all petty thrill-shit either. I've helped take down a few scumbag executives and politicians, too, paying gigs that helped pay the rent. You'd be surprised what people will say and do when they think nobody's around to hear it. Secrets are our bread and butter."

"I bet. What do you do in the winter? Stay home?"

"That's the much darker side of being invisible." He leaned forward in his seat and lowered his voice. "Our skin is very valuable. Traditionally, when one of us dies, we're skinned and our hides are tanned. Well, not exactly 'tanned' but it's a similar process. The leather has lots of uses, not the least of which is extra clothing for us so we can keep warm. The skin retains its ability to reroute light even after removal. Gruesome, isn't it?" He leaned back, slouching into his seat. "Hair can be woven into a variety of objects, too. We try to keep skins and such in the family. A little more practical than keeping an urn full of ashes on the mantel, though certainly more macabre by most standards. We also have very strict taboos about hunting others for the value of their skin." He held up his age-spotted hand. "It's why this is such a concern to me. With these marks, it would be very easy for someone outside our community to hunt me down. And there are hunters who do it for a living. Like shooting elephants for ivory."

Hamilton grimaced, thinking of Nazi atrocities during World War II. The difference here was that the invisible culture had risen to expect it, and that the intrinsic value of their skins became an inheritance for their children. It was hard to wrap his head around it. "I can't do a lot for you that you can't do with over-the-counter medications," he said. "Hydroquinone is good for this sort of thing, but it will take a few weeks to clear up your skin. Retin-A works well for wrinkles and spots. I could give you a prescription for both."

"I've tried the two-percent hydroquinone before. It didn't help much. I was hoping you might have some more original ideas. Repeat business, you know. None of my people are getting any younger."

"Do you have a sample of the makeup you're using for your face?" Hamilton asked.

"I have some right here, in fact. I keep it handy for

touch-ups." He pulled a small vial out of his coat pocket and handed it to Hamilton. Hamilton opened the vial and sniffed at it, but its odor was too faint to tell him anything useful. It was a flesh-colored liquid. "Do you suspect the makeup for some reason?" the man asked.

"I'm not sure. Some creams increase melanin production in the skin. Can you get me a list of the ingredients for this?" He put the vial on his desk. "And can I take a sample for testing?"

"All the ingredients are commercial, so getting a list shouldn't be a problem. And please take whatever you need for a sample."

"Just to clarify things, you are human, right?" He put the vial to the side of his desk.

"More or less. We can have sex with regular folks, we just don't produce any offspring. Just some sort of divergent evolution, I guess."

Out front, he could hear Chopra and Olgebright leaving the clinic, talking to one another, unaware he was still in his half-built office. They were alone. Hamilton leaned back in his chair, thinking about the age spots. In regular people, age spots were just high-density clusters of melanin gathered under the skin. But if these cells were actually transmitting light collected from the opposite surface of the hand or body, then maybe this was just a matter of a dirty projector lens. "Let me see your hand." The man held his hand out. Hamilton looked closely at the floating spots on the back of the man's hand, then turned it over to look at the palm. There, he could still see the spots, but they moved around based on his viewing angle. Transmitted images, rather than the actual age spots.

"There's laser treatment for age spots," he said.

"Doesn't work. Others in our community have tried that already. It just permanently damages the cells so they don't transmit the light, then you have to cut them out and stitch it up."

"Let's try the Retin-A, anyway. I'm guessing that the melanin you have in your skin normally stays hidden behind the light transmitter cells. Melanin is a regular pigment for your whole body, so it must be hiding someplace. If we clean off the lens, so to speak, by breaking down the pigment into clear molecules, then we might have a chance at getting them to disappear. If there's no improvement in a week, you can drop back in and we'll try something else." He opened his desk and pulled out a prescription pad. "I'll need your name."

"Raoul de Lambert," the man said.

Hamilton spent a minute scribbling out the prescription and handed it to Raoul. "See you next week, then?"

The prescription slip disappeared into his pocket. "I hope so," Raoul said.

After he ushered Raoul out the back door, he realized that the vial of makeup was still sitting on his desk. He snatched a plastic coffee cup lid out of the trash, tipped a sample onto it for testing, then ran to catch Raoul before he exited the alley.

As he stepped out onto the cement stoop in the narrow alley, he spied Raoul lying on the ground, apparently dragging himself across the payment toward a car near the end of the alley. His arms were held strangely in the air. "Raoul!" he shouted.

Someone else, someone invisible to him, said, "Shit." A woman's disembodied voice, echoing on the alley walls. Raoul's arms dropped to the ground, and Hamilton heard footsteps approaching. In a panic, he opened the vial of pigment and threw its liquid contents in the direction of the footsteps. A streak of spattered flesh-colored pigment appeared suddenly on the woman's chest and up across her neck. She stopped, presumably to take in the mess he'd made of her skin. "God damn you, peasant, you are so dead."

Less dead than he was just a few seconds before, he thought. At least he could see her coming, now. The woman strode toward him again, a knife flashing into existence in one invisible hand, but a piece of rebar suddenly flew up off the ground and smacked into her forehead. She dropped onto her back like a rock. Hamilton heard a sudden exhalation of breath. A car farther down the alley started suddenly and pulled away quickly, the lights not coming on until it had turned the corner out of the alley.

A young girl's voice spoke out of the darkness. "Fast thinking, doctor. I wasn't sure exactly where her head was, before. Can you help my dad? She hit him on the head pretty hard."

His eyes darted nervously around the alley, but the young voice echoed off the brick walls, making its location ambiguous. "I can try," Hamilton said to the air. "He's a big guy." He looked down the alley to see if anyone was nearby using a phone to record the evil doctor dragging the corpse into his laboratory to experiment upon. It was dark. No one was close by, except for the ones he couldn't see.

He grabbed Raoul by the shoulders and pulled him

toward the secret lab…the clinic, dragging him inside. The crazies were starting to get to him. He passed through the doorway and was ready to close it when the young voice spoke again, close behind him. He jumped in the air. "Pull him in further. You have to bring the woman in, too."

"What's going on?" he asked, pulling Raoul in further to make space for the woman, then checked to make sure he was still breathing. "Do you know who attacked him? Or why?"

"I was supposed to be on watch while dad was inside. I don't know how they got here before us—that car must have been there the whole time. The woman—she's a Hunter. She's a skin hunter."

"But she's invisible. Isn't she one of your own?"

"No. She's wearing someone else's skin."

Despite having been through medical school, Hamilton had to fight to keep his lunch down. He didn't want to touch the woman. Her knife was lying near her in the alley, and the hood of her extra skin was askew so he could see part of her neck. He slid the hood off, then regretted it. Now it looked like a head was lying in the alley, a gash in her forehead where the kid had struck her with the piece of rebar. He grunted, thinking that the sloppiness of the construction guys might have saved his life. He picked up the woman by the armpits and dragged her into the corridor with Raoul. There was a cell phone floating in the air, and the young voice was telling someone how to get to the clinic.

He attended to Raoul. Pulling the hoodie back, there was a confusion of invisible head and visible blood pouring from a cut to his scalp. A swollen lump rose on the back of his head outlined only by the blood on it. "I can't really see how much damage there is," he said.

The young voice paused in talking on the phone long enough to say, "Get his makeup vial and smear some makeup around the wound. That'll show you the outline."

Hamilton went out to the alley, retrieved the near-empty vial, and returned. The kid's phone had disappeared into an invisible pocket and he lost track of where the she was. He knelt and applied some of the makeup around the wound, enough so he could tell that stitches would be needed. Two nights in a row. He retrieved his stitching gear and set to work. "What's your name, kid?"

"I'm not a kid." She was indignantly silent for a few seconds, then said, "It's Jennifer."

"Well, hello, Jennifer. You've got a good batting arm." He heard her snort and could imagine her reluctantly smiling. "What's going on with the woman?"

"She'll be dealt with. She's a cold-blooded killer."

"A skin hunter, you said."

"Yeah. We have some people coming to pick her up. Help me peel her skin off, doctor."

"There's no way in hell…oh, *that* skin. Let me finish up with the stitches."

"I have to say, Doctor, you seem amazingly casual about all this."

"Working in Sudan makes you 'casual' about a lot of things. The things you can do something about, you get down and do it. The things you can't," he shrugged, habitually wincing as he tied off the last stitch and snipped it off, "you just try to forget." He checked Raoul's pulse again. "Could have a concussion. Not much I can do about

that. Keep an eye on him for behavioral changes, severe
dizziness, vomiting and such. When he comes to, he'll need
some painkillers."

He went over to the woman and lifted her up while
Jennifer wriggled the invisible skin off her body. The
woman seemed to materialize inch by inch. There was a
sharp rap at the rear door, and a voice called out,
"Jennifer?"

"Hang on." Jennifer opened the door, and a
slender, medium-height woman with long, straight, black
hair walked in. She glared down at the unconscious woman
on the floor, her lips tightening.

She glanced over at Hamilton, green eyes sweeping
briefly over him, dismissing him as non-threatening.
Hamilton suddenly felt nervous. She leaned over, grabbed
an arm of the woman on the ground, and lifted her across
her back as though picking up a small bag of potatoes. "Tell
Raoul he owes me some coin," she said, then walked out
the door. Hamilton heard a trunk slam shut, then a car door
slam. She drove off.

Raoul groaned and tried to sit up. Jennifer helped
him. *Convenient,* Hamilton thought. *We won't have to carry him.*
"Now what? Do you have someone to pick him up?"
Hamilton asked.

"We have a car parked out front. I can drive well
enough. I'll borrow dad's hoody and use some spray-on
makeup. We'll get home okay, if no one checks me for
pants. Can you pull the car around back for me? It'll save
some hassle." The invisible Jennifer pulled some car keys
out of Raoul's pocket and tossed them to Hamilton. Raoul
tried to sit up, his hand on the back of his head.

Hamilton hesitated, thinking of the two invisibles alone in the clinic, wondering for a moment if they might steal something, then realized how completely irrelevant that was compared to everything else going on. "Yeah. I'll pull it around. Give me a minute."

When he was in the car, he just sat still and breathed slowly, key in the ignition. Was there blood on the floor to clean up? Supplies missing that had to be accounted for? Witnesses? He took a deep breath and let it out, calming himself, staring dead-eyed down the street. This was not what he signed up for. He started the car, pulled out into traffic, then drove around to the alley, parking behind the back door. He looked up and down the alley before entering the clinic.

Half-supporting Raoul, he helped him into the back seat. Jennifer had pulled her hood up and had sprayed her face with a skin-tone, but bobbed along on invisible legs. Large parts of Raoul's head were still invisible, making him look like some abstract porcelain sculpture with garish red and flesh highlights.

Jennifer took Hamilton's hand, startling him. "Thank you, doctor. Sorry it went this way, but things can be confusing in the community. You probably won't get used to it."

"I somehow don't feel reassured."

Jennifer giggled. She let go of his hand, leglessly bobbed over to the door of the car, got in, started the car and drove away. She didn't seem to have any trouble driving. *They must start early*, he thought.

Going back inside, he looked at the old linoleum floor. Fifteen minutes and a little bleach would take care of it. The construction crew would be tearing it out soon anyway. And once that was taken care of, he could clean up everything else. He sat down at his desk. Jennifer or Raoul had left the vial there. The coffee cup lid into which he'd dribbled the pigment sample still sat on his desk. He reached for the vial, but his arm bumped into something else first, something invisible that clinked. Frowning, he felt around for it. His hand came to rest on a small leather bag. An invisible bag made of human skin, he reminded himself. It was unexpectedly soft, but still made him sick to think of its origins. Lifting the bag, it clinked again, and he dumped its contents out. There were two more of the golden coins he'd received, and one smaller half-sized coin. His breath caught in his throat. There was going to be no easy way to turn them over to the clinic billing department. There was the lack of patient forms to explain, and, of course, the gold coins themselves.

But the bag; that was a sign of trust. That wasn't given to him as a reward, or payment, he realized. That was a contract. Or perhaps an obligation.

The gold he could stash somewhere, or possibly get a safe-deposit box. At least the clinic was giving him a regular paycheck, so he didn't have to worry about cashing in the gold.

He cleaned up the mess and left the clinic, walking back to his apartment, trying to understand this new world he'd been dragged into, constantly looking over his shoulder for the Hunter's driver that got away.

Chapter 4 - Kraken Finds a Foe

Joey Grice shivered, his mind feeling naked in front of the man they all called Kraken. He'd seen Kraken absorb other people into his body like rolled dough and feared the same horrible death every time he was in the same room with him.

Kraken wasn't fat, though. It seemed that even when his mass increased, it increased in proportion to what he started with, and he had been a strong man when Joey first started doing jobs for him.

They were in Kraken's Manhattan Beach warehouse, since Kraken never allowed his "help" to visit him at his home. The man owned a number of buildings in the area, mostly industrial structures, including a lab where he performed unpleasant experiments; Joey was just as glad that he'd never been there.

"So you left the Hunter Pamela in the alley?"

"I saw her pull a knife on the dude. Well, I saw the knife in the air; she was invisible. The man just swung his hand in the air, and the knife fell to the ground. Then I heard this thump, like a body hitting the pavement. The dude started looking around, and I hightailed it. He's got to be a sorcerer or somethin'."

"The alley was fairly dark, was it not?" Kraken asked.

"Well, yeah."

"And you were looking in your rear view window?"

Kraken was standing uncomfortably close. *Dear God,* Joey thought, *please don't touch me.* As if he could hear his thoughts, Kraken put his hand on his shoulder and squeezed it. Joey winced and held his breath, but his flesh wasn't dissolving yet.

"Yeah. Maybe he threw something at her that I couldn't see at that angle."

"Perhaps." Kraken took his hand off Joey's shoulder. Joey breathed again. "Still, if he *was* a sorcerer..." He walked around to the back of a large mahogany desk and sat down in a chair custom-made for his massive stature. The chair still creaked when he settled into it. "You were chasing down a glass person for me, correct?"

Joey shivered. He and Pamela had been freelancing that night, hunting down the glass man to harvest his skin and sell it on the open market. The man they were tracking, Raoul de Lambert, had visited the sorcerer, come back out, and then the sorcerer followed him, somehow sensing that something was wrong, waved his hand, and took down Pamela even though she'd been invisible. He wasn't about to tell Kraken they were freelancing that night, though. "Yeah. We wanted to get a glass guy for you. You said you wanted one."

"If you had succeeded, that would have been an exceptional accomplishment. I would have been quite happy." He wasn't smiling, though, and obviously wasn't happy. He leaned back in his chair and stared at Joey from dark eyes under a thick brow. "Tell me more about that night and this…so-called sorcerer."

Joey swallowed and nodded. "We had a tip and an address, Pamela and me, and we staked it out. We saw this guy come out all bundled up like it was winter, right? And the invisibles, they do that a lot, so we figure the tip was good and we tail the guy. He pulls up in front of this curio shop and parks, then gets out real slow, looks at the junk in the window and then walks next door to the clinic. All the lights are out in the curio shop, but there's still a couple of people in the clinic. It looks like they're closing up for the night. He looks like he's gonna go in. I pull around and park in the alley, Pamela gets out, expecting to walk around to the front, and, hey, we got lucky. The guy is walking around to the back door of the joint."

"Which joint?"

Joey looked down at the floor, grimacing. "I'm not sure. There was the clinic, the junk store, and, uh, some business I didn't catch the name of. He seemed interested in the clinic, so we figure maybe it was the back door to that."

"Was the glass man a junky, by chance?"

Joey shrugged. "I don't know. He went in, he came out, Pamela whacked him and was dragging him to my car, and then the other guy comes out. Maybe a doctor? Anyway, he waves a hand at Pamela, she goes down, and you know the rest. I took off."

"Well, I don't really know the rest, because you took off. What did the doctor-sorcerer do to the glass man? Why was he there? Is this sorcerer so capable as to take out a trained Hunter with a wave of his hand? And what happened to your partner afterwards?" He leaned forward, and Joey started sweating an ocean. "Aren't you concerned about her?"

"Hunting supernats has its dangers and rewards, Mr. Kraken. Sometimes we meet things that aren't worth screwing with."

"And you believe this fellow is one of those things?"

He looked up at the ceiling. "Pamela was a great partner. I'd love to see someone take the guy down. But if he's that powerful, I'm not going to mess with him. If an opportunity comes up to kill the bastard, I'll take it, but the odds better be in my favor."

"Well, Mr. Grice. That's just a matter of good planning, isn't it? Let's see if we can find out where this mysterious doctor-sorcerer lives. If he's serving the community, it should be fairly easy to find out who he is. I've got an idea. I could use a decent sorcerer, especially if he were my servant."

Chapter 5 – A Medium-Sized Ghost

Hamilton rapped at the exam room door, then walked in without waiting for an answer. Sitting in a chair in the room was a small, frumpy looking lady with an old sweater hanging loosely over her shoulders. She had tied her gray hair into a thick ponytail behind her head and she stared at him over a pair of wire-rimmed reading glasses. She gripped a small purse on her lap. His first impression stereotyped her into the mass of elderly scraping by on nothing but social-security checks.

"Agatha Noone? I'm Doctor Hamilton."

"It's pronounced Noo-nay, not Noon. And sure as hell not no-one."

He smiled professionally. There went the stereotype. At least she seemed to be human. "Alright," he glanced at his clipboard, "Mrs. Noone. The nurse tells me you're having a lot of lower back pain."

"That was just a load of crap so I could get in to talk to you. My back is as good as can be expected at this age."

The words erupting from the frail-looking woman momentarily stunned him. He leaned against the wall and put the clipboard on the edge of the sink and considered her. Her eyes looked very bright. Like scalpels. Despite her shoddy appearance, she seemed to exude confidence and self-assurance. "All right," he said, "you've got my attention. Are you having some issue you didn't want to tell the nurse about?"

"You're the doctor been working on changers and glass people, right?"

He crossed his arms and pursed his lips, then said, "I'm not sure I know what you're talking about."

"Oh, come on, Dr. Hamilton. We all know each other. We may not all like each other, but that's beside the point. Part of the other community." She waved a hand. "You know."

Hamilton looked her over again, wondering if he'd missed something like lizard skin or fangs. She still looked like a frail old woman. "What is it, exactly, that you wanted to see me about, Mrs. Noone?"

She fiddled with her purse without opening it, nervous energy occupying her hands. "I have a sick friend I want you to see."

He looked down stupidly at her purse. "Your purse is alive?"

She glared at him sternly and said, "Don't be a fool! Of course my purse isn't alive. Why would you even think that?"

"Right, of course. Why would I?" He spread his hands apart apologetically and sighed. "Why don't you tell me where this friend of yours is, what's wrong with him, and we'll see if I can help or not."

She took her glasses off, wiping the lenses with the

tail of her blouse before saying anything. She perched her glasses on the tip of her nose, peering over the tops of the lenses at him again as though they were only there for decoration, and said, "Well, fundamentally, he's dead. But that's not actually what's wrong with him. He's a ghost, but he's a sick ghost."

Hamilton rolled his eyes and ran a hand through his thick brown hair. Yesterday, hoping for some cheap enlightenment, he'd picked up a book at the local bookstore called, "A Supernatural History of California". The one thing that California had was a lot of unprovable folktale ghosts. He sat down on a stool in front of her and said, "Mrs. Noone, you have to understand that I'm a doctor who was trained to work on living humans. So far this week, I've only had to work on bullet wounds, cuts, and age spots. Though these people have come from what you call your community, their problems are relatively normal ailments that I can deal with. I haven't been trained on werewolf mange or ghost physiology. So I'm not sure I can help you at all."

Agatha wouldn't look him in the eye. "You've got to try to help. I just know that. Trust me. It's important."

He leaned back on the stool. "Why is it important, Mrs. Noone?"

She held up a hand, "Please. Call me Agatha. You will, eventually, anyway."

And what did that mean? Hamilton wondered. "Agatha, why is it important? The ghost is already dead."

"I can't tell you. Not yet. It will change things."

Of course, Hamilton thought. *She couldn't be normal, could she?* He sighed softly. "Where is this ghost, then?"

"His house is…was…in Venice Beach. About an hour's drive if traffic is tolerable."

He nodded. "All right. I get off here about 4PM today. We can take a look then."

***

Traffic was average, and they arrived at the Venice Beach house just after 5PM. The yard was nothing but dead grass up to a chipped and faded pale-green picket fence, blackened in parts by the fire that brought the house down. Part of a chimney had toppled and all of the wood remaining in the structure was charred black, crisscrossed beams making a crucifix of death from the skeleton of the house. A kid, maybe ten years old, rummaged through the debris for anything interesting. He ran away when they got out of the car and approached the burned out husk.

Hamilton sniffed at the wet charcoal smell of the air. It had drizzled that afternoon, and the ground outside the fence was slick. Black soot stained every surface. "The fire killed him?"

"Oh, no. He was dead twenty years ago. His ghost was occupying the house all that time, since he was tied to it. The only reason a ghost sticks around is if something ties them down when they die. Some task or riddle or desire left unfulfilled." She shook her head. "There are a lot of OCD ghosts out there."

He glanced down at the top of her head, unsure whether she was joking or not. "I'll bet. What was his reason for hanging around?"

"He was killed here in his home. He was stuffed in the crawl space underneath the house in a rolled-up carpet. Rats got to most of him before he really started smelling the place up." She rubbed her nose as though remembering the smell.

"You lived here after he was killed?" Hamilton asked.

"Oh, god no. But I knew Corwin Abercrombie long before he was murdered. He was a stage magician of minor talent and didn't have a lot of friends. We dated for a while, off and on. After he was murdered and stuffed like a petrified corndog under his house, his payments stopped and the bank foreclosed on it. After a while, they auctioned off the house. It went through a number of owners. Then it mysteriously burned down while the current owners were off on vacation. I'm fairly certain they arranged to have it burned down."

"Why?"

"They probably believed it was haunted. Of course, they were correct. But they were very religious folks and couldn't see selling a cursed house to another unsuspecting buyer."

They walked slowly around the perimeter of the charcoal husk of the house. "Give me time," she said, "he has to be broken in slowly."

"What's that?"

She glanced at him. "Oh, sorry, you can't hear him, can you?"

"I suppose you're going to tell me you were talking to the ghost," Hamilton said.

She pointed at him and winked. He found himself irritated by the gesture. "What am I supposed to do for this ailing ghost, Agatha?"

"Rains are coming. Where his desiccated, slightly

chewed corpse had some staying power, holding him here, there's nothing but ashes left, now. In another month, as his ashes wash into the sewers, leaching away from his…" she waggled a hand, "…let's call it his burial site, then he'll fade away. Just as we've grown fond of our corporeal existence, he's grown somewhat attached to his incorporeal condition. His consciousness in the ghostly realm. He doesn't wish to be dissipated."

"Worried about hell in the afterlife, is he?"

She tilted her head. "Aren't you?"

"I'm a humanist. There is no hell or heaven dreamt of in my philosophy."

She smiled. "Even with that philosophy, you might understand why he wished to continue his nebulous existence, though tied to the foundations of an old house. Nobody likes the idea of ceasing to exist. What he'd like you to do is to transport his remaining ashes somewhere else. Some place out of the rain. Some new haunt."

He stopped and studied her suspiciously. "Why haven't you done this yourself? Or coerced someone you know to do the job? Why me?"

"I could, but it wouldn't work out. I can't tell you why yet."

"You're hiding something."

"I'm just not telling you something yet. I can't. You need to gather some of his ashes."

"I didn't bring a sample container."

"I brought something," she said. She pulled a garden trowel and a small peanut-butter jar out of her purse.

"You two didn't get along very well, did you?"

She smiled grimly. He took the jar and trowel from her and she directed him to a spot of dirt and ash that looked like all the others. How was it that she knew where the body was all these years without telling the police about it? Her face betrayed nothing. She wasn't acting anxious about his questions or probing. Curious. He squatted down in the debris and scooped ashes into the jar until it was full. Just ashes. This was all that Corwin Abercrombie had become; a Jiffy jar full of dirt, charred wood, and burned flesh. In a moment of distracted thought, he pinched a bit of the dirt on the ground and brought it to his nose, smelling it. He heard Agatha behind him say, "Ahh!"

"Agatha! You brought someone new! And he's sniffing me." The loud voice suddenly manifested behind Hamilton, startling him, and he stumbled forward into the ash and mud. "And wearing me!" The voice laughed.

Hamilton picked himself up out of the damp ashes and tried to brush himself off, a futile effort that spread the damage even further. He glared at the ghost from a lowered brow. The ghost wore a sky-blue vest and a gray fedora, hovering a few feet off the ground, full of himself. "You must be the ghost," Hamilton muttered.

"He's not an idiot!" the ghost cried, feigning surprise.

"Sort of is," Agatha said. "He thought my purse was alive. Dr. Hamilton, meet Corwin. And vice-versa."

Hamilton looked up and down the street, concerned that others might see the floating apparition, but nobody turned an eye their way. "How is it," he asked, "that we can see him and nobody else can?"

"You touched his remains. You created a link with

him," she said.

The ghost drifted closer to Hamilton, frowning as he approached. "You put my remains in a…a peanut butter jar?"

"Actually," Agatha supplied, "it was a jar for storing my old bacon grease. The peanut butter was gone a long time ago."

Corwin scowled and crossed his arms. "Agatha, you wound me yet again. Wasn't murdering me enough?"

"Old fool. You know I didn't do anything but leave you."

"And yet, here we are together again, except for the mediocre sex."

Agatha rolled her eyes and licked her lips, ready to join battle, but Hamilton stepped between them. "Hey, sorry to interrupt the lover's spat, but now what?"

"Now we need to find a new home for the ashes. Something more stable than a house."

"Yes! A new home!" echoed the ghost.

Hamilton held up the jar and said, "I still don't understand why you needed me, of all people, to do this. You easily could have done this yourself."

"The Oracle?" Corwin said. "Oh, no, she can't take part in the events that whirl around her, only act as a bystander, as she always has."

"Shut up, ghost," Agatha grumbled.

"Oracle, huh?" Hamilton muttered. "It figures. For just a moment, I thought you might be a normal person."

"Normal?" said Corwin, "no, nobody that Agatha knows is normal." He glanced mischievously at her. "Do you know why she really doesn't want me to disappear?"

"Be quiet, Corwin."

"Arr! The treasure! She's been harping at me ever since I died to find my treasure!"

"It's not a treasure and you're not a pirate, Corwin. Let's get back to the car. Doctor, what do you suggest we do with the ashes? Something permanent, where Corwin isn't going to get accidentally flushed down a toilet someday."

"Can't we just bury the ashes, or stick them in an urn in a mausoleum?"

Agatha shook her head. "That would raise the question of how I knew where his body was. My abilities as an Oracle have put me in a position of having information that I could only have if I was prescient or guilty. Which side do you think the law puts their faith in? His ashes must be permanently interred, but completely anonymous."

He thought about it as they walked back to the car, but in the back of his mind, he was wondering if he was the patsy destined to trigger some curse while the leader ran off with the pirate treasure, whatever it was. "It's ash and mud. Mix it with some clay, bake it, and you'd have a nice brick," he suggested, "and the brick could be part of a building. You can't get much more permanent than that."

Agatha looked thoughtfully at him. "I wouldn't want him in some stranger's building." She took a breath, then said, "The clinic has brick walls, doesn't it?"

Hamilton said, "Ha, ha, ha! I knew this was going someplace I wouldn't like. No, your pet ghost is *not* going to be haunting the clinic."

They climbed into the car. Corwin shrank down to a few inches in height and hovered near his jar in the back seat. Agatha said, "There's a craft shop on Sepulveda about a mile from here. They'll have red clay."

After a minute of driving in silence, she said, "Any ideas what to do with Corwin's brick, then, once we have it?"

"We could drop it off at any number of construction sites," Hamilton suggested.

"Bricks are notorious for being stolen from construction sites," Agatha said. "And I'd have to buy the place once it was built. My finances are somewhat limited."

"An Oracle, huh? If you can see the future, why aren't you rich?"

Agatha sighed. "It doesn't work that way. I can't see the future when I want. I can see it when it's important for me to see it. I'm just not sure what that trigger is. Sometimes I get irritatingly vague hints at possible futures that require a bit of imaginative interpretation."

"Like a horoscope," he said.

"Hopefully a little more useful than that. On very rare occasions, someone can ask me something and I'll just know, out of nowhere, what the answer is." She looked out the window of the car. "That has some advantages and some disadvantages. I've been threatened a number of times when someone wanted an answer I just didn't have or gave an answer they didn't want to hear."

"What did you do? I mean, how do you get out of situations like that?" Hamilton asked.

"I'm an Oracle. There's always a way out. Not always convenient, but there's always a way." She was fretting with her purse again. Hamilton dropped the questioning. Agatha pointed. "Turn there. There's the store."

They picked up the clay and some cardboard and tape to hold the shape while it dried. Returning to the car, Agatha suggested, "The building next to the clinic is brick, too. There was an army surplus store there a couple of years back, but it's been vacant ever since. We can put the brick there."

Hamilton drummed his fingers on the steering wheel, still feeling like he was getting roped into something he didn't understand. "The ghost…Corwin, he's going to be tied to the building his ashes are in, right?"

"Of course," Agatha said.

"So he won't be drifting around the clinic moaning and shaking chains all night, right?"

"Of course not."

"So all I have to do is break in, chisel out an existing brick, slap some new mortar on Corwin's brick, slip it in, and sneak back out, right? Then your ghost is all 'healed'."

"If you do it tomorrow night, I can arrange for someone to get us inside the building."

"Great. I'll bake Corwin into the brick tonight." And close this case tomorrow. He looked over at Agatha, wondering if that would be the last he'd see of her. Probably not. She was still hiding something, using him somehow. He shook his head.

***

The next evening found Hamilton and Agatha at the back door of the vacant brick building adjacent to the clinic. The two buildings shared a common wall between them, and it was obvious from the brick used that they were built at the same time. The back door of the building was painted steel, and a dinged and rusty roll-up door stood a few feet away facing a narrow cement loading dock. It looked as old and rickety as the building and rattled lightly whenever a breeze came by. Higher up on the building he could see dirty windows with cobwebs arcing across the panes. The building had been empty for quite some time.

Agatha glanced at her cell phone. "She'll be here soon."

A dark-blue Prius arrived after a couple of minutes and parked next to the building. As the driver climbed out of the car, Hamilton immediately recognized the long, straight, black hair. Her eyes were hidden in shadow. "You again," he said.

"Why, hello, doctor," she said softly. "You seem to be getting into a lot of trouble lately."

"Yeah, thanks to…" he waved a hand around as though to encompass confusion, ending with a snort.

She walked up to the metal door of the building, pulled some small tools from a back pocket, and opened the door after only a few seconds. "There you go. Lock up when you're done!" She gave a little wave, got in her car, and drove away on battery power, silent as death.

Agatha watched her drive away. "You know her already?"

"She came by to pick up a body the other night. At the clinic."

"You sold a body?" Agatha whispered, horrified.

"Actually, I think she was still alive when that woman took her. Raoul said she was a Hunter."

"Oh!" Her eyes widened, and she backed through the doorway, her glance darting up and down the alleyway.

He stepped in behind her carrying a small bag; an old visiting doctor's bag a patient had gifted to him in Sudan. A perfect size, as it turned out, to carry one brick and a few mortar tools.

It was dark inside. Hamilton pulled a small LED flashlight out of the bag and examined the room in which they found themselves. The perimeter walls were red brick and the inner walls were drywall and two-by-four frames, a temporary structure to divide the wide space into smaller rooms. Through an open door in the rear room, they could see the front of the store nearly sixty feet away, the glass panes painted over with white paint. Two raised alcoves behind the front windows, normally for displays, were stacked with empty boxes and some wooden scraps. The length of the dusty wooden strip flooring was interrupted by an old wooden stairway with a broken handrail clinging to one wall. Debris from the surplus store littered the floor. Stained clothing that might be doubling as a rat's nest lay in the corner of the room, and a clothing rack lay on its side in front of a scratched wooden door. "Probably to keep the zombies out," Hamilton mumbled to himself.

"What?" Agatha said.

Hamilton smiled but didn't reply. He lifted the clothing rack and pushed it out of the way, then opened the door that it had been blocking. There was a large walk-in closet with dark wooden paneling and wainscoting. An old olive-green coat hung on a hook next to a few dozen wire coat hangers. Hamilton grunted, looking around the small closet, thinking that this one room might be salvageable.

In the front half of the building, they located a small bathroom, but both the toilet and the sink were missing.

Hamilton squatted down and tapped the floor.

"What is it?" Agatha asked.

"Probably asbestos tiles. These old buildings have a lot of that kind of stuff in them."

"Did they install that so the bathroom floor didn't catch on fire?" Agatha said.

Hamilton laughed. "You think Corwin is going to like being tied to this place?"

"This place is a dump. I'm being banished to warehouse hell." Corwin said from behind him.

"I'll visit you regularly, Corwin," Agatha said.

"And now threats!"

Hamilton sighed. They picked a spot where the mortar already looked like it was beginning to soften and crumble and loosened a brick with a small chisel and hammer. One came out after a few minutes of chipping and tapping. Their new brick was several shades of crimson darker than the existing worn bricks, but it filled the hole reasonably well. Hamilton mixed up some Quikrete and cemented the brick in place. As he stepped back from his work, Agatha suddenly clutched her head and moaned, "Ahhhh! Ah, Corwin, you son of a bitch."

Corwin laughed and spun around in the air. "Twenty years you left my body under that house!"

"Twenty years," she said, "that money of yours has been waiting in a trust. And now I see it! Now I see it! Why did my Oracle abilities fail me until now? And why didn't the damned lawyer holding the trust try to find me?"

"The trust was written very carefully, dear Agatha, so that only an Oracle could find it. It was always written for you, my dear, but the instructions for the lawyers were to retain the funds without seeking you out until you came for it, and not until you had put my remains in a final, secure resting place, since I knew you would find me no matter how I died." He floated next to the brick and laughed maniacally, but theatrically, his hands crooked like grasping claws, the way you'd expect a ghost to do. *Very vaudeville,* Hamilton thought. "What I didn't expect, exactly, was to be murdered, or that you would refrain from revealing my corpse to the police for fear of being accused of the deed."

"Oh, Corwin," she said. She shuffled some of the broken mortar around with her toe. "Why couldn't you just have stayed alive?"

"And part of my trust accents the 'secure resting place,' which I had always assumed was going to be some gravesite or mausoleum. Not a wall in an old building, though I guess it will serve. You will have to buy it, of course."

"I can't afford…how much money is in that trust?"

"Enough. Still, I suspect you will need a renter, too."

They both looked at Hamilton.

He rubbed his forehead. "I knew I was getting sucked into something," he said. "I need to get one thing straight. You said you were murdered, right?"

Corwin nodded.

"So did they catch the guy?" Hamilton asked.

"I don't know," Corwin replied. "After I died, I lost all my memories of who did it and how it was done. Or why."

"So he says," mumbled Agatha irritably. "I think

he's still hiding something, just like the damned treasure."

"Not a treasure, my dear. An inheritance."

She growled.

Hamilton looked back and forth between them and frowned. "So there isn't any chance that some guy is going to come looking for Corwin's ghost to finish what he started, right? No reason for someone to pursue a post-mortem vendetta?"

Agatha shrugged. "My Oracle abilities have seen nothing to that effect."

Corwin's ghost bobbed up and down. "Whoever murdered me has not, to my knowledge, ever returned to the site of their wrongdoing. They must have been satisfied with my death, for whatever reason they had."

"How would you know if you don't know who the murderer is?"

Corwin shrugged. "I would think I would have at least recognized the fellow lurking about on occasion, if I had known him. And there has been no one around the house from my prior circle of acquaintances."

"Hmm," Hamilton muttered. "So as far as you're concerned, there's no pressing need for you to seek vengeance against this unknown attacker. No personal grudge. Correct me if I'm wrong, but aren't ghosts supposed to disappear once their issues are put to rest? Go to their final resting place?"

Agatha raised one eyebrow sharply and glared at Corwin. "That's a very good question, Corwin. Why do you linger so?"

"Perhaps something will lead me to my killer. Who knows? It's an unresolved mystery," he said. "Perhaps I'm stuck here forever."

"Maybe it's worth a little research," Hamilton suggested.

Corwin seemed agitated. "Maybe I like it here, and don't want to do a little research, and get sent to…to who knows where. Let's just drop it, okay?"

Hamilton glanced at Agatha, who seemed to be stiffening up like an oak board, perhaps preparing to engage in more verbal swordplay with Corwin, but she opened and then shut her mouth without making a sound.

"Fine, Corwin," Hamilton said. "We'll drop it. For now."

Corwin glared angrily at the two of them, then turned into a fine gray mist and retreated to his brick, ending the conversation.

Hamilton shot Agatha a look, and she returned it, grim-faced. Whatever Corwin was hiding had to be resolved. It was clear that neither of them was prepared to drop it.

***

Back at Hamilton's apartment, curiosity sent him to his laptop where he Googled Corwin Abercrombie, stage magician, and found a brief Wikipedia entry about him. He went by the poster-filling name of 'Captivating Corwin, Master of Magic'. There was a picture of a marquee poster with Corwin looking dark and mysterious, but dressed much like Corwin the ghost, which explained his gaudy taste in deadwear. Just as Agatha had mentioned, he wasn't very well known, but then had a sudden surge in popularity with a new stage trick where he flew around over the audience. There was conjecture that he'd stolen the idea from another magician, Ivan the Illusionist, who did something very similar in his own show. Corwin disappeared two shows after he started flying, then Ivan's show picked back up. Then, he too disappeared. Neither magician was ever heard from again, and the secret of the flying magicians was apparently forever lost.

Hamilton leaned back in his office chair and tapped his fingertips on the desktop. It was definitely a mystery. So why wouldn't Corwin talk about it? Had he really stolen something from Ivan the Illusionist?

He wanted to grill Corwin about it, but it was late, the building was locked up, and until Agatha bought the building, they'd have to pick the lock to get in. He would just have to wait.

Chapter 6 - Chopra Gets a Soul

Hamilton put down his pen and stood up at his desk in his unfinished office, stretching his back, tired from filling out the day's paperwork. Pembrook Clinic was closing for the night. In the quiet office, he heard MacDonald and Olgebright talking as they left, the bell above the door jingling. In an exam room, he could hear Madesh Chopra finishing up with his last patient, discussing a prescription. Hamilton walked toward the lobby, where Carol was just getting ready to lock up for the evening.

A small, nervous man entered the front door.

"Can I see Dr. Hamilton, please?" the man said. He had a thick Spanish accent and wore a baseball cap with a hoody over the top of it. *Day worker,* Hamilton thought. One of the guys that hung out in front of the Home Depot waiting for someone to come by looking for temporary laborers. The man pushed the hoody back, took his cap off, and brushed a tangle of black hair from his forehead.

"We're actually closed for the day. If it's an emergency…" Carol said. She glanced over to Chopra, who ushered another patient out the lobby toward the door. Chopra continued for her, "para una emergencia, vaya a

Memorial Hospital o llame al 911." His Spanish wasn't perfect, but this was one phrase all the doctors had memorized.

"¿Dr. Hamilton no está aquí?"

Hamilton overheard from his back office and stuck his head out "I'm here. What's the problem? ¿Cómo puedo ayudarte?"

The small man glanced anxiously between Chopra and Carol, then, continuing in Spanish, said, "My friend in the car out front…his soul has been stolen."

Hamilton sighed. Chopra became rigid, his lips tightening. Carol said, "Can you guys handle this? I've got a date."

"Go ahead, Carol. We'll see you tomorrow. Madesh, I can handle this if you want to take off."

"I will stay for a moment. You may need help."

"Really, take off. I can handle it."

"I will stay."

Hamilton bit his lip, looking back and forth between Chopra and the nervous man, hoping that this was just a normal guy with a delusion, but if it wasn't, then Chopra would be in for a surprise. Somehow, he'd have to work around that. In Spanish, he asked, "Let's see your friend."

The three of them walked out to the car, parked near the front of the clinic. Hamilton looked in the back seat. Another Hispanic male was lying there prone, mouth gaping, his eyes staring unfocused at the ceiling of the car, one leg folded beneath the other. His skin looked ashen.

Hamilton opened the door to the car, leaned over the man, and checked his pulse. "Pulse is about fifty. Skin is dry, body temperature seems cool. Breathing slow." He pulled out a penlight and looked at the man's eyes. "Eyes dilate okay. I can't tell if his soul is missing." He looked up at Chopra to see how he would react.

Chopra ignored his statement. He opened the opposite car door and leaned over the man, cursorily examining him. He stood, shaking his head. "I think I've seen something like this before. Let's take him inside."

They fetched a wheel chair from the clinic and positioned it curbside, dropping one of the arms and setting the brakes. The three of them struggled to move his limp body from the narrow confines of the car to the chair. They rolled him into the clinic and into an exam room, then transferred him to the exam table. His arms flopped off the sides.

"Now," Hamilton asked the other man, "what's your name?"

"Carlos Hernandez."

Hamilton looked puzzled for a second, as though struggling to remember. "I've heard that name before."

"It's like John Smith," Chopra said in English. "You will hear it a lot, as long as immigration laws are as they are."

"Ah." He nodded. "All right. Carlos, why do you think your friend's soul is gone?"

Carlos crumpled his hat in his hands. "I...I made a deal...I borrowed money from a Macachati to pay rent for our two families. The Macachati said there would be no interest, but if I failed to pay him on time, then Jose's soul would be taken for payment. I...I thought that its soul magic was not real, a child's story. And I knew that the foreman would pay us today anyway, but a new man was there who did not know us and refused to pay our wages. When the Macachati came to collect his money, I could not pay him. Jose fell and I could not wake him. I had not told him what I had done. I did not tell him!" he cried.

Hamilton glanced at Chopra and shrugged his shoulders, at a loss. Souls. Stitching up supernatural creatures was one thing, finding lost souls quite another. After a minute, Carlos' broken sobs subsided.

"The Macachati are not to be trifled with," Chopra said. He wouldn't look at Hamilton when he spoke, only Carlos. "Dr. Hamilton, you may wish to leave now. This might be out of your realm of comfort."

"He asked for me," Hamilton said, wondering how much Chopra knew about this business.

Chopra's brow wrinkled as he frowned and scratched his neck. "Carlos, why did you ask for Dr. Hamilton?"

"When I asked my grandmother for help, she told me to seek out Hamilton. That he might be able to help."

"And why did your grandmother think Hamilton would know how to deal with lost souls?"

"She knows many secret things. She passed across the barrier twenty years ago."

"Your grandmother is dead?" Chopra asked.

Carlos nodded.

Chopra looked critically at Hamilton. "You have dealings with ghosts?"

Hamilton rubbed his neck and looked up at the ceiling. "One," Hamilton said. "From a couple of days ago."

Chopra rolled back and forth on his heals. "You know about the dog?"

"Yeah."

"You have barely been here a week." He shook his head. "Do you have any idea what you are getting into?"

"Not a damned clue. I wouldn't mind some help," Hamilton said.

Madesh Chopra sighed heavily. "They drove me from my practice in San Dimas and threatened my family with physical harm. I thought I would be far enough to be safe…"

"The Macachati?"

"Yes. In the Aztec culture, they were spirits of the dead, but in modern Hispanic cultures, they are small demons that feed upon spirits." Chopra seemed tired, slouched shoulders bent as if under a heavy yoke. "When I started helping the farm workers there…"

"You can help us?" Carlos interrupted, hope lighting his eyes.

"Possibly," Chopra said. "Is your friend Jose a heavy drinker?"

Carlos regarded the unresponsive Jose, as though asking for permission to tell, then slowly nodded. "Yes, he is."

"That weakens the link between the soul and the body," Chopra continued. "It makes the work of the Macachati easier. A strong spirit link cannot be broken. By strengthening that link, the soul can be brought back to the body. If there is enough of it left. How long ago did this occur?"

"Today," Carlos said.

Chopra nodded. "Good. There is little chance that they've fed on it or that the soul has been used in a device."

"A device?" Hamilton asked.

"A tool. They have things that can be powered from souls." He gazed at the floor in thought. "Unpleasant things. But they sell souls and barter between themselves. This I have learned. A soul will not degrade for many days after it has been stolen because it has not been marketed or evaluated yet. At least, it is unlikely." He turned toward the door of the exam room. "I think I have the ingredients for an injection that should return the soul to its body, stealing it back from the Macachati demon. I kept some handy from my stint in San Dimas, though I never truly expected to use it again."

"You have it here?" Hamilton asked.

"In my personal fridge. Behind the Pepsi. I'll fetch it." Chopra left the exam room and returned in less than a minute with a small syringe. There was less than a milliliter of dark fluid in it.

"So how is this supposed to work?" Hamilton asked.

"Pain brings the soul back. Alcohol dampens the connection to your soul, while pain creates thick bungee cords to it, jerking you back to the bridge from which you leapt." He smiled grimly, tipping the needle up and squeezing the plunger to excise the air. A dark drop appeared at the tip. "This is mostly tarantula hawk venom, from a wasp that lives here in California, plus a stabilizer. This wasp is purported to have the most painful venom in the world, guaranteed to make you scream, but the effect only lasts around three minutes. It is also, oddly, not harmful to humans, except for potential damage from flailing around or biting your tongue." Chopra nodded toward a towel on the counter. "If you would be so good as to stuff that in our patient's mouth before I inject this, then perhaps the police won't come by to see who we are torturing." He considered Carlos. "You may wish to wait outside for this."

Carlos shook his head and didn't move. His squeezed his crumpled hat, gazing at Jose.

"Very well," Chopra said. He swabbed an area on Jose's upper arm and jabbed the needle into the muscle tissue, injecting the venom, then put the expended syringe on the counter. Returning to Jose, he grabbed his left arm and directed Hamilton to grab the other.

"How long does this take?"

"The Macachati will sense the new tension pulling at the stolen soul. It will fight it and it will lose. It may take a minute."

"Is it going to know who did the job?"

"It will know…"

At this moment Jose began to scream, the towel in his mouth dampening most of the sound. His back arched as he writhed. Hamilton and Chopra kept hold of his arms as they jerked convulsively. For three long minutes, Jose howled while his wide eyes stared forward like he was standing at the gates of Hell. Sweat covered his forehead. Hamilton glanced over at Carlos whose eyes were squeezed shut, his skin also glistening with sweat. He was mumbling something over and over to himself, but it couldn't be heard over the din of Jose. Finally, Jose's body relaxed, his muffled cries fading into a fast pant. His eyes darted around the exam room until they came to rest on Carlos.

Carlos cried into his hands. Whether it was with joy, shame, or relief, none could tell.

"As I started to say," Chopra continued, "it will know where the soul came from and who made the deal. It will come back to Carlos and ask him who took back the soul. Then it will come for me or those close to me."

Hamilton frowned. "So you'll have to move again."

"Or fight. There are other possibilities." He turned to Carlos. "You have a couple of choices you can make. The Macachati, the little demon, will come back to you. You can leave this city. The Macachati are fairly limited, physical creatures, so they aren't very good at tracking people. That might keep them from finding you. Or me. A second option is that you can kill the Macachati. Despite being demons, they have a corporeal form and can be hurt. A baseball bat, knife, gun, whatever, will end the pursuit as certainly as moving away. There would be no legal repercussions as the body always disappears once the thing is dead."

Carlos nodded slowly and thoughtfully. He said, "I do not think we wish to move."

Chopra smiled grimly and pulled a plastic case out of his lab-coat pocket. He opened it. "This case contains two more doses of the venom. If they are preying on your community, now you know how to use them. I have a source for this, so if you need more, let me know. Also, remember the name of the insect; the tarantula hawk. There are many tarantula populations in Santa Maria and Santa Margarita north of here, and this is where the wasps can be found. Tell your friends that this is a way they can fight the

Macachati."

***

After they helped a wobbly Jose back to Carlos' car, they returned to the clinic, locked the front door and turned off the lobby lights, retiring to Chopra's small office. "So, now you know," said Chopra. "When I saw you with that gold coin, I knew that their community had touched you, but I didn't know if you realized it or that they would continue to seek your services. When I came to this clinic, I hoped I had left all that behind."

"It would seem that they've adopted me," Hamilton said.

Chopra sighed. "I must admit, the gold is nice, but the evil you encounter exists at a whole new level, personified by the creatures you must deal with."

Chopra surprised Hamilton by pulling a bottle of Glenmorangie from his locked desk. He tipped a shot into Hamilton's empty coffee mug, while pouring himself a double-dose into a clear whisky glass. Hamilton sipped lightly, savoring the taste of the Scotch in his mouth before swallowing.

"When I was working in Sudan, I had a friend smuggle me some eighteen-year-old Glenmorangie inside a bottle labeled 'disinfectant' just so no one would steal it. It made it to the health center where I worked, but the sad thing is, our supplies were so stretched that I actually ended up using a lot of it as disinfectant." He shook his head sadly and took another sip. Chopra chuckled. After a moment, Hamilton said, "Speaking of evil, have you run into any Hunters before?"

"Hunters? I'm not familiar with them."

Hamilton explained his encounter with the invisible man, Raoul and the woman wearing the human skin. Chopra shuddered. "Every time I come into contact with their community, there is some new horror," he said.

"We've just come to accept drug addicts, wife beating, and gunshot wounds as normal, is all. There's plenty of horror in the human community."

Chopra swirled his Scotch in his glass with his nose over the rim, breathing in the fumes. "I suppose so. At least I know how to treat those things."

"Speaking of which, how did you ever learn that wasp venom could bring a soul back to a body?"

"Hmm. That's a bit of a story." He put his glass on his desk and folded his hands together. "I think when I first encountered a soulless person, there were rumors that sometimes, if you punch them or slap them hard enough and often enough, or break an arm, the soul would come back. There were some very strange rationalizations for this, depending on the affected person, but I was able to find the common ground. That common ground was pain. A lot of pain. So I began to look for chemicals used for torture and such, things that wouldn't damage a person, but would cause an agony to the body so extreme that the soul could not avoid feeling it, even though departed. Luckily, I stumbled upon the wasp; severe pain without damage. I began advertising in the Santa Maria Times for fresh samples of the wasp. Two dollars for dead ones, and five dollars for live ones. From my first ad, I gained only ten dead wasps. They are not as common as I would like. From that, I produced ten samples of the anti-Macachati injections. I maintained the contacts I made for future needs. The venom worked unexpectedly well, although I wasn't prepared for the screaming."

"You need an EpiPen version," Hamilton suggested. "You could be rich."

Chopra laughed, but Hamilton saw that he was thinking about it. They were both lost in their own thoughts for a minute while they quietly nursed their whiskeys.

"I have a theory about souls," Hamilton said.

"Do you?"

Hamilton nodded. "It's a bit mechanistic. But if we are to deal with the supernatural world, we'll need to create models that describe that world so that we can provide remedies. Like 19th century doctors, we should be ready to dissect the corpses so that we can understand how they function. Figuratively, anyway."

"Raiding the supernatural graveyards, so to speak."

Hamilton chuckled. "Hopefully not."

"So tell me this theory of yours about souls," Chopra primed.

"I think that the human mind learns continuously from the time it's born, and the brain is a map of everything it's learned. That's what we think of as the soul. When a person dies, there's some transformation of the electrical pattern in the brain that defines who you are that maps onto some other substrate, something we haven't defined yet, something alternate universe with its own rules of physics. So the mind can maintain its pattern outside the brain."

"That's not substantially different from the conventional religious view. You are merely trying to quantify it by comparing it to other objects."

"That's how we define everything, isn't it? Mass is only understood when we compare it to another mass. Likewise the plethora of subatomic particles; all their properties are defined based on how they react with other particles; they have no self-evident properties otherwise," Hamilton said. "The conventional religious view is that the soul has a unique existence without requiring a relation to anything else. I'm saying we can define it based on its relation with known objects, like discovering the shape of a dinosaur by looking at stone fossils."

"An interesting thought. If we could define the supernatural world in your terms then, with some logical structure, you think it would help our profession."

"Exactly."

"Well, Dr. Hamilton, we can only wish for good luck in learning such things. For me, my glass is empty, and I'm more than ready to go home."

Chapter 7 – Gordon's Golden Clinic.

A week later, Hamilton tossed a handful of gold coins on Michael Gordon's big oak desk. Hamilton watched his eyes carefully to see how he reacted, but Gordon remained very still, eyes slightly widening, locked on the coins. Finally, he picked up one of the coins and examined it closely. "Gold coins," he said.

"Yeah," Hamilton said. "People keep paying me with gold coins. It's a little problematic since they aren't regular patients and they haven't filled out any forms—I can't just turn these in to the billing department and tell them there's no paperwork to go with the money."

"These patients—is there something odd about them that they wouldn't want their data recorded? Their medical issues?" He looked at Hamilton with one of the blandest, disinterested looks Hamilton had ever set eyes on. It certainly wasn't the reaction he expected. Gordon knew something.

Hamilton reached out and tapped a coin. "This was for a bullet in a dog's leg. These here were for some stitches in a guy's head after he was mugged and helping him with his rare skin condition. This one here was supposedly for lower back pain, but it turned out that the lady just wanted help moving something. And other stuff."

"Those sound like…very mundane cases." He leaned back in his chair, locking his hands together over his stomach. "I wouldn't think there was any reason the patients would insist on anonymity in such situations or pay with gold coins."

They sat and stared at each other for a good half-minute, waiting each other out, Hamilton tapping the desk top with the edge of a coin. "They also seem to prefer coming in the back door of the clinic," he added.

Gordon leaned forward, frowning, and put his elbows on the desk. "Matt, do you believe in the supernatural?"

"Not per se. Werewolves, ghosts, invisible people, sure, but I think there's a logical explanation behind all of it. Nothing supernatural."

"Ah! Now we get somewhere. Being candid is so difficult when you're concerned that someone else will think you're crazy. You've met some people from the community."

"The community? So you know already."

He shrugged broadly. "I've had suspicions. They lay low, keep to themselves, and stay away from places like hospitals and clinics for the obvious reasons." He sighed. "I am not disinclined to accept the extra funds, even if the currency has to be laundered somehow." He picked up a gold coin and let it clunk to the desk's surface. "If they have adopted you as their pet doctor, we will need to create a space isolated from the normals, perhaps cordon off the front of the clinic from the rear. At least add a soundproof door."

"I thought you needed the extra space for the regular clinic."

"We do." He sat back again, thinking, then raised a finger. "Now that I think of it, the building next door is vacant. We could probably rent it from the owner and add a door between the two buildings. I believe they have a common wall. That would give us plenty of space for both the normal clinic and the "backside" clinic."

Hamilton had to smile. *Agatha,* he thought, *you wily Oracle, you. I never had to say a word. You must have planned this from the beginning.*

"Also, since you're already working with unusual cases, I have a cousin with an issue you might consider looking at that's a little exceptional."

"As long as it's about stitches and age spots, I'm your guy," Hamilton said.

"She's possessed," Gordon said. "Exorcism has had no effect, and since you seem to believe that everything has a logical physical cause, I'd like you to examine her. See if you can 'logic out' the demon." He pushed the gold coins back to Hamilton. "Keep these for now. You might actually have need of them if you're dealing much with this crowd. I'll have to figure out some way to make the finances work. It's going to be hard to rationalize the expense of the new building unless it's generating income that I can actually declare."

"What if we pay for it with gold? Keep separate books?"

"I doubt that the owner of the building would go for something that fishy."

"I'm fairly sure she would."

Gordon's eyebrows lifted. "You know this person?"

"She had me rescue a ghost last week. Before that, I never met her. She put in an offer on the building a few days ago."

"This seems unusually convenient for her." He rubbed his chin thoughtfully.

"She's also an oracle. So the ghost says."

"Ah. An oracle. Someone who predicts the future in the most ambiguous way possible?"

Hamilton chuckled. "Something like that."

"Hmm. Well, I'll have my uncle schedule an appointment for his daughter—the possessed kid—and we'll see about getting that door installed and finish one of the new exam rooms before then. In the meantime, maybe we can have you work a split shift, afternoon in the front clinic, and evenings in the back, after everyone else has gone home. You can shut off the front area lights and continue to use the back door for patient access. The community needs medical care just as much as anyone else. Probably more."

"Okay. I'll get a safe-deposit box for these." Hamilton scooped up the coins into his skin-bag. Gordon's eyes widened.

"Is that…an invisible bag?"

Hamilton grinned and held it up, jingling the coins hidden inside. "You don't want to know." He turned and exited the office, leaving a mystified Gordon behind.

***

Hamilton sat on the rear cement stoop with the alley door of the clinic cracked open, staring without seeing at the garish urban graffiti and toppled trash cans. A cat meowed not far from him. The clinic had closed for the evening and he'd poured himself a shot of twelve year-old Glenlivet, nursing it slowly as he considered what life had dumped in his lap.

How big was this supernatural community? How was it that they survived in a city without being noticed? Sure, the oracle, werewolves, invisibles, even the bloody hunters, could pass themselves off as normal humans, but how about non-humans? The ones that couldn't hide? Giants and dragons?

He swirled the small dram of whiskey at the bottom of his tumbler. Maybe there weren't any. Maybe only humanoid creatures could survive close scrutiny in the city. Either way, did he really want to be the guy that monsters went to when they caught an interdimensional cold? Or ate someone that gave them a tummy ache? Could he just run away from the problem and start a new practice in a new city? He sipped his whiskey. He didn't like running away from anything. And if they really needed a doctor of the unusual, well…

A drunk turned into the short alley and stumbled toward him, taking awkward steps as he approached. Hamilton wondered if the man had smelled the Scotch before he turned the corner. Maybe he'd have to get another glass, he thought, smiling. Then again, maybe this was another freak out to finish the job from the other night. Come to fetch their skin back.

He stood up on the stoop and stepped toward the door. The stranger whispered, "Dr. Hamilton?"

Tumbler in one hand, bottle in the other, he turned

to examine the man. Overcoat, broad-rimmed fedora, poor-fitting shoes twisted at an odd angle and loose slacks. Eyes hidden under the brim of the hat.

"We're closed," Hamilton said. "Can it wait until tomorrow?"

The man looked up and down the alley. "I'd rather not be out in the light, where someone might see me better."

Hamilton let out a long and exasperated sigh. "What?"

"What?"

"What's your problem?"

"You've not much of a bedside manner."

Hamilton laughed dryly. "Long day," he said. He pitched back the last sip of whiskey, then waited for the man to say something.

The man looked a little embarrassed. "So, I've got this itch."

Hamilton started laughing again, then got himself under control. The man frowned. "I'm sorry," Hamilton said. "That was rude. What are you? Are you human?"

The man lifted his hat and exposed two small horns. "A satyr, if you please." The satyr's penetrating, vivid green eyes riveted Hamilton glistening like a spring meadow in morning dew. Almost hypnotic. He shook his head to clear it.

"A satyr with an STD?" he asked.

The satyr shrugged ruefully.

"Do you drink Scotch?"

"I'm a satyr. I'll drink anything. But I do appreciate a good Scotch."

Hamilton nodded and waved with the bottle of Glenlivet. "Come on in. I'll see what I can do for you."

After a quick exam, Hamilton issued the satyr some antibiotics and a three-pack of sample condoms. "If the antibiotics don't seem to be helping after three days, come back in and we'll do a culture. But they should clear you up."

"Thank you, Doctor," the satyr said. He didn't leave immediately, but slowly sipped his Scotch instead. "If you don't mind me asking, what made you decide to become a doctor for the supernatural community?"

"Decide? I didn't decide. I pulled a bullet out of a dog, and then it was decided for me." He snorted and poured himself another shot, then sloshed a bit more into the satyr's glass, happy to have the company.

"A dog?"

"A werewolf, I guess."

"Ah." He sipped, closing his eyes. "Well, don't imagine that your services do not go unappreciated, Doctor Hamilton. We are all part of the same community, even if we aren't all human. I hope you stay."

Hamilton stared into his glass. "Not everyone wants me here," he said.

The satyr sighed. "There are those who hunt us down for their own reasons. To use us, enslave us, or just kill us out of their hatred for the unknown, hatred for everything that's different. Do not think that you are alone, Doctor. As you help us, we will help you."

Chapter 8 - The Secret Door

Construction on the door between the two buildings began shortly after Agatha Noone and Michael Gordon signed the lease contract.

Gordon described what he wanted to Vince Brogan, the general contractor, the same one who'd been working on the existing clinic construction. They stood amidst a pile of debris inside Agatha's building.

"The door goes here," Gordon pointed, "in the wall between the buildings, as near the rear as possible. I want a closed room built adjacent to the door, so it appears to have no access to the rest of the building. A secret door…"

"Wait, wait. Hold it right there," Vince interrupted. "We can't do secret doors. This is a permitted installation. Everything goes on the plan, all the details. We're not some fly-by-night outfit."

"I'd be willing to pay an extra $500 above your standard costs," Gordon said.

The man chewed his lip and stared silently at Gordon, considering. Gordon fidgeted.

"A thousand, then," Gordon said, breaking first.

"Two thousand," Vince replied instantly.

"Fifteen hundred, and keep the modification off the plans."

"Done." Vince said. He grinned and shook Gordon's hand.

"Did I mention that I need the inside of the new building fitted with some offices and exam rooms, too? On the sly?" He held onto Vince's hand.

Vince's smile disappeared. "That…will cost a lot more."

Gordon watched Vince's face twist as he tried to figure out how he was going to retrofit the inside of a building without being seen or heard by the inspectors, while simultaneously coming up with a bloated cost estimate for the job.

"I hope we can work something out," Gordon said, and wondered just how much gold Hamilton had stashed away.

They discussed the design. From the side of the original clinic, there'd be a locked door labeled "supplies". Inside, it would look just like a supply room, with shelves and boxes and cabinets. As Vince explained it, anyone who put a strong magnet next to a certain spot on the rear wall would toggle a latch allowing the rear wall to swing out a few feet, thus gaining access to the rest of the leased building. There were no levers or buttons to accidentally discover. The magnet could be hidden away almost anywhere in the room.

Two days later, the construction crew added to the general cacophony of the ongoing effort to add offices and exam rooms by cutting a hole in the brick wall for the new doorway.

MacDonald, who'd been kept out of the planning process, wore a surgical mask to keep from choking on the dust and suspiciously examined the doorway. "What's this for, then?" he asked Chopra.

"Storage," Chopra said. "We're renting some room in the vacant building next door so we can have more space here for offices."

"Why not rent the whole building? It's vacant, isn't it?"

Chopra rubbed his thumb and forefinger together. "Expensive per square foot. The board doesn't want to pay for more than we need."

MacDonald glanced over at Hamilton. "We could always just get rid of dead weight. That would free up some space."

"Piss off, MacDonald." Hamilton had heard it before.

MacDonald faced him. "You come in late every day and then hang around after the clinic closes. I've been watching you. I don't know why Gordon hasn't tossed you out on your ass already."

"Maybe he likes working with people who aren't dicks," Hamilton replied. MacDonald flushed red.

Chopra frowned. "Down, boys. Don't you both have patients to attend to?"

As if on cue, Carol stuck her head back in the construction area and said, "Dr. MacDonald? Your two o'clock appointment is here."

MacDonald gave Hamilton one last glare before he left.

Hamilton chewed on a knuckle. "Even after the door's installed, MacDick will be a problem. If he sees one of us go in there and not come out for an hour or two, he's going to figure it out."

Chopra shrugged. "We'll just have to be very careful. Maybe we can use the back doors of both buildings to go in and out."

"That would look even more suspicious, going out into the alley all the time."

"Perhaps we could have Gordon assign you to the new building permanently. No running back and forth under MacDonald's prying eyes. Minimize the use of the secret door."

Hamilton nodded. "We might have to do that."

***

Construction went slowly in the new building. To keep the noise down, the workers used screws and screw guns instead of nails. They worked at the same time as Vince's other construction team on the other side of the wall so that the noise from that construction effort would blanket their own. They left work early each day so Hamilton could continue to treat the community, if any new patients came by.

Late one evening after the regular clinic closed, Agatha and Hamilton stood inside the new building, admiring the construction progress. Corwin hovered around, worried that his brick might be too close to the work area.

"We'll have to put something on the rear door so people stop rapping on the Pembrook's back door," Hamilton said. "Some kind of sign, like, 'Supernatural

Creatures Knock Here.'"

"Mark the door with a diamond shape," Agatha said. "Everybody knows what that means."

"Everybody but me, apparently," Hamilton said.

"It just means, 'we do business with the supernatural community.'"

"Why just a diamond? Why not a pentagram? Wouldn't that be more appropriate?" Hamilton said.

"Hmm." Agatha rubbed her chin as though deep in thought. "A dark alley with a mysterious door with a pentagram on it. Hmmmm."

"No need to be sarcastic, Agatha. So it's a crappy idea."

"Word of mouth might work well, too, of course. That is, after all, how you acquired your first few customers. Your…ah…someone is coming up the alley," Agatha said.

Hamilton glanced down at her. Her eyes were closed, one hand was splayed out in front of her as though fending off a breeze, and the other hand rested lightly on her chest.

"Is that pose for the rubes, or does it actually help you see things?" Hamilton asked.

She opened one eye and frowned at him. "Force of habit, I'm afraid. I sense that the man outside is looking at both the doors, unsure. Almost certainly a fresh customer for you."

Hamilton raised his eyebrows. He went to the back door, opened the deadbolt and cracked the door open. "Hi, can I help you?"

The man shuddered and scanned the alley nervously. "I hope so! Are you Dr. Hamilton?"

Chapter 9 – A Farewell to Arms

Hamilton brought the man in to one of the partially constructed shells of Backside's new exam rooms. They'd recently stocked a small white roll-around cabinet with some basic medical supplies, which was the only medical item to speak of in the room. "Sorry, we aren't furnished completely," he said. An understatement; besides the small cabinet, there were two folding chairs in the room that the construction workers had brought in, and a number of woodworking and drywall tools scattered around. The stranger's eyes darted suspiciously between a hand-saw and a drop cloth spread out on the floor. "I can pop next door for medical supplies if we need them," Hamilton said reassuringly. "What's your name?"

"Muh…my name is Gary Lumley. I—I wasn't even sure I should come here. First, I saw a normal doctor, but he wanted to take me in for observation, and then there were cops he was talking to, so I snuck out. Then I saw an herbal healer and she wouldn't get near me when she saw the infection, and then she sent me to a—a witch, and she said she'd never seen anything like it and she looked scared, and your name came up. She sent me here and told me to use the back door, so no one would see me go in. Is this like a secret lab?" he asked.

Gary Lumley sweated like a snowman on a summer day. Nervous, his eyes darting around the room, hands shaking. If Hamilton hadn't seen so much weirdness in the last few weeks, he would have been nervous himself. "Not very secret, apparently. What are your symptoms?" he asked.

The man pulled up the sleeve of his tee shirt. At the shoulder junction, there was a dark line, and at a break in the line, a dozen small tentacles writhed as though straining to reach the air. Hamilton involuntarily scooted his chair back a few inches. "I see."

"And look!" the man cried. He pulled up his other sleeve. A similar dark line, minus the writhing tentacles, circumscribed his shoulder joint. "There are lines on my legs, too! What is happening to me?"

Hamilton took a breath, pulled a cotton swab out of a cabinet drawer, and leaned in close to poke around the area. The tiny tentacles snatched the swab from his hand and started flailing it around wildly like a crazed conductor's baton. He grabbed it and carefully pulled it away from them, placing the swab in a sterile plastic baggie. "Nothing like this has ever manifested before, I take it."

"I don't think so. I would sure as hell remember if it had."

"How about family history? Anything you can't explain? A disappearing relative or something?"

"I'm afraid I don't have much to go on, there, doctor. A homeless man found me next to a burning house when I was a baby. His name was Robert Lumley, and he sort of raised me until Child Protective Services discovered me. I was five years old then. Robert died just after I turned ten. He told me once that there were a lot of shouting, angry people around the burning house. That was in Innsmouth, Massachusetts."

"That's a long way from California."

"This is where the jobs are," Lumley said. "And Innsmouth was a good place to leave."

"What have you tried to get rid of these, um, tentacles."

"I tried cutting one, but it hurt like hell. It's like they're a part of me," he whimpered.

"Let me take a look at this swab with a microscope and see what it tells me. Relax, and I'll be back. If you need something, talk to Agatha out on the loading dock. She can come get me."

He left the sparsely furnished exam room and headed toward the secret door between clinics. Agatha was reading a magazine, sitting in another folding chair. "If you need my help with anything, just let me know," she said.

Hamilton nodded his thanks, opened the panel, and stepped into the storage room, passing through to Pembrook Clinic. He headed down the dark hallway to their small lab room. Corwin appeared suddenly next to him, startling him.

"What are you doing over here?" Hamilton growled at him. "I thought you were confined to the other building."

"It's kind of all one building, now, for haunting purposes. Another odd case, Dr. Hamilton?"

"They're all odd. Why can't supernatural creatures get colds?" He entered the lab and sat down at the bench, then swabbed a slide, put a coverslip on it, and placed it under the microscope.

He turned on the light on the microscope, focused it, then memorized the major features of the cell. Looking up from the microscope, he pulled down a reference book and thumbed through it. "Hmm. Fairly normal cells. Kind of a primitive design, like early eukaryotes." He bookmarked a page in the book, scribbled notes in his personal notebook, then closed it and reached for a book on bacteria and primitive multicellular organisms. After five minutes, he was tapping a page thoughtfully.

"What have you found?" Corwin asked.

"Sponges. His cells most resemble sponge cells. Some shapechanging characteristics, but all the shapechangers have colonial cell arrangements, so that's not a surprise." He was looking at biological characteristics of sponges when a scream of undiluted horror came from the other building. Hamilton dropped his book and ran from the lab, back through the storage room, and nearly crashed into Agatha coming the other direction.

"Your patient is screaming," she said calmly.

"My arm!" Gary cried from the exam room, "My arm has come off!"

His arm crawled slowly across the floor, fingernails scratching at the linoleum, the wriggling tentacles at the other end of the arm trying to crawl the opposite direction, but with no discernable purpose or destination. Hamilton turned to look at the stump of Gary's shoulder, where a matching group of tentacles wiggled and closed in on each other, blending into a smooth surface that resembled raw muscle. No blood oozed from the stump. Gary cringed away from his own crawling arm.

Hamilton returned his attention to the arm, deep in thought. The thing began to change shape. It looked like a face was forming in the flesh near the shoulder stump. He wondered what sort of monster it might turn into, then remembered the book he'd just been studying.

"Augh!" Gary howled. "What is happening to me? He reached down to his upper thigh with his remaining hand and clutched at the tentacles that had suddenly manifested there. Hamilton could see them wiggling under his pants.

Gary panicked, but Hamilton calmly said, "I think I know what's going on."

Gary looked down hopefully at his crawling arm, and said, "You can reattach my arm?"

Hamilton bit his lip and shook his head. "You are budding, like a sponge does. I believe that you're giving birth."

Gary reached up with his remaining hand as he felt another tentacle punch through the skin of his other shoulder. Hamilton caught him as he fainted, laying him gently on a drop cloth on the floor.

"Agatha?"

Agatha was standing at the doorway, watching the bizarre scene. "Yes?"

"Can you sneak over a couple of cribs from the regular clinic's storage? Maybe some cardboard boxes and towels if we don't have enough. I think we'll have quintuplets on our hand here, pretty soon." He retrieved some scissors out of the cabinet and cut away Gary's pants, exposing the tentacles forcing their way through the skin at the leg joints. On the crawling arm, the swell of a head began to form. All the hair on Hamilton's body was standing on end and he wanted to run away screaming, but it wasn't every day you got to deliver quintuplets. Or quadruplets, depending on whether you counted Gary's original head and body as a child or the parent.

***

Two hours later, all the pieces of Gary were distributed in baskets, boxes, and bassinets. The original Gary had regained consciousness, grimacing as much of his own torso mass had redistributed to form tiny legs and tiny arms. His other disconnected limbs were working hard to reshape themselves into baby shapes. "Are you telling me," Gary asked, "that this is *normal* for me?" He waved his tiny legs and arms angrily. Quintuplets it is, thought Hamilton.

Hamilton hid a bemused smile behind a hand. "Apparently your cell structure is closer to that of sponges than humans. Sponges reproduce asexually by budding new colonies of cells. Other shapechangers can repurpose cells like this but reproduce via more conventional methods."

"Asexual, huh? That explains why I never found women—or men—particularly attractive."

"It is curious that every generation should have four offspring," Hamilton said, "so you would think that the world would be overrun with your body type at that rate. But then again, I can also understand a pretty high attrition if you were trying to live in a regular human community."

Gary looked down at his body as well as he could and grunted. "When Robert found me next to the burning house, you think it was my real parent's house, don't you? Burned to the ground because of this?"

"Humans react badly to lesser differences than this. Your real father—or mother, as it might be—must have thrown her arm or leg out the window before the attackers burned down the house, hoping you would live. You were lucky that the mob didn't find you. Even luckier that you'd already reshaped yourself into a baby when Robert Lumley discovered you in the grass."

"Dad—my human dad—always said I was shaped a little funny when he found me." Gary looked around at the other cribs around him. "He must have been a real saint."

"I'll bet he was. Do you have someplace I can take your, uh, offspring?"

Gary's face clouded over. "No, I don't. None of my friends would, uh—" He glanced around at his strange, warped-looking offspring.

"The witch," Agatha said. "The witch will help him. The one he saw before he came here." She crossed her arms and leaned against a wall. "Not for free, of course."

***

Agatha delivered the 'children' to the witch and called Hamilton afterward. He'd already returned to his apartment and was writing more notes in his notebook while feasting on a microwaved chicken pot pie.

"The babies are delivered," she said. "Henrietta seems nice enough. We're hoping that Gary's main body will put on weight fast enough to look like a small adult in a few months, once the new arms and legs fill out a little. This is new to Henrietta. She seemed exited."

"That's good. My first case in the new clinic, and I didn't really have to do anything at all but watch."

"You talked to the poor man and figured out what

was going on. You did what you could and helped him. You didn't burn his house down or chuck him out a window. No one could ask for any more than that."

Hamilton laughed. "When you put it that way—"

"The clinic will do fine, Matthew Hamilton."

"So says the Oracle?"

"Just a good feeling," Agatha said. "Just a good feeling."

Interview with a Golem

"So that's how the Backside Clinic got started," I said.

The golem nodded and leaned back. "That is how it happened."

"The murder of Corwin Abercrombie; did that ever get resolved? The murderer captured?" I asked.

"Hamilton had just started gathering clues to that mystery, though the solution to it nearly fell in his lap later on. I will get to that part of the story soon."

"Was Corwin a part of the supernatural community when he was alive? That is, was there something special about him, or were his magic tricks just tricks?"

"He was a fairly talented magician when alive, if you can give his stories credence. Mundane trickery, however, sleight of hand and showmanship. Not actual magic."

I scribbled extra observations on a notepad while the digital recorder recorded silently. "Dr. Hamilton seems to handle unusual situations pretty casually," I observed.

"His prior experiences in Sudan trained him to react calmly to the unexpected," the golem said. "Even the most terrifying situations seemed only to spark his interest instead of causing panic. Each new case, no matter how bizarre, was a new lesson on the empirical analysis of the supernatural world."

"I noticed that Chopra got involved in that story. I gather he's part of the regular staff at Backside now?"

"Ever since the encounter with the Macachati, yes. All the staff eventually became involved in some way, except for MacDonald, of course."

"Was this patient, Gary, at all like any of his other encounters?"

The golem thought for a moment, staring up at the ceiling. "Only by coincidence. Due to his escalating conflict with the monster Kraken, there was the mysterious crawling finger he needed to deal with. This occurred shortly after his discussion with Michael Gordon on creating Backside Clinic, about four weeks after he started work at Pembrook."

Chapter 10 – Fingered Out

Hamilton's apartment was near enough to the clinic that he could walk there in twenty minutes. He usually did walk unless it rained, leaving his Corolla parked in his designated parking space at the apartment. Today, the rain had been coming in sporadic cloudbursts, and thunder and lightning were playing off the coast a few miles away. Hamilton gazed at the overcast sky and thought how great it would be to loaf around reading a book while sipping hot chocolate on his day off.

He struggled up the stairs to his apartment with two grocery bags in one hand and his house keys in the other. His apartment was on the second floor of the white-stucco complex at the end of the walkway, and he considered himself lucky that he shared only a single common wall with one other resident who was quiet most of the time. Once inside, he took his groceries to the kitchen and stowed them where they belonged, then heated a cup of water in the microwave, afterwards ladling generous spoonfuls of powdered chocolate mix into it.

He picked up the hot chocolate and a worn copy of The Three Musketeers, then headed out the front door to the walkway just outside his front door. The second-story walkway was fairly wide and covered overhead, so he could enjoy the muggy breezes, intermittent thunder, and the soft sound of sporadic showers without actually being out in it. A week ago, he'd set up a beach chair and a small, ugly rattan table near his front door just for this purpose. He sat. Light rain pattered on the leaves of the palm trees in the complex's small courtyard.

Two sips and a few pages in, something bumped his chair and mrowled at him.

He looked down. A black cat prowled around the base of the beach chair, looking up at him expectantly. It was soaking wet.

"You can't have my hot chocolate, cat." He tried to go back to reading his book, ignoring it. The cat sat in front of the chair and meowed again, unconcerned with 17th century French politics. Hamilton put down his book and stared at it. The markings were strange. At first glance, it appeared all black, but there was a thin band of white around its neck, like a collar, and a small patch of gray and white hair on its chin. It stared back at him, looking forlorn with its matted wet hair. "So who do you belong to?" The cat jumped up on his lap.

He shook his head and dumped the wet cat off his lap. "You aren't going to let me enjoy my day off, are you?" He stood up, turned and opened the door to his apartment, and the cat dashed in ahead of him. Hamilton stayed there with the door open for a minute, thinking the cat would eventually realize he was in the wrong home and come back out. The cat meowed again from somewhere deep in his apartment. Hamilton sighed. He carried his book and

chocolate to his small dining room table and set them
down. In his bathroom, he retrieved a dirty towel out of the
hamper and started looking for the cat. The cat was in front
of the refrigerator. It meowed again.

He rubbed the cat semi-dry. The cat seemed unable
to decide whether it loved or hated the rubdown. Hamilton
was used to being owned by a cat; his parents always had at
least one in the house. He opened the fridge, pulled out
some 2%, and filled a saucer. The cat lapped it up noisily.
Hamilton went to sit on the couch with his book, but
moments later the cat was calling his servant again. "What
now?" He returned to the kitchen. The cat sat in front of
the cabinet containing canned goods. Hamilton opened the
cabinet. In the front was tuna. The cat pawed at a can and
looked up at Hamilton hopefully.

"There's no way in hell you could know…" he
started, then remembered how the last week had gone. He
pulled a can of tuna out while the cat pawed at his leg and
meowed louder. "Hang on, cat, hang on." He dished out
half the can on a fresh plate and put it on the floor. The cat
dug in, purring loudly. Hamilton stood watching it eat, then
took a fork and started eating the rest of the tuna out of the
can himself. They finished at roughly the same time.

After putting all the dirty dishes in the sink,
Hamilton retired to the couch with his cooling chocolate
and book to relax. The cat nudged its way onto his lap and
started purring again. He lodged the book up against the
side of the cat as a book rest. The cat didn't seem to mind.

Thirty pages in, he heard a loud crash outside,
followed by a burst of mild profanity. The cat jumped off
his lap and started exploring the apartment. Hamilton rose

to investigate the noise.

Two apartments down, a young woman picked up groceries off the walkway. A paper bag with a wet torn-out bottom sat off to the side. Her short blond hair was wet and straggly from the rain; she must have been caught out unprepared, but despite that and a tacky waitress uniform, he could still see that she was quite pretty.

"Can I help you with that?" he asked.

She glanced up at him, a loaf of bread in one hand and a small bag of apples in the other. She tried to flip a strand of wet hair up out of her face, looking up at Hamilton. He was wearing a green tee-shirt with a giant recycle symbol in the middle of it and worn blue jeans. She smiled briefly. "Please," she said.

It took only a minute to move the armloads of groceries into her kitchen, and Hamilton couldn't help but look around. There were lots of candles. The smell of incense. Pagan wall hangings, and cute little knit pentacle coasters. A patterned Indian throw rug brightened the center of the room. "Comfy," he said.

She pushed her wet hair back with both hands. "Thanks. I take it the decor doesn't freak you out?"

"Naw. Should it?"

"Some people get offended." She shrugged.

"Are you waitressing around here?"

She looked down at her uniform, which was also still wet. "Oh, yeah. You should come by sometime. It's, like, three or four blocks from here. Cord's Cafe. The food actually doesn't suck."

He laughed. "Good recommendation. I'll do that. It's on my way to work." He moved toward the door. "Oh, my name's Matt, by the way."

"I'm Maggie. And thanks for the help. See you around?"

That, he thought, is a great place to put a question mark. There's the "see you around" dismissal with a flat delivery, and then there's the hopeful question mark that intimates some slight interest. "I'm just two doors down. Give me a shout if you need anything," he said. He smiled and lifted his hand as he left but stopped suddenly in the doorway when he heard the screech and yowl of a surprised cat fighting in his apartment. A lamp crashed to the floor, followed by a more satisfied growl. After a moment, the cat came trotting out of the apartment with what looked like a mouse in its mouth. He sauntered proudly over to Hamilton as Maggie watched from behind him, and then dropped the squirming thing at his feet.

He leaned over to look at the mouse, then stepped back, bumping into Maggie. "I think it's a finger," he said. Despite himself, he glanced down at his own hands to make sure it wasn't one of his.

"But it's still moving," Maggie said.

He looked up at his open apartment door nervously. "Where's the rest of it?"

Maggie stared at the squirming finger and swallowed. There was a multi-colored thread wrapped around it, like a demonic friendship ring. "Voodoo," she whispered.

Chapter 11 - I Find Dead People

The crawling finger had been indecorously and carefully transferred to a Tupperware container with a pair of tongs. Maggie and Hamilton sat in his apartment staring at the thing as it tried to scratch its way out.

"We could trim its fingernail. A post-mortem manicure. Probably have less chance of escaping," Maggie said.

"How is it you're so cool with this? A crawling finger?"

She said, "I could ask you the same thing. You act like you've seen this before."

He grunted. "Not this, exactly. You're dodging my question."

"There's magic in the city. I've seen some strange things."

"I don't believe in magic. Magic is just science waiting for an explanation."

"But you've seen strange things, too, true?"

He nodded. "Yeah, I guess I have. This week has been...odd." He crossed his arms and stared at the wriggling finger. "You know, salt can make a dead limb jerk."

"Lick the stump, see if you can taste any."

He gave her a dirty look. She grinned back.

Behind them the black cat had taken up residence on the couch, managing to sleep and purr at the same time. Hamilton suspected this was going to be a permanent arrangement. "Why do you think the finger was here?" he said.

"In Haiti, there's a belief that if you leave the finger of a dead man under a pillow, then someone who sleeps there will be susceptible to the will of the bokor, the zombie controller."

"Like a tooth fairy from hell."

"Just like that. Do you have any idea who might have hired a bokor to attack you?" Maggie asked.

Hamilton thought back to the Hunter that was knocked unconscious in his clinic, and the fact that the driver got away. Was there a connection there? "I might have a guess. There was a couple I—uh—had some trouble with at the clinic a few weeks ago, right after I started there. One of them could have tailed me back to the apartment." And the other one might be dead.

"If the bokor had taken over your body, he could have done anything he wanted to you. If it wasn't for your cat—"

"Not my cat." He glanced over his shoulder at the beast. It opened a lazy eye at him, then shut it again.

"Right. Not-your-cat saved your ass."

He'd already named the cat in his head; Old Man. The gray patch of hair on its chin just made him seem like one. "Bit of a coincidence that this cat should show up and invade my apartment the same day zombie-finger shows up. Think someone sent the cat, too?"

"I think the cat might have sent itself." She looked at it as though she'd seen it before. It ignored her. "I might be able to figure out whose finger this is."

"Let me guess. A magical tracking spell."

She forced a laugh. "No, of course not. Spells! Ha, ha! I have a friend that's a cop. He might be able to run the prints for me. Or print."

"Isn't the crawling finger going to freak him out?"

"Just the print, not the finger. I'll call him from my apartment."

"And I guess I'll go get some cat food. You okay with that, Old Man?"

The cat yawned and went back to sleep.

After Maggie and Hamilton left his apartment, the cat got up, jumped onto the windowsill, turned into a crow, and flew away.

***

Hamilton carried a bag of milk, tuna, cereal, sourdough bread, sharp cheddar cheese, and mayo back to his apartment. Some damned crow seemed to be following him. He glared at it a couple of times, but it always landed when he did, poking around in the grass for bugs. *Pretending,* Hamilton thought. *Or I'm just becoming paranoid.* But with all the other weirdness going on, he couldn't dismiss it as a coincidence. The crow disappeared as he opened the door to the lobby, likely off to pester someone else.

He went inside and opened the door to his apartment. The cat was right where he left it. It looked at him groggily and went to sleep again. Well, at least it was low maintenance. Except…he slapped his forehead. Cat litter! Another trip to the corner store. "Dammit," he muttered. He left the apartment and nearly ran into Maggie. "Matt!" she said, "I've got an address. It's about two miles from here."

He took the slip of paper from her. "That was quick. Say thanks to your cop friend for me."

She brushed an errant strand of hair behind an ear. "He just owed me a favor."

He looked at her askance, raising an eyebrow. She half-smiled at him. His heart thumped. "Well," he said, clearing his throat, "now that we have it, what do we do with it? We can't go to the cops with it, and we can't go in with guns blazing." He walked back into his apartment, dropping the note on his coffee table. The cat stood and stretched. "How do we plan this? If this is some voodoo priest…"

"Bokor."

"Right, a bokor, and some voodoo slave, at a minimum, then how can we deal with that? For all we know we're dealing with some army of undead."

"Let's go look at the place. Maybe you'll get an idea."

He hesitated, unsure of the possible dangers. Still, simple recon, what could possibly go wrong with that? "Okay, let me grab my keys and put out the—where did the cat go?"

Maggie shrugged. "Nature calling, maybe?"

He did a quick check of the rooms. The cat was nowhere. He raised his arms in surrender and left the apartment.

Chapter 12 – Bring Out Yer Dead

"It's still here and it hasn't moved at all in the last hour," Maggie said. "It's right where it was before. Of course, if it's a dead guy…"

"You said a cop gave you the address." He was scrutinizing the arrow-charm hanging between them, locked onto an invisible target in the building.

She frowned. "I didn't exactly tell you the truth. I thought you might be all weirded-out if I told you I did magic stuff."

"I pulled a bullet out of a werewolf a few weeks back. You are not going to weird me out."

She stared at him with a mix of surprise and admiration. "You were acting so coy about magic."

"Coy boy, that's me," Hamilton said.

She wiggled the charm and the needle didn't move. "Still pointing to the guy. At least whoever is in there isn't moving. If nobody living is in there, maybe we could sneak inside and look around."

"Maybe we could be cut to pieces by a crazy zombie priest with a machete that doesn't show up on your doohickey. Maybe we should leave this to the cops."

"And tell them what? We have this crawling finger,

and we used magic to find out where the body is?"

"Or we saw someone drag an unconscious person into a warehouse, and here's the address," Hamilton suggested.

"That doesn't tell us who's after you, or why. If they're not there right now, this might be our only chance of finding some information about them. See who's in charge. And I've got this." She pulled out a small canister of pepper spray.

Hamilton felt better for seeing it. *And we can always run like hell.* He looked up at the dark windows of the building, where the arrow pointed. There was no sign of light or movement. "I know I'm going to regret this," he said.

They left the car parked where it was out of the line of sight of any of the building's windows. They circled around to the back of the old industrial building out of view from the street, passing through the dark shadows cast by the setting sun.. The parking lot around the building was empty of cars and enclosed by a chain-link fence with a locked gate, but a smaller personnel gate was propped open with a chunk of cement. Many of the building's high windows had broken panes, and tan paint peeled from its metal siding like skin from a bad sunburn. Weeds grew up through cracks in the cement. It looked abandoned. At the rear of the building was a single personnel door next to two steel roll-up doors on a broad loading dock. Hamilton tested the door. "No surprise. Locked," he said softly.

"Hang on," Maggie said. She pulled a small piece of paper with a glyph drawn on it, rolled it up into a tube, and put it inside the keyhole. She bent over, whispered something to the keyhole, and was rewarded with a click. She removed the paper and returned it to her purse. "Try it now."

He opened the door. "I'm impressed," he said. The hinges screeched like a dying banshee as he swung the door open. Hamilton winced. Opening it slowly didn't make any difference; it just made the squeal last longer. "If they didn't know someone was coming in, they sure do now."

They stepped inside. The door opened onto a broad cement loading dock, cracked and oil-stained, empty except for a few pallets and a stack of folded cardboard boxes. After standing in darkness, listening for a few minutes, Hamilton pulled out an LED penlight that was attached to his keychain and removed it from the keys. The jingle of the keys sounded like cathedral bells in the open area. Maggie pulled out her cell phone, turned off the ringer, and activated the flashlight app. They crept as silently as possible to the far door of the room, though both realized it was probably too late for silent creeping to do any good. Hamilton reached for the doorknob, and whispered, "Do you have an oil spell for squeaky hinges?"

Maggie shook her head.

He turned the knob slowly and pulled the door open. It moved quietly. He let out a breath that he hadn't realized he'd been holding.

Beyond the inner door was a large warehouse or work area, taking up most of the rest of the building. To the side was an open stairway leading up to two dark offices on an upper floor that only took up a quarter of the floor space. A storage area occupied the area below the offices, filled with more empty pallets, some fifty-five-gallon oil barrels, and a recent-model pickup truck. No lights were on and nothing made a sound.

"I think we're alone," Maggie whispered.

"Maybe. Keep your pepper spray handy."

They explored the inside of the truck, finding nothing of interest, then crept slowly up the stairs, each creaking loudly enough to wake the dead. While Maggie stood ready with her pepper spray to blast anyone who might be waiting to ambush them, Hamilton threw open the door. "Ah! Holy crap!" she cried.

Hamilton looked inside, shining his penlight. On the floor lay a man dressed in layers of bright cotton clothes with a huge variety of beaded jewelry and feathers decorating him. It was hard to tell whether the bright colors were from his blood or the clothing.

"Someone beat us to it. I'm guessing he's the bokor." The man looked like his skin had been shredded and stabbed a thousand times. Spatters of blood painted the walls and floor of the small room. Though he was lying face down, his head was turned to the side and they could see that both his eyes were empty sockets. Much of the blood seemed to come from deep gouges and tears on his throat. "Death of a thousand cuts. And then some."

"Bad mojo." Maggie stepped into the room, then immediately stumbled back into Hamilton, raising her pepper spray again. He grabbed her to keep them both from falling.

"What is it?"

She was shaking, her arms rigid on the spray trigger. "Someone in a chair. I think...I think he's dead, too."

Hamilton stood quietly, listening. His arms were still

wrapped around her waist. She put her free hand on his. "You can let go now."

"Oh, right. Sorry." He reluctantly let her go, then shined his penlight around the door jamb. The light played across a pale man sitting in a chair, unmoving. Not cut up like the other man. On one of the man's hands, a bandage covered the stump of a missing finger. "Looks like we found the finger guy, anyway."

He stepped into the room. A window was open to the outside, letting in a light and welcome breeze. A desk was covered with what must have been voodoo implements; candles, a mortar and pestle, small jars of herbs and tiny bones. He stepped over to the man in the chair, shining his LED flashlight in his unblinking eyes with a doctor's care. The pupils shrank. Hamilton moved back suddenly. "He's still alive."

Maggie shined her phone on him. The man sat perfectly still, hands on his thighs, staring straight ahead without blinking. "He's still under control of the bokor."

"The dead bokor?"

"Yup."

"We can't leave him here for the police to find."

"Or the bokor's gang. Whomever he's working for."

He swept his light across the still form of the man. "Hey, buddy, we've got to get you out of here. Can you stand up?"

The man didn't move. He jostled the man's shoulder to no effect.

"There's probably some totem linking the bokor to him." She reached toward the bokor, her fingers twitching above his corpse as she tried to find a spot where she wasn't touching flayed flesh. "Eww. Can you help me roll him over?"

Hamilton glanced around the office and saw a knit shawl hanging on a coat-rack. "Let's use this." He pulled it off the rack, and with the shawl between their hands and the bloody shreds of his body, they succeeded in turning him over onto his back. "There," she pointed. Two small tassels of bloody hair wrapped in copper wire hung on leather cords around his neck. Maggie removed them, cutting through the cords with a pocketknife, careful to avoid the blood still oozing from the bokor's neck.

"He was killed pretty recently," Hamilton observed. "The blood hasn't completely congealed yet."

"Hopefully the killers are on our side." She handed the locks of hair to Hamilton. "Try making him move now."

"Stand up!" he commanded. The man stood slowly. Down below, they heard a clatter. "Oh, crap," Hamilton whispered.

Maggie shook her head and sighed. "Of course. There are two tassels."

Hamilton examined the tassels in his hand. One was bleach-blond, the other brunette. "Oh."

"Let's get out of here and pick up the other one on the way out."

"Wait. We still don't know who the bokor was working for."

The sudden, happy strains of "Don't Worry, Be Happy" made them both jump. It came from the bokor's vest pocket.

"What a freaking twisted bastard," Maggie said. She plucked the phone out of his pocket, memorized the incoming number, then muted the ringer. "We have your clue, now let's get the hell out of here."

Hamilton wiped fingerprints off the door handles as they left. They didn't leave nearly as quickly as desired, as the controlled man followed them with a plodding, stumbling gait, and needed to be led carefully down the stairs. Down below, they found a woman standing still in one of the fifty-five gallon drums, the lid lying to the side where it had fallen. Hamilton lifted her unresisting form out of the drum. "Follow me," he said to them. The two of them followed complacently. They made it back to his car without incident, both awkwardly bumping their heads on the top of the door frame when they got into the back seat.

"Hang on, I need to arrange a place to put these two before we leave." He unplugged his own phone from the car's stereo and called Agatha Noone.

She answered on the first ring. Of course, Hamilton thought, she was probably expecting the call. "Hello, Doctor Hamilton. I suspect you need to get into the clinic building."

"Hi, Agatha. You could at least let me ask first."

"I'm already here. Drop by when you wish. Gin!"

"What?"

"Sorry," she said "playing Rummy with Corwin. I think he cheats."

In the background he could hear Corwin, "This, coming from an Oracle."

Hamilton sighed and disconnected. "Let's go. They're waiting for us at the clinic."

Driving back, Hamilton kept looking in the back seat, expecting the zombies, or whatever they were, to lunge forward and take a chunk out of his neck. They sat still and blankly stared forward.

"When we get back," Maggie said, "remind me to glyph our apartments. Maybe the cars, too. People won't notice our cars when they look for them, if they don't already know where they are." She looked irritated. "Good for avoiding stake-burnings. Not so good for pizza deliveries."

"While you're tossing around ignore-me glyphs, how about making one for the back door of the clinic? Or the whole alley, for that matter. If there's going to be increased traffic…"

Maggie nodded. "Maybe something more permanent than a yellow sticky note, huh? That's going to cost you."

"The clinic has coin," he replied.

***

Inside the clinic, Hamilton made introductions, then they scrounged some old wooden chairs that had been left behind in one of the front rooms, setting the two voodoo-slaves in them. Agatha put her hands on her hips and considered the two of them as they stared into space.

"That's a mismatched pair. At least you might have a chance fixing the man."

Hamilton looked with dreadful anticipation at the woman, feeling that the floor was about to drop from underneath him. "What's wrong with the woman?"

Agatha sniffed, wrinkling her nose. "She's dead."

Chapter 13 - Dead-end Jobs.

Hamilton handed the unresponsive man his lock of hair and said, "Wake up, you're free." He wasn't surprised when nothing happened.

"I'm sure there was a combination of chemicals or drugs to sap his will, too. That's the way voodoo works. You might just have to let the drugs run their course before he becomes aware of his surroundings," Maggie said.

He knelt in front of the dead woman. "I suppose this one is a little more complicated. How do you animate a corpse? Can a corpse have willpower?" He handed the woman her own lock of hair, half-expecting her to keel over on the spot. Instead, the woman's hand curled slowly around the lock of hair. "Oracle, do you have anything?" Hamilton asked.

She smiled and closed her eyes. After a minute of communing with the whatever, she opened them and said, "I see you throwing money on a grave."

"That's...not really very helpful."

"That's what I saw. Take it or leave it."

"Okay. Let's think this through. You know I'm trying to quantify all this mumbo-jumbo into a scientific model that's consistent with what I've observed so far. It's my best bet for treating the ailments I'm dealing with." He walked around the chair of the dead woman. "She doesn't have any blood flow to carry oxygen to any part of her body, so the voodoo guy must have replaced or added some chemicals to the body that allow some other form of energy transport. Chemical diffusion or capillary action seem to be out of the question because they wouldn't move chemicals around fast enough to do any good, and her heart isn't pumping anything. That still leaves electricity as a possible source, suggesting that her body chemistry is more like a large battery than a biological engine. That would also allow for some sort of mental activity, so she could at least follow the bokor's commands. In that case, there could be some chance for independent thought." He sighed. "On the other hand, she's dead, and will probably start decomposing, for which there's already a bit of evidence."

"She smells," said Agatha. "And even with independent thought, she might be of animal-level intellect."

"I…am not," croaked the dead woman. Her head bent down to stare at the twist of hair in her hand. "I am…" She closed her eyes, and opened them slowly, and said in a small, choked voice, "I cannot cry." She slowly put both hands to her face.

Agatha's eyes widened. "Okay, she can talk. But she will still have to be kept here for awhile," Agatha said. "She can't go on the streets this way."

Hamilton squatted down so that his eyes were level with the woman's. "What was your name?" he asked.

She frowned slightly. "My name *is* Medjine

Herivaux. My family comes from Port-au-Prince. What year is this? Where am I?"

"We're in Redondo Beach. It's near Los Angeles, in California. And the year is 2015."

She choked and gasped. "Five years! Five years gone. The bokor came and took me because my family owed him money." She looked at her pale hands. "And now, now what am I? Have I ceased to be a human? Can I ever bear a child?"

"You are changed," Hamilton said. "We have yet to define your limits." *And figure out what you eat to maintain your battery—hopefully not brains or babies.* Subconsciously, he put his hand on the back of his head. "If you've been this way for five years, the bokor must have had someway of maintaining you. Maybe we can go back to the warehouse and find out what he used. Maybe improve on it."

"But what can I do in this…changed body? I cannot live life as I have. My old job is gone. I can no longer face humanity this way. Before, I used to work as receptionist at a convention center; such work will be impossible for me now."

"You were…are a receptionist?" Hamilton said. Agatha, Corwin and Maggie looked at him knowingly and suggestively. Medjine nodded. *Throwing money on a grave. Or paying a dead employee. Mostly dead, anyway. Okay,* now *it makes sense.*

He rubbed his forehead and winced. Talk about equal opportunity employment. Somehow, he knew he'd regret this. Somehow, they'd need to deal with the smell. "How'd you like to work at Backside Clinic, Medjine?"

Her lower lip trembled and she looked up at

Hamilton with the first sign of hope.

***

Maggie and Hamilton met back at her apartment. He pulled out the phone that he'd retrieved from the dead bokor and fiddled with it. "Dammit. It's got a passcode on it. Who does that on their phones?"

"Spies, secret agents, assassins, politicians, kids with parents…"

"It was a rhetorical question, okay?" He started to randomly punch passwords into the phone.

"It'll lock you out if you do that too often. I saw the last caller's phone number. That might help us. We can do a reverse call lookup online."

Five minutes later, they both stared at the computer screen. "Unregistered. Maybe a burner phone?" Maggie suggested.

"Hmm." Hamilton scratched his head. "We could maybe do that…what did you call it? Sympathetic magic with the phone."

"That would only work if the phone were part of him. Like attracts like, so hair leads you to a body. A cell phone would lead you to a phone manufacturer."

"So this phone does us no good at all."

"You could always wait until you get another call. Or call the number that we saw on the phone. Maybe pretend to be the bokor?"

"Yeah, maybe." He pocketed the phone. "We'll see how that goes."

Interview with a Golem

"I take it this was the first time Dr. Hamilton met Maggie?" I asked.

"It was," the golem said.

"The start of a romance?"

"Dr. Hamilton has always been a romantic in both senses of the word. But in his position, it wasn't easy to develop or pursue a romance, and the great number of changes and supernatural revelations in his life were a severe distraction at first. Though that doesn't mean he didn't think about it. With Maggie, it became a little complicated." He tapped his leather chin thoughtfully. "In the other sense, being a romantic is just part of his nature, caring for people, helping them, believing that there was good in everyone."

"Hamilton made a lot of friends, from the sounds of it," I said.

"He has," said the golem. "In the beginning, this was not so. Kraken and his Hunters were beginning to learn more about him and finding him to be a thorn in their collective side. And it was only going to get worse. Allow me to elaborate."

Chapter 14 – Ozman's Bookstore

Benny Osman originally named his bookstore "Benny Osman's Occult Book Store" until someone pointed out the unfortunate abbreviation to him. He wondered why school kids would stop, point, and laugh in front of his store each day. More irritating because he'd only put his name on the store to avoid having to file for a fictitious name. Knowing that he'd end up paying one way or the other, he just had to go for a cool name, weeding possible names down to Oddman's or Ozman's. Ozman's won out because it had the L. Frank Baum spin on it, and it sounded more like his real name. Ozman's Occult Books and Paraphernalia.

He didn't feel cool, though. The appeal of magic to Osman was like a drug addiction for a drug that was no longer on the market. The addiction ended up not being the drug itself, but the attempt to acquire it, an obsessive-compulsive intensity that affected everything he did. Like opening an occult bookstore just so he could meet people who could do magic, or who might be magic. He didn't expect the store to make money; the store was a money pit eating away slowly at an inheritance from his parents. Fortunately, there were also other people who had offered him money in exchange for any unusual information he acquired from his customers, not only reinforcing the idea that magic existed, but that he was a useful cog in discovering that world.

He waited for the magic to come to him, and passed that information on to those who could pay for it. It helped pay the bills.

A man walked into the store, the customary bell above the door jingling as he entered. An unfamiliar face. A new customer.

"Good morning!" Osman declared. The man was taller and broader than Osman and had a head full of hair. Osman subconsciously smoothed what little hair he had left across the spotted skin of his head. He peered over the top of his thin wire-rim glasses at the stranger.

The man nodded. "Good morning. I'm looking for any sort of book about supernatural creatures, maybe historical, or about their biology."

"Biology? That's pretty specific. Any particular kind of supernatural creatures? Ghosts, dryads, vampires?" Osman asked. The question was more information-gathering than helpful; most of Osman's books were about magic, not creatures, and the breadth and depth of his shelves were not significantly larger than the public library's, few dating before 1950. He guided Hamilton toward the tiny section of books concerning mythical creatures.

"No, nothing in particular. I'm, uh, gathering data for a fantasy novel I'm writing," he said. Osman could tell he was lying.

"Really? Are you local?" he pried.

"I'm in Redondo."

"You'll have to come back and tell me when your

novel gets published," Osman said. "Here we are."

The man browsed over the two dozen books on the shelf. "Dictionary of Mythical Creatures," he mumbled, squinting at a spine. He took the book from the shelf and thumbed through it. Osman was familiar with the book. It was crammed with historical references and origins for hundreds of creatures, including demons and angels. Most of the creatures were so obscure that he had never heard of them, like the Ciquapa from the Dominican Republic. Harbinger of death. Like so many books of this sort, most of it was just fabricated nonsense or myth, but there were always tidbits of truth buried in the volumes. The man nodded to Osman. "This looks useful."

"You looked pensive."

"Filling out details of the plot in my head. Lots of potential with a this many critters to choose from." He picked out another book, "California Myths and Legends – Fact or Fiction?" He kept glancing at Osman, as though nervous that he was looming over him, watching. Well, it was his bookstore. Shoplifters could really kill profits, and the margins were already negative.

A thin black leather-bound volume appeared when the man slid the second book from the shelf. He picked up the small black volume and looked at the cover. "The Name of Things," he read.

"What?"

"The Name of Things. Wow, this looks really old." He flipped it open. "And the contents aren't even in English."

Osman snatched it away from him, snapping it shut. "I've been looking around my store for this volume since the day I acquired it. I thought I'd lost it. I had a customer who wanted it badly."

"Wouldn't do me any good. I can't even read it. Curious that the cover is in English, though."

"Yes," Osman said, chewing on his lip. "Very curious. I could swear…"

"I'll get these other two, I think."

"Very good. Let me ring you up." He took the two books from the customer's hand.

They went up to the register and the man pulled a credit card out of his wallet. He looked up into Osman's eyes, hesitated, then put the card back in his wallet. "I think I'll pay cash today."

Osman hackles rose, but he pasted on a smile. The man dug a twenty out of his pocket and handed it to him. While Osman turned to the cash register to make change, he said, "Do you need a bag?"

"No, thanks" the man said. He seemed anxious to leave, "I'm good. It's not raining."

"Great. We hope to see you again!"

The man hurried out, but looked over his shoulder as he went.

Osman rushed back to the shelf to check on the thin volume of The Name of Things, happy that he'd finally be able to make the sale to Mr. Hunter. It was strange when he'd first acquired the volume from another collector; it had arrived in the mail, he'd put it down on a shelf behind the counter, called Mr. Hunter to tell him that he had it, and then couldn't find it afterwards. He knew it was in the shop. It just wasn't where he remembered putting it. He thought he was losing his mind.

He looked around, lifting volumes and shifting books around. Now, where had he put it this time? Had the last customer stolen it from him, right under his nose? If he'd lost it a second time, Mr. Hunter would be furious. He ground his teeth in frustration, standing in the middle of his shop, slowly turning in circles. Where could the damned thing be?

Chapter 15 – Cord's Cafe

Cord's Cafe was situated midway between the clinic and Hamilton's apartment. Four city blocks either way. It wasn't the first time he'd stopped in for breakfast in the morning on the way to the clinic, and dinner in the evening on the way home. But it was the first time he'd come in at 5AM. Work at the clinic had snipped away at his ability to sleep soundly, until waking up in the middle of the night, sweating, was a regular occurrence. This morning, he sat at one of the two-seater tables eating ham, scrambled eggs, and some sourdough toast saturated with butter. He was already into his second cup of coffee. To the left of his plate was a book titled, "California Myths and Legends – Fact or Fiction?" He caught Maggie's eye as she came by with a coffee pot.

"Top it off for you, Matt?"

"Thanks, Maggie, please. I won't make it through the day otherwise."

She filled his cup slowly, lingering over the table. "What'cha reading, anyway?" she asked.

He held up the book so she could see the cover. She pursed her lips and tilted her head. "Huh. Learning anything useful?"

"Do you know anything about werewolves? I mean,
myths about them? Maybe local stuff?"

Maggie laughed. "In the city? Naw. Nothing to hunt
here, 'cept maybe fried chicken and meatloaf. In the
country, I bet they're all over the place."

Hamilton smiled. "Very funny."

"There's a lot of weirdness around here, Matt. You
just take it as it comes. Some crazies around, and sometimes
strange stuff just happens. You can't explain it." She waved
her coffee pot to encompass the whole restaurant. There
was an average-looking middle-aged couple eating a meal
big enough that they'd need a take-home box, a homeless
guy who was probably hoping they'd leave it there, nursing
a cup of coffee until they left, and three teens with various
deserts on the table, paying more attention to their phones
than each other, obviously lingering leftovers from last
night's bar crowd. "See?"

After learning she was a witch and receiving her
help with the undead, Hamilton now found her to be a
master of the facetious, too. It was hard not to like her.

The bell on the door jingled, and they both glanced
over at it. A young woman with long, straight black hair
came in and sat at the counter. She hung her purse on the
chair next to her, warding off strangers who might wish to
sit there. "Hey, Maggie. Coffee, please."

Hamilton immediately recognized her. She'd gotten
rid of the Hunter's body and picked a lock for him. He
sipped his coffee, watching her. Either she hadn't seen him
yet or she was ignoring him on purpose. Either way was
okay by him. She seemed like a dangerous person to know.

"Hi, Clare. Big party night?" Maggie pulled out a cup from below the counter, did a quick check for lipstick on it, then poured her some coffee.

Clare shrugged. "Naw. All-nighter studying for Spanish finals at the CC. Just wanted to grab a bite and go back to the books."

"Still taking night classes?"

"Yup. Seems like you can't get a job in California without being bi-lingual. How about the six-ounce steak, rare, and eggs, over easy?"

Hamilton glanced at the two girls as they talked. They were both a few years younger than he was. Could have gone to school together. Clare was dressed in a California suit; blue jeans, sandals, and a t-shirt. Light makeup. Attractive, he thought. Maggie wore an obligatory Cord's Cafe outfit; jeans again, but a blue shirt with the cafe name blazed across the back in red and yellow letters trimmed in black. The letters were shown on a bed of coals, and were supposed to be suggestive of a barbeque, but looked more like they were burning in a pit in Hell. Maybe suggesting that their barbeque was damned good?

One of these days, he thought, he had to get away from the clinic and meet some people. Normal people. Maggie was nice enough and lived in the same apartment building, but that might be a little stalky. Of course, him coming here a few days a week might give her the same vibe. Clare, well, that woman was just scary. He went back to his book. It wasn't a big rush.

The book didn't have a lot to say about werewolves. There were a lot of stories about ghosts. Some American Indian spirits and gods, like Coyote. There was Bigfoot.

Shape-changing bears. Even mermaids luring sailors to their deaths on California's rocky shores. But really, these were just stories passed from one generation to the next, either to try to explain the unexplainable, or to scare the bejesus out of misbehaving children. Quite a few lost gold mines, too, usually with more ghosts.

He put the book down and rubbed his eyes, then looked in his cup. Maggie had topped it off again while he wasn't looking. The teens had left. Someone who could only be described as a thug had taken up residence in one of the nearby booths. Hamilton sipped his coffee and let his eyes drift, unfocused, but watchful. The thug had a dark blue beanie and black jeans, with a worn, loose leather jacket. He kept glancing over at Clare. Clare and Maggie talked quietly for a minute, then Clare shifted her attention to Hamilton.

She walked over to his table. "Hi, Dave," she said. *Dave?* Hamilton thought. *Ah, a fake name for the extra set of ears listening in. Not a bad idea.*

She said it like they were old friends. She studiously ignored the other guy that watched her. "I was wondering if you could give me a ride to my place. I need to get home a bit sooner than I expected." She glanced sideways at the thug without turning her head and gave Hamilton a tight-lipped smile.

Hamilton smiled back hesitantly. "I'd love to, but I walked. Where's your car?"

Her face fell. "I walked here, too."

Hamilton raised his eyebrows curiously. It was 5AM and still dark outside except for the perpetual twilight glow from Los Angeles' lights, not exactly the safest time to be strolling around Redondo Beach, but then, from what he'd seen already, she could probably take care of herself. He saw a smug smile stretch across the thug's face. What a dick, he thought. He pulled out his cell phone. "I was going to get a cab anyway. Why don't you ride along, and I can have him drop you off?" The smiles and frowns swapped between Clare and the thug. Really satisfying, Hamilton thought. The thug tossed a couple of dollars on the table for the coffee, then left the restaurant. After making the call for a taxi, Hamilton slipped the phone into his overshirt pocket.

"So what's the deal with the guy?"

Clare looked over her shoulder at the front window, squinting to see into the darkness outside. "Not totally sure. He's been stalking me all night, everywhere I go."

"Does he know where you live?"

She shook her head. "Not yet. I hope." She looked over at the door. "We need to get out of here before he comes back with his friends."

"Unless he's just waiting out there for you. We can just hang here until the cab gets here."

"When?"

"Maybe five minutes."

She blew her breath out, turning sideways so she could keep her eye on the doorway. "You should leave a good tip for Maggie."

Hamilton grinned. "Guess I should pay before the taxi gets here, anyway." He left cash on the table with the check. He waved at Maggie as he left with Clare, and Maggie frowned at him. He paused at the doorway and looked back at her. What was that about? She turned away from him and started wiping the counter.

A taxi finally pulled up in front of the restaurant. As they approached the door, Clare said, "Wait," and put her hand in front of Hamilton. "I can see someone standing across the street. Like they're waiting."

Hamilton peered into the darkness. The glare from the taxi lights washed out most of the shadows behind it, and the reflection off the restaurant window blocked the rest. "I can't see anything."

She pulled his hand and they made a run for the taxi, getting inside quickly. Across the street, he caught a glimpse of a man putting a phone to his ear. The man was in the shadows; it was hard to tell if it was the same guy as the thug in the restaurant. "One fifteen Tardis Street!" she said. The taxi pulled away.

"And after that," he said to the taxi driver, "if you could take me to 1602 Harbor Street, I'd appreciate it." The taxi-driver nodded to the rear view mirror. Hamilton felt somewhat smug about the neutral way they'd just exchanged addresses, but maybe it was an accident. Maybe Clare didn't see him as anything but a safe ride home. And she was still a pretty scary person, so maybe that was a good thing. He suddenly regretted mentioning his address at all before the taxi dropped her off.

Clare turned around, peering out the back window.

"Are we being followed?" Hamilton asked.

"There are a lot of cars behind us. I can't tell," she said.

Hamilton glanced up at the taxi-driver. His eyes were narrowed with suspicion.

They arrived at her place. "Can you do me a favor

and come inside?" Clare asked. Hamilton raised his eyebrows, but she saw the look on his face and said, "I'm not hitting on you, dork. I just need your help."

Hamilton ran his hands through his hair, wishing he'd had more coffee. "Yeah, sure, when you put it that way."

She gave him something bordering between a smirk and a frown, grabbed his hand, and pulled him out of the car. Not gently. He almost stumbled. With his free hand, he struggled to take a twenty from his pocket and hand it to the driver, meaning to wait for change. Clare glanced around the street at the parked cars nearby. She said, "Shit," and pulled him toward the apartment at a near-run. The taxi wasted no time disappearing. She pulled keys out of a small purse and barely slowed down as the key speared the keyhole and the door swung open. Turning around inside the lobby area, she scanned the light traffic visible through the glass door. "If they saw us come in here, things will not go well."

"Who is 'they'?" Hamilton asked.

Clare darted up a stairwell and said over her shoulder, "Hunters. You know that bitch that was wearing a skin? Like her. But more of them. C'mon, don't just gape."

He followed her up the stairs. The hallway carpet was faded, but not worn through, and there was a faint smell of mildew mixed with new paint. Humidity and age had taken their toll, but it wasn't a total dump. The wall sconces were clean, decorative, and none of the bulbs were burnt out. A few doors down, she unlocked her apartment door and went inside. "Leave the lights off," she said.

Her furniture was older than he expected it to be, a

mismatched collection of 1950's kitsch. She had stripped curtains on her windows and a dozen throw rugs with muted gray and brown colors. A fifty-inch television hung on the wall across from a depressed leather couch. Clare immediately crossed to the window and looked out. "Someone is parking," she said.

"People do that."

She gave him a quick scowl. "Two men just got out. They're crossing the street. They looked up this way. Someone else stopped their car in the street and is talking to them. I think he's looking for a space to park." She spun around to face him. "What time is it?"

Hamilton pulled out his cell phone. "Five-thirty. If you think these guys are after you, shouldn't we get out of here?"

"They might be after both of us. You said one got away at the clinic, didn't you?"

"Yeah. All the more reason to get out of here, then."

She glanced up at the horizon, which was just starting to brighten. "No time. They'll come in here when the sun is up." She bit her lip, looking at her bedroom door. It was much darker than the rest of the apartment. "Look, you're a doctor, do no harm and all that crap, right? I'm going to have to trust you with something."

Hamilton looked a little puzzled. "You're not human, I suppose."

"There's more to it than that. I'm going to be totally out of it when the sun comes up. I need you to guard me. And keep me out of the sun."

"I'm...not much of a fighter." His mind drifted

back to his time doctoring in Sudan, and he knew that it was a lie. He just didn't want to be put in that situation again.

She pulled a pendant from around her neck and tossed it to him. "You don't need to be. Put that on."

He caught it and studied it. It was an old pendant, maybe 1930's, with an ornate metal holder around an azure stone and tiny runes carved in its surface. As he dropped the chain over his head, she punched him in the face as hard as she could. He slammed back against the wall and said, "Son of a *bitch*!" He put his hand up against his face but realized that he wasn't in any pain.

"A fireplace poker would have made a better point," she said, "but it's all electric heating in here. It gives you immunity to most types of kinetic damage. Those clowns would just wait until I slept, come in, take it off me, and drag me into the sun." She growled. "It'd be a big coup for them. They don't know the pendant exists yet."

"Drag you into the sun?" Hamilton repeated.

She looked at him in disbelief. "Really? You hadn't figured that out yet? Yes, I'm a vampire. Anyway, take care of the pendant. And keep me out of the sun."

He looked down at the pendant, fiddling with it, wondering what made it work, then tucked it down inside his shirt.

She walked into her bedroom and came out with a baseball bat. "Here. It isn't much. But if they rip the pendant off you, you're a dead man, so be liberal handing out the home runs." She reached up behind his head and kissed him on the cheek, looking him in the eyes. "Don't hold back."

Hamilton opened his mouth to ask her why she had a baseball bat, but she suddenly slid down his front and fell flat on her face onto one of the throw-carpets. He stared down at her unmoving form for a minute as sunlight started to creep through the window. Down the hall, he could hear voices in the lobby. Hell, he thought. And he was due at work in three hours. He lifted Clare by the armpits and dragged her into her bedroom, depositing her on a mattress lying on the floor. Paisley sheets. Tacky.

Coming back into her living room, or not-dead room as it was shaping up to be, he heard footsteps in the hallway. The baseball bat felt heavy in his hands, but he'd been in fights before. *Take the fight to the enemy,* he thought, *attack where you aren't expected.* He opened the door and stepped into the hallway, startling two men. One was the thug from the restaurant. The other was taller and heavier with short stubble hair, clean-shaven, wearing a sports coat. He glanced up at the baseball bat slung over Hamilton's right shoulder and immediately reached into his coat. Hamilton reflexively brought the bat down to knock the gun from his hand. The gun tumbled to the ground between them. The man glanced at the bat and the gun, then lunged for the gun. Behind him, the thug from the restaurant had pulled out another gun with a fat silencer on it and fired at Hamilton from four feet away. It made a soft "poonk poonk" sound as it fired, and Hamilton stumbled back a few feet. He put his hand on his chest, amazed that the pendant worked. Two bullets dropped from his coat onto the carpet.

"Hell, he's got a vest on." The thug aimed at his head. Hamilton ducked behind stubble-head just as the guy was getting his own gun off the floor and rammed him hard in the face with the end of the bat. Stubbles fell back into the other thug, the shot going up into the ceiling. *Great*, Hamilton thought. *People in other apartments will be getting shot. Time to end this.*

He brought the bat down toward the thug's head, but the man blocked with his arm. Hamilton heard a bone crack and a howl from the thug. His gun dropped to the carpet as he clutched his fractured arm. Stubbles was flat on his back, out for the count. He took another swing at the thug from the restaurant, but the man ran down the hall. Hamilton stepped over Stubbles to pursue, but then heard glass shatter behind him in Clare's apartment. The door was still ajar. He tucked the bat under his arm, picked up both guns off the carpet, and ran back into the apartment.

Someone was climbing...no, *flying* into the apartment through the shattered second-story window. The man raised a gun toward the bedroom while he hovered in the air. Hamilton could make out the vague shape of Clare where he had left her. It suddenly occurred to Hamilton that the flying dude might think that he was one of his own thugs, busting in the door. He brought up the two silenced guns and shot him in the chest, twice. A wild shot went off from the flyer's gun as he jerked in the air. He slowly raised his gun toward Hamilton and Hamilton put two more slugs in him. The man tilted over and lay still, suspended in the air four feet off the carpet, dripping blood.

Just like Sudan, all over again, he thought. But messier and much weirder. When the Sudanese hospital had been invaded, they had already begun to evacuate their patients due to increased paramilitary activity in the area. It wasn't clear what group was attacking the hospital, or why, but when one of the members systematically began shooting the patients, his Army training kicked in and he managed to brain the guy with a steel rod from an IV stand. The unconscious attacker had guns, and Hamilton knew how to use them.

With the aid of a couple more doctors with military backgrounds, they were able to hold the fort until the Sudanese Army arrived. But that was a long, long time ago.

He lowered the guns, grinding his teeth miserably, and looked around the room. He was a doctor. He was supposed to be keeping people alive. Not this.

The police would undoubtedly arrive soon.

He went over to the floating man and started stripping off anything that could be removed, trying to discover what allowed the man to stay airborne. When an ornate leather bracelet slipped off his wrist, the man fell to the ground. Hamilton picked up the bracelet and took a moment to examine the complex and almost hypnotic pattern woven into it, then put it in his pocket.

It wouldn't be long before the police arrived. He turned on the light in Clare's bedroom. There were two partially packed suitcases and a duffel bag near the bed. It looked as though she might have been expecting trouble, ready to leave in a hurry. He glanced back and forth between the duffel bag and Clare, deciding that she'd fit inside, then retrieved the leather flight-bracelet from his pocket and slid it onto her wrist so she'd be easy to carry. He slid his arms under her and lifted her, light as a feather, then folded her carefully into the duffel bag. He tossed one of the two guns in with her body along with the bloody baseball bat, and zipped the bag shut. He grabbed one of her suitcases and closed it. She'd want a change of clothes.

He snatched a wide-brimmed felt hat from the body in the living room and snugged it onto his head, anxious to obscure the view of his own face from any prying eyes, and checked for people in the hall. Luck favored him—gunfire and a man lying on his back in the hallway kept the residents from sticking their heads outside unnecessarily. Hamilton did a quick wipe of the doorknob and stepped over the unconscious Stubbles, dropping one of the guns he'd used next to him. Just in case. Let Stubbles explain the silencer and the dead man inside to the cops.

He left the apartment building, walked a block, and hailed another taxi. The taxi driver tried to help put the duffel bag in the trunk, but Hamilton intervened with, "It's fragile. Let me handle it." He placed Clare carefully in the trunk and they headed back to his apartment. He could hear sirens in the distance as early morning shadows crept up the street.

Chapter 16 – Custody and Possession

Hamilton returned to his apartment with the two bags and went about the task of turning his bedroom into a darkroom, assuring that the curtains wouldn't allow stray beams of light to sneak in. Old Man meowed at him and pawed at the cat-food cabinet. "Hang on, cat." He took a minute to open a can of tuna and fill a bowl of water for Old Man, then resumed preps for the bedroom.

A bloody vampire, he thought. *I'm helping a vampire. What do I know about vampires, besides popular media? Although, a lot of the basic stuff seems to be true; sunlight issues, down for the day, and stalking around at night. And she kissed me. I let her kiss me!* He rubbed his cheek where her lips had touched and wondered what actually kissing her would be like.

He found himself smiling, despite the chance that he might be wanted for killing one of the thugs and despite his possession of the murder weapons and a bloody baseball bat tucked away in the duffel bag. And there was what appeared to be a dead girl on his bed. Or undead, not that the police would make that distinction.

On the plus side, there was a decent chance that the bad guys didn't actually know who he was, even though two of them could identify him if they saw him again. At least they hadn't seen his car. And they didn't know he had a pendant that could stop bullets; the one thug thought he was wearing a bulletproof vest. If Maggie had some spell to make him look different, then he could travel back and forth between the clinic and his apartment without too much hassle.

On the downside, the police would have some information on Clare's apartment and who was living there, unless she was living there under a false name. Which, considering everything else about her, seemed likely. The one thug, Stubbles, was going to have some serious issues dealing with the police; it'd look like he was part of a gang war. The loose thread would be Clare's involvement. But before tonight, there was no connection between him and Clare, so it would be difficult for the cops to track her location down to his own apartment.

He pulled Clare out of the duffel bag and laid her out on his bed. Her body was already cold, and he wasn't sure she needed a blanket, but he tossed one over her anyway. Old Man jumped up on the bed and sniffed at her face, then backed up and hissed. Hamilton picked up the cat and tossed it outside the bedroom. "She's a guest, leave her alone," he said, and closed the bedroom door. The cat stared at him questioningly, or accusingly, but the nuance of the cat-glare was lost on him. He ignored it.

He left a note on the bedroom door telling her to raid the fridge as needed and that he'd be back by 5PM if nothing turned weird at the clinic. Of course, if it was still daylight outside, she would still be dead to the world.

And speaking of weirdness at the clinic, Hamilton

thought, *Michael is bringing in his possessed cousin today. How do I prepare for something like that?*

As he left his apartment, he remembered that the first thug had seen Maggie and Clare talking together at the restaurant. He rapped at Maggie's apartment door. She should be off her shift by now. "Maggie?" he called, "it's Matt." He heard some movement inside and then the door opened. She looked bleary-eyed. "I was just about to hit the sack. What happened with Clare? Did she get home okay?"

He opened his mouth to say that she was in his bedroom but thought better of it. "I took her to her apartment, but that thug in the restaurant and a couple of his friends were waiting for us. We got away okay, but you're probably in danger. They saw you two talking together at the restaurant."

"Did you call the police?"

He hesitated. "You remember how the bokor thing turned out?"

Her brow creased suspiciously. "Yeah…"

"It was like that, but a lot worse. The one thug you saw in the restaurant got away. The others, not so much."

"Oh crap, Matt. I don't want to quit my job." She turned around and looked at her apartment. "And I'm not going to let them make me move. I just moved in a year ago." She turned back to Hamilton, teeth gritted and anger in her eyes. "If they want a fight, then they'll get a fight. But now I'm not going to sleep worth a crap. I may as well prepare."

"You already have the ignore-me glyphs on our apartment doors."

Her lips tightened to form a thin, angry line. "I can

do much better than that."
***

Hamilton drove his Corolla to work, driving a roundabout route to avoid passing by Cord's Cafe, just in case the thug or one his associates was out looking for him. The one that got away at least knew that he was associated with Clare and Maggie. He couldn't think of any immediate association with the clinic, his car, or his name. Clare had called him "Dave" at the restaurant instead of "Dr. Hamilton," so the thug didn't have that to go on either.

On the other hand, Clare had referred to the thugs as Hunters, and he'd already had dealings with the Hunters, like the one that escaped during Raoul de Lambert's invisible visit to Pembrook. If the Hunters talked to one another, he would probably be pegged as a problem that had to be dealt with.

At the clinic, Hamilton checked in, dealt with a half-day's worth of human ailments, then went to his back office. A door had been installed in the side where the two buildings had a common wall, leading to a storage room in the new building, but the door was kept locked. Hamilton verified MacDonald was busy with a patient, unlocked it, stepped through, and locked it behind him. He pulled the hidden magnet from a structural tube in one of the storage racks, opened the secret door, and stepped into the rough and unfinished lobby of Backdoor Clinic. "Is the pastor's daughter here yet?" he asked Medjine.

Ventilation fans had been installed behind the desk where Medjine sat. She had covered her face except for her eyes, and incense burned nearby. "She is in the regular offices of Pembrook Clinic. Her father insisted on coming along with her, and Michael Gordon felt that the less her father knows about this extension building, the better."

"Oh. Of course." Hamilton went back through the storage room and headed to the front of the original clinic.

The pastor and his daughter were waiting in the lobby. The pastor wore street clothes but was identifiable by his collar. He eyes wandered disdainfully around the lobby area, grimacing to show his disfavor. His glare settled on Hamilton. Hamilton nodded and said, "Reverend Orley, I'm ready to see you and Lucy."

He nodded curtly. "Michael Gordon tells me you are quite good at dealing with extraordinary cases like my daughter's. May we speak privately?" The tone was sharp and condescending. Hamilton watched the girl out of the corner of his eye. She seemed scared and trapped, looking around the clinic anxiously.

"Certainly. Right this way."

He led them into one of four normal exam rooms and closed the door, turning to face the two. The father started talking immediately. "I've seen some of the best experts in the church, and none of them have been able to get rid of this demon. But I don't know why Michael thought a medical doctor could do any better than the hand of God."

"Reverend Orley, I'm not sure I can do much good, either. I've had some luck with other unusual cases, so Mr. Gordon has come to expect it, I think."

"Luck. I see." Orley sniffed but deflated a little with Hamilton's self-deprecation. "I hope you can do something. This demon infesting her soul has broken the discipline of our household." He stuck out his chest a bit and said, "To date, this clinic has done some good work, and we would see it continued, but I needn't remind you that without our organization's support, this clinic would collapse."

Curious turn of phrase, and a not-so veiled threat, Hamilton thought, glancing at the girl. Her eyes flicked toward her father, her lips tight. Was she scared of him? And where was this demon supposed to be? The girl wasn't exactly spewing split pea soup around the room.

"What can you tell me about this demon, Reverend?"

"It's a rebellious imp! Each action upon the girl is reflected back – each lesson, each disciplinary action is cast back upon the teacher!" He gritted his teeth angrily, fists clenched. *Ah,* Hamilton thought. *I wonder how many times the girl has been subject to those same clenched fists?*

"So, say you needed to slap her for misbehaving, you would feel the slap yourself?" Hamilton asked.

Orley grimaced, feeling his cheek, as if remembering some pain. "Yes. Yes! That's correct."

"Well, that's bad. If the child can't be punished, how can she be trusted? How can she learn?" He tried to keep the sarcasm out of his voice, but it was difficult.

"Exactly!" cried Orley.

"When did this problem first arise?"

"Nearly three months ago, when her mother left our home. She was a witch! I told her to never return, but she brought this devil into my house and my daughter was possessed with its hideous powers!"

Hamilton got the picture. Abusive dad, mother is forced out, but not without leaving the daughter with some way to protect herself. The mother was a witch? He wondered if that was real or a fabrication from the father. Still, if she was possessed by a demon, it had to come from somewhere, and the convenience of having a demon so helpful seemed unlikely unless someone with an interest in the possessed person's welfare had a hand in it. How did this man ever get custody?

"Can I speak to your daughter alone, Reverend?"

He didn't move. "Anything she has to say may be said before the eyes of God. I will remain."

Well. That would make things a little more difficult. He rubbed the back of his neck, thinking. "Okay. Lucy, can you tell me where your demon came from? Did your mother send it to you?"

She looked trapped. Her father's glare curtailed her words. "I don't know," she mumbled.

"Speak up so he can hear you, girl!" He grabbed her arm hard, then winced and let go, massaging his own arm.

"I don't know!" she said.

He couldn't slap her, but that didn't keep the psychological torment from being slathered on. Hamilton shook his head sadly. If this demon were ever forced out, the girl would be powerless against Orley.

"Lucy, can I talk directly to the thing possessing you?"

She looked up at Orley as though asking permission, but he just stared at her accusingly, rubbing his arm. She turned to Hamilton and nodded. It didn't take long. Her eyes rolled up a little in her head, then returned to normal. She had a wicked little half-smile and gripped the edge of the seat like she was ready to throw it at someone. "Doctor," it said. "I've heard so much about you." Orley stepped back away from Lucy.

Hamilton raised his eyebrows. "I doubt that. I haven't been here that long."

Lucy shrugged.

"What name do you go by, Demon?" Hamilton asked.

Lucy cackled. "Not so dumb as that, am I! I would not easily give up my name to a mortal, lest I give away my own will."

"Considering you're here, I think that boat's already left the dock."

"It was a mutually beneficial arrangement between friends. I protect the girl, and I get to inflict a special kind of misery over this damned soul. It's a payment few but a spirit like myself can appreciate." She gestured at Orley, who bared his teeth at her. She grinned back at him humorlessly. Hamilton got ready to intervene physically if Orley lunged at the girl, punishment or not. "At least," added the demon, "she is not likely to ever be *raped* by this man."

The thing had referred to itself as a 'spirit' instead of a demon, though there was likely no semantic distinction between the two in Orley's mind, Hamilton thought. "I suppose it would be futile to ask you to leave, then."

"My contract lasts until she turns eighteen, Doctor. After that, we'll see. I have a long waiting list, and I wouldn't want to deprive my other customers of their just deserts."

"Well, we all must do what we must do. My job is to cure people of their ailments." He surreptitiously winked at the spirit. "Reverend Orley, I think I can resolve this problem. Please excuse me for a few minutes, I'll need to set some things in motion. I'll return shortly."

He left the exam room and approached Pembrook's receptionist at the front desk. "Carol, can you please call Amarita at Child Protective Services?" It hadn't surprised him when he'd learned that the supernatural community had their own representatives in CPS, considering their unique and often violent society. "If one of them can get down here in the next fifteen minutes or so, I need someone to interview one of my patients. And her father."

"I'll take care of it," Carol said.

"Thank you, Carol." He turned back toward the exam room and snorted like a bull at a red flag, then reentered the arena.

"Reverend Orley," he said, closing the door. "I'm afraid I'll be unable to release the demon from Lucy's body."

Orley looked down his nose at Hamilton. "Sadly, that does not surprise me."

"Unfortunately, I also won't be able to release Lucy from the clinic.

"What? She's *my* daughter. You have no right."

"We have notified Child Protective Services that there might be an issue here. They'll be down to interview you shortly, if you don't mind sticking around."

Orley's face darkened to crimson. "You…you! The Board will remove any funding that this clinic has received! We will see your damned clinic closed before the end of the week. Conspiring and colluding with demons to steal children away from their masters…their fathers! You and your ilk will burn in hell." Spittle flew from his mouth as his fiery speech ended, his finger pointing at Hamilton in damnation.

Hamilton looked at his iPhone. "Another ten minutes, and you can tell that to the CPS, too." He thought about the twenty-five gold pieces the clinic had stashed away in their new wall safe in the last few weeks. Closing the clinic down wasn't a realistic threat. Not anymore. Pembrook or Backside; the new clinic could pay for both.

Orley sputtered and stumbled from the clinic, his face a mask of pulsing red veins seemingly ready to explode. Hamilton watched him go, satisfied with the outcome, but aware that the repercussions from this case would follow the clinic for years to come. He considered Lucy. "So if you aren't a demon, what are you?"

Lucy rolled her shoulders. "Spirit of revenge, actually. Whether I'm demon or angel depends on which side you're on. That's why their pitiful exorcisms didn't work."

"So who hired you for the job?" Hamilton asked.

"Well, that I can't tell you. Private contract, you know. But let me just say, Orley's divorce wasn't a pretty thing."

***

The afternoon wore on and evening came. Hamilton quit for the night and poured himself a small shot of Laphroaig, kicked his feet up on his desk, and hoped nobody new would come tapping at the door. He was writing notes in one of his notebooks when the ghost appeared.

Hamilton looked up from his notebook, then glanced over at the bottle of Scotch. "Hi, Corwin. I'd pour you a shot, but then I'd have to drink it."

"Hello, doctor," Corwin said. He seemed more somber than before. "Do you remember when you and Agatha were talking about my murder? About a week ago?"

Hamilton put his notebook down, using his pen as a bookmark, and leaned forward, swirling the Scotch in his tumbler. "How could I forget?"

"I have a confession to make. I'm fairly sure why I was murdered, and who did it. I just didn't want Agatha to know. She would…I'm not sure…be very angry, at least. Perhaps she would leave me, and I couldn't live, that is to say, exist, that way."

Hamilton wondered how much he should give away as to what he'd already guessed at. "Does this have to do with some bauble you stole from Ivan the Illusionist?"

Corwin jerked back from the desk. "What? How…?"

"You have your own page on Wikipedia, Corwin."

"I what?"

Hamilton sighed, pulled his iPad out of his backpack and fired it up. "Hang on for a second." Once the page loaded, he turned the tablet around and pushed it toward Corwin, who eagerly began to read. "Oh, that was a terrible poster of me! What? Minor magician? And Ivan! Oh, I'm undone!"

"You're dead. I don't think you have much to worry about."

"But what if Agatha sees this and comes to the same conclusions you did?"

"Who says she hasn't?" Hamilton asked.

"How will I ever find out?" Corwin cried.

Hamilton shrugged. "So you want to tell me the rest of the story?"

"Let me finish reading this. The bottom of the screen is cut off."

Hamilton scrolled down for him and Corwin continued scanning the text.

"Ivan is missing?" he asked.

"You didn't know?"

Corwin was distraught. "I stole the bauble from Ivan. He knew I'd been lurking around…I'd seen his show a half-dozen times, trying to figure out how he had engineered that flying stunt, but there was just no way to set the wires for what he did. It was impossible! I researched his acquisitions during the period before the flight sequence was added to his show and found out about this bracelet he had."

Something clicked in Hamilton's mind. "Wait a second. A leather bracelet? With a very complex woven pattern running through it?"

Corwin stopped talking and just hovered, staring at Hamilton for a minute, dumbfounded. Finally, he said softly, "You've seen it, haven't you?"

Hamilton nodded. "I think I have. Tell me the rest of your story, as far as you know it."

"Okay. I planned carefully for weeks before I found a way to steal the bracelet from Ivan. He had no idea at the time who stole it, but in an act of foolish arrogance, I incorporated the bracelet into my own show. He discovered how I had stolen it from him, snuck into my home, and killed me to retrieve it. I would guess, from your computer information, that someone killed Ivan, too, to claim the flight-bracelet for himself. I can't say I feel badly for his death, serves him right for stuffing me under the house. Anyway, if you saw the bracelet recently, you may know who Ivan's killer is."

Hamilton snorted and took another sip of whiskey. "He's dead, too. I didn't get his name."

"And the bracelet?"

He thought about Clare lying on his bed wearing the bracelet, waking up and wondering what it was. "Clare has it now."

"Clare?"

Hamilton rummaged around in his mind and realized that Corwin hadn't met her yet. "A vampire who's helped out the clinic a couple of times. Before Backside was open for business."

They sat in silence for a few more moments, then Corwin said, "I hope you understand that I don't wish for Agatha to hear any of this."

Hamilton knocked back the last of the whiskey. "I can keep secrets. But she'll find out eventually if she doesn't know already."

"Maybe."

"I'm headed out," Hamilton said. "I'll see you tomorrow if you haven't passed over yet."

Corwin scowled at him, then disappeared.

***

By the time Hamilton reached his apartment, it was dark and Clare was gone. There was a note on the counter. He picked it up, depressed and relieved all at the same time. The note read, "Matt, I'm off to a safe house until things settle down and I can get a new place. You're still in danger, so keep that little item I loaned you close by. And thanks for the bracelet. Flying around is kind of cool. Sorry about the lamp cover in your bedroom. Be careful, XOXO, Clare."

He glanced up at where the glass lamp cover on his bedroom ceiling should be and saw that it was missing, making a mental note to not walk around barefoot in case Clare didn't find all the glass shards.

Her bags were gone, along with the gun and bloody baseball bat. *Nice of her to haul away the incriminating evidence*, he thought. Old Man was missing again, but he was getting used to that. He might have run out when Clare had the door open.

He clutched the pendant, the 'gift' from Clare. The way things were going, he would have to wear it 24/7.

Interview with a Golem

Considering what I already knew about Clare and Maggie, it was good to hear their 'origin story'. "So that's how he got involved with Clare. This is before she and Maggie had their little…well, war."

The golem nodded. "Oh, yes. Well before that."

"Hmm." I scribbled a note or two. "And judging by the story about Ozman's Bookstore, your book, The Name of Things, seems to have some say regarding its next owner."

"That is true, though this had nothing to do with my own will. The book has occult mechanisms built into it of which I am unaware. How it decides where to go, or whom to deceive, I do not know, but it does seem to have a will of its own."

"And the Reverend Orley, what became of him?"

"First, he unfortunately encountered Dr. MacDonald as he departed the clinic, a story I will relate in a moment. As for his daughter, he lost her to Child Protective Services, yet he somehow avoided jail time. The lack of any new scars or bruises on the child due to the spirit's intervention regrettably worked in Orley's favor. He succeeded in removing funding from the clinic, and likely believes that it's tottering on its last legs, begging for funds from other sources. Eventually, he will learn that this is not true and no doubt seek some other form of revenge."

"So Orley and MacDonald are still in the picture?"

"In a manner of speaking. A story about Medjine will enlighten that subject."

Chapter 17 - Medjine Goes Shopping

MacDonald knew something weird was afoot, and it had to be that troublemaker Hamilton at the root of it. When Reverend Orley stormed out of the clinic, MacDonald dropped his lab coat on the back of his office chair, dashed out the front door and caught up with the man at his car door to see what happened. Reverend Orley wasn't about to commiserate with one of the staff from the despised clinic, but MacDonald quickly convinced him he was on his side. "I knew something was off about Hamilton," he told Orley. "He's a disgrace to the clinic."

Orley, standing with one hand resting on the open door of his BMW, paused and scrutinized MacDonald. "We're going to cut off the subsidies to the clinic," he said. "But I think the Board of Regents can see fit to keep one staff member on the payroll, if you can report back to us. The man is in league with Satan, and communes with demons."

MacDonald assumed that Orley was speaking figuratively but nodded his concurrence. Hamilton had disobeyed MacDonald the first day there, taking in that filthy dog. Now he'd done something stupid to take their funding away. Gordon, their lack-wit administrator, wouldn't take any action; Hamilton was his golden boy, for some unknown reason. MacDonald was furious, and too angry to see that Orley's main interest was seeing the clinic shut down entirely, whether MacDonald was a casualty of that process or not.

"I'll see what I can turn up for you, Reverend."

Reverend Orley just smiled grimly, patted him on the shoulder, got in his car, and left.

The next matter of concern was this strange woman in a headscarf that kept appearing near the clinic. He saw Hamilton talking to her once on the sidewalk. They disappeared around the corner and he tried to follow them from a distance, but when he came around the corner, there was just the empty street. And that was doubly strange, since he was fairly sure there was an alley behind the clinic. By the time he returned to the front of the clinic, the thought of the missing alley was only a vague blur in his mind, like a dream that couldn't be remembered.

Today, he left the clinic, and here she was again, the mystery woman with the all-encompassing dress, walking down the street not fifty feet from the clinic. Coincidence? Not bloody likely. Hamilton probably had dealings with the terrorist community, he suspected, probably his connections from Sudan. Just add it to the list. MacDonald followed her at a distance, determined to see what she was up to. He picked up the pungent scents of acid and incense and frowned. *Foreigners and their strange smells.*

***

After the first few times she'd gone shopping, Medjine became used to people avoiding her. The smell was

very difficult to hide, though the electrolytic solutions
they'd been playing with had improved the situation a lot.
The bokor's little chemical lab had offered up vinegar and
baking soda, which seemed to keep her battery charged by
drinking the baking soda with water and bathing her skin in
white vinegar. A selection of herbs were blended together
in a sachet to mask the odor, and they experimented with
things like flavored antacids and citrus juices to replace the
vinegar, though the ascorbic acid didn't seem to work as
well as the ascetic acid. Some of the acidic exfoliators
seemed to improve her skin quality, repairing some of the
decay, and after the first week, she found she could expose
most of her face without scaring off people. Still, people
tended to stay away from her.

So she jumped when someone tapped her on the
shoulder from behind, and spun around. The man
confronting her was slightly shorter with neatly groomed
black hair, a black beard hovering between being stubble
and being short, and round, frameless glasses. He was
dressed neatly with a conservative sports coat and light-gray
shirt, with polished black shoes offset by worn blue jeans.
He stepped back as she turned around. He gave a bare
sketch of a bow and said, "I'm sorry to startle you."

Medjine was sure she would know this man if she
had met him before. Strangely, there was a new scent in the
air beside her own, an earthy smell, as if it had just rained.
Was that coming from this man? She was unsure what the
actual scent might have been; since her body chemistry had
changed, nothing smelled or tasted the way it used to. Acrid
odors that would have wrinkled her nose before now
seemed like floral arrangements.

"It's quite alright," Medjine said. "I just wasn't expecting anyone…"

"Did you know you're being followed? Don't look around, he might notice."

She immediately glanced down the street, then caught herself.

"He's about a half block up to the north, standing at the window at the cleaners." The small man laughed pleasantly. "Because there are so many interesting things to see in the window of the cleaners."

Medjine already liked the manner of the man but felt suspicious. She frowned and asked, "Why are you following a man who was following me?"

The man turned a little red, not easy to see on his swarthy skin. "Well, you see. I've seen you around here before," he motioned casually at the small shopping center, the drug store, the outdoor cafe, "and just noticed you again a few blocks north of here. I may have noticed you a bit longer than would be considered appropriate, and thus observed the other man trailing behind you, paying even more attention than myself. I felt it my obligation to make you aware of that fact, and an opportunity to introduce myself to you."

She noticed he stood a little closer than most people would, considering the smell that normally accompanied her. She nodded to him. "And you are?"

"My name is Naga Padoha. My parents thought it would be amusing to name me after the serpent-dragon of Indonesian mythology. Someday, I might forgive them." He smiled when he said it.

"I am Medjine Herivaux," she said, "from Port-au-

Prince, originally."

"I am very pleased to meet you. Would you care to join me for a cup of tea? The day is pleasant, and the outdoor seating at the cafe next door is nearly empty. Also, there are few locations around where your stalker can linger that won't be uncomfortably exposed. We can make him suffer at our leisure."

Tea, she thought. She was grateful for his suggestion. She could handle clear liquids, even if her new body chemistry changed the flavor of everything she drank. Spiced chai tea now had overtones of spicy chicken curry. Not a terrible conversion, but not her first choice. She avoided bakeries now; walking past an apple fritter was pure torture, since solid foods were off her list.

They took a table at the edge of the cafe's borders. A nearby couple, sipping idly at their coffee, suddenly paid up and left. Naga glanced over at them. "A little problem I have, I'm afraid, is that the smell of sulfur often drives others away. Outdoor cafes and light breezes abate the problem, but don't eliminate it completely. Does it bother you?"

Medjine almost laughed. "Does the smell bother *you*?" She left the statement ambiguous on purpose. She might have been speaking of him or herself.

"My genetic makeup precludes the ability to smell anything. Part of where I come from, I imagine. Having a sense of smell there would be a serious detriment. A pity, since I do wonder about how things taste. I can only take pleasure in the texture of things."

Was that flirting? Could this be real, she thought? But her, basically an undead semi-organic battery, with a human? How would that work? She shook her head sadly and looked away. Such flights of the imagination would only end in regret.

"Did I say something wrong?" Naga asked.

"No, no, it's not anything. Nothing." His hand rested on the table and she reached out to touch it placatingly, then noticed a small spot of discolored flesh on the back of her own hand and jerked it back. They sat in silence for a moment, then she asked, "What does the man look like?"

"Ah, I should have thought to show you." He seemed relieved that she had changed the subject. He took out his cell phone, selected a photo, and slid it across to her. "I took a picture of him as I passed him. Do you recognize him?"

Medjine stared at the image and pursed her lips. "Doctor MacDonald." She leaned back in her chair. "He is a detestable man. He works at the clinic where I am employed."

Naga glanced in the general direction of the clinic. "Pembrook?"

She took a moment, then rolled her eyes, and took a hesitant breath. "Yes." She could see him trying to look through her, reading the facial clues.

"Or Backside?" he asked.

They were both quiet for a minute, Medjine trying to figure out if there was some chance that he was non-human, and whether that would improve the odds of a relationship or not. "Backside has barely been open a month. How can everyone know about it already?"

"The community is small, but well-connected,"

Naga said.

"Are you human?" Medjine asked.

It was his turn to look away. "Not quite. Mostly. I'm a contract lawyer."

"That's still human. Mostly." She smiled at him.

He laughed softly. "My father is from a nearby dimension. Humans would call me demon-spawn, but they call anyone from another dimension by that name. Not just lawyers."

"And what does this contract lawyer do?"

"I create contracts that can't be broken. Or, let me say, such that an intentional breach by either party would be very unfortunate. The contracts sort of protect themselves, one might say."

"You use magic, then?"

"Not magic so much as minor curses. I'm very good at seeing the potential paths people might take and creating contracts such that the paths detrimental to either party are not taken. Diversions from the contract tend to be proportionate to the…strength of the effect. Like a Pinocchio clause, you might say." At this moment, a waiter approached the table, sniffing curiously at the air. He arrived, fortunately, just as a slight zephyr carried the bulk of the scents away. Naga said, "Two teas, please, one oolong and a spiced chai." He turned back to Medjine, who was gaping at him. "Oh. I should mention that I'm also very good at knowing what people want at the moment, which is quite valuable in contract negotiation."

Medjine blushed, but Naga seemed not to notice, perhaps on purpose. "What do you think MacDonald wants?" Medjine asked.

Naga glanced over his shoulder. Over the last ten minutes, MacDonald had surreptitiously drifted over to a newsstand set outside a hardware store across the street from them, pretending to read the headlines. Not within hearing distance yet. "I'd have to talk to him, face-to-face. Does he know that you know who he is?"

"I don't think so," she replied. "We have never talked, and I never go in the Pembrook Clinic front entrance to go to work. I doubt that he even knows that the Backside Clinic exists. Dr. Hamilton mentioned that he keeps nosing around at the storage room between the two clinic buildings. Usually we avoid using that door now and use the rear alley entrance. There are permanent ignore-me glyphs mounted at both ends of the alley, so few notice our comings and goings. Only those who know the word to momentarily disable a glyph can find the clinic's door."

"He dislikes your Dr. Hamilton?"

Medjine nodded sharply.

"Do you think that Pembrook and Backside can be turned into separate entities?"

"I believe the administrator is already working on that. Backside is supposed to make charitable donations to support Pembrook from the gold it gets. It will make bookkeeping much easier, I think."

"And how many weeks notice does Pembrook give you in case of a termination?"

She looked at him curiously, wondering where he was going with this line of interrogation. "Two weeks notice."

"Good. I can work with those facts." He scribbled something on a napkin, then pushed it over to her.

"What is this?" she asked, picking it up like a cocked mousetrap.

"A small contract. If I get MacDonald out of Hamilton's hair, you agree to go out with me for dinner?"

She stared at him blankly. After a moment of uncomfortable silence, he reached out slowly, pulled the napkin from her rigid hand, and said. "Sorry, terrible idea." He wadded up the napkin and tossed it over his shoulder, where it caught fire like flash paper and disappeared in a puff of smoke and ash. "Let me try again. Would you please honor me by accompanying me to dinner some night this week?"

If her heart were still beating, it would have fluttered. "That's better," she said. "I'll think about it." She fought to keep a smile off her face. It would have to be drinks instead of dinner; food still wasn't an option, unless Dr. Hamilton had some idea as to what she could consume safely.

Their tea arrived and they quietly sipped at it for a minute. "I suppose I should go talk to the fellow and get this over with." He pulled a quarter-folded sheet of paper from the pocket of his sport coat, unfolding it and smoothing out the creases on the table. It was blank. He stood up, smiled at Medjine, took the paper, and casually walked across the street toward Dr. MacDonald. As he walked away, Medjine surreptitiously added a spoonful of salt to her tea.

***

As Naga approached MacDonald, MacDonald glanced up and caught his reflection in the window of the hardware store. He turned suddenly and hurried further along the sidewalk. Naga called out to him, holding up a hand, "Mister MacDonald, I have a proposition for you!"

MacDonald stopped in his tracks. "That's *Doctor* MacDonald."

Naga nearly laughed at how easy that was. "Right, of course, Doctor," he said, approaching him with the blank paper in his hand. "My name is Naga Padoha. I was hoping we could come to a mutually satisfying agreement. I understand you have some dealings with that horrible man, Matt Hamilton?"

Naga watched the distrust and anger play in the man's eyes. He barely needed his special ability to see what the man wanted. But the hook was set; he perceived Naga as a potential ally.

"A piece of work he is." MacDonald ground his teeth then spat on the sidewalk. "Who's the woman?"

Naga glanced over at the table where Medjine sat. "Her? Poor girl, Hamilton has been extorting money from her for oxycodone. Hasn't been caught yet, but you know, it's only a matter of time. But I have contacts. Friends in low places. I'll make you a deal." Naga could feel the man succumb to desire.

"I knew he was up to something. He needs to be dealt with. Removed from the clinic."

"Indeed, indeed!" replied Naga. "I can arrange that he immediately be removed from Pembrook's employ. Well, within two weeks and a day, anyway."

"Fired?"

"Let's just say not employed there anymore." He waved a pen loosely above the sheet of paper out of sight of MacDonald, words appearing in neat script on its clean white surface. "In exchange for that, just so that rat Hamilton doesn't get suspicious and come after me, you will agree not to pursue any damaging actions against Hamilton."

MacDonald licked his lips, his eyes shifting back and forth. He looked doubtful. "Are you working for Hamilton?"

"Would it matter? He gets fired. Things at the clinic go back to normal. Hamilton goes on with his life somewhere else, you go on with yours."

He stood quietly for a moment, thinking. "I guess not," he muttered.

"Then sign here, and it'll all be taken care of. I've already signed my bit." He handed the brief contract to MacDonald. MacDonald slowly read it, nodding and nodding until he reached the end.

"What's this?" he asked, turning the contract toward Naga and pointing to the last paragraph.

"That's the enforcement clause. If either of us fails to meet the terms of the contract, then the enforcement clause kicks in."

"It says I'll void myself if I fail to meet the terms of the contract. What the hell does that mean?"

"Yes, in different degrees. Small infraction, you might pee yourself a bit. Bigger things, well…"

"How is that enforceable?"

Naga closed his eyes and spread his hands wide. "Think of it as the power of suggestion. Like telling a person that he might have an itch on his left arm, just below the elbow."

MacDonald instinctively reached over to scratch his

left arm, then caught himself. He slowly smiled. Naga could see that he didn't believe that the contract had any power at all. How do you make a person void himself? Certainly not by signing a contract.

Naga kept a straight face while MacDonald signed. He could just take the contract to the clinic administrator, show it to him, and MacDonald would be fired instead. In MacDonald's lust to see Hamilton terminated, he hadn't realized the power of the contract to which he applied his signature. But Naga would never do that. Unlike MacDonald, he knew the strength of the enforcement curse, and wasn't about to abuse it himself.

Grinning, Naga returned to the table with Medjine, sliding the contract over to her. She perused it while he sipped his now cool tea. Holding the cup in both his hands, the tea slowly came to a boil. Medjine glanced over at his cup and he shrugged nonchalantly. "I hate lukewarm tea."

She dropped the contract on the table. She looked angry. "You're going to see that Dr. Hamilton is removed from his job at Pembrook?"

He waggled his hand. "Sort of. I expect he'll have his hands full running the Backside Clinic, shortly." He lifted his cup and took a long sip. He watched contentedly as Medjine's angry frown slowly metamorphosed into a broad smile.

Chapter 18 – The Missing Alleyway

Despite the contract, Dr. MacDonald, peeping out the front window constantly like a neighborhood busybody, saw Medjine the next day as she strolled past the front of the clinic on her way to the obscured alley entrance. Perhaps it was just part of Naga's effort to dismiss Hamilton; continue the illicit sales of drugs to the strange woman to build a case against the man.

He dropped his white smock across the back of a chair and said to Carol, "If anyone asks, I'll be back in a minute." He stepped out the front door of the clinic just in time to see the woman turn the corner. He followed her. Somehow, he'd lost her before, so he jogged to make sure she didn't disappear again.

As he came around the corner, she was gone. He stared down the street and ran a hand through his red hair, flustered. Did she turn down the alley?

He hurried down the block and once again, couldn't find the alley. There *was* an alley. Wasn't there? He ground his teeth together and walked back to the clinic, thinking *alley, alley, alley.*

When he came in the front door, he said, "Carol. There's an alley behind the clinic, isn't there?"

Carol smiled cheerfully. "Why, of course, Dr. MacDonald. The back door of the clinic opens up to it."

MacDonald rubbed his forehead. Of course! The back door. Why didn't he think of that?

He walked down the short hallway and into the construction area at the back of the clinic. He considered the back door, making sure it was really there, and then opened it up, stepping out into the alley.

***

"Aw, Hell," Hamilton muttered. He was in his regular office filling out some paperwork and caught MacDonald out of the corner of his eye as he walked out the back door. He glanced at the time on his phone and figured out what was going on. Medjine was due in, and MacDonald had seen her. And now he was in the alley. Hopefully, Medjine was already inside the other clinic, out of view.

He waited for ten seconds for MacDonald to come back in, but he didn't reappear. Hamilton jumped out of his seat, went to the back door, and saw MacDonald standing at the far end of the alley, staring contemplatively at the cars as they drove by. He was shaking his head. Then he stepped out and turned the corner.

"Crap flakes," Hamilton cursed, and ran down to the end of the alley. He uttered the magic word that Maggie had said would momentarily neutralize the ignore-me glyph, at least for the person saying it, and the placard appeared. It was attached to the brick wall just inside the alley with silicon, a temporary installation until they bought some screws that would work in brick or found someone in the community who knew what sort of fastener was appropriate. Fortunately, it was no longer in the line of sight with MacDonald. The glyph placard was just above Hamilton's head, and he reached up and jerked it down off the wall, strands of silicon dangling from it, just as MacDonald came strolling back around the corner.

MacDonald peered into the alley and frowned. Hamilton opened his mouth to fabricate an explanation, but saw that MacDonald wasn't looking at him. MacDonald strolled past him into the alley, looking around at the walls, rubbing his chin thoughtfully, looking as confused as a man could look.

Hamilton looked down at the glyph he was holding. The ignore-me glyph. Apparently all-purpose. He stood still and hoped that MacDonald wouldn't try to walk through him.

MacDonald walked back to the rear door of the clinic, opened it, and just stared at the alley for a minute, frowning. Then he went inside, shut the door, and locked it.

Hamilton hurried over to the Backside Clinic door and knocked. A latch was thrown and the door opened, Medjine peering out. She looked around for a second, and Hamilton realized she couldn't see him. He put the sign down. "Medjine, it's me."

"Oh! That's strange. I didn't see you there."

"That was the glyph. Hey, the silicon RTV, is it still there? The stuff we used to put up the glyph placard?"

Medjine looked behind her. "It's still behind my counter."

Hamilton came inside with the placard and closed the door, retrieving the tube of silicon, stripping off the old bead of silicon from the sign, and adding a fresh bead along the perimeter of the back. "I'll need some tape to secure it while the RTV cures."

Medjine found some masking tape left by the construction crew and handed it to him. He added tape to the sign, crossed his fingers, and opened the rear door a crack, peering out. The alley was still empty. He reached out, applied the glyph to the outside surface of the door, smoothed down the tape, and closed the door. He was sweating. It was very likely that MacDonald had gone back out the front door of Pembrook to check to see if the alley was there.

"You moved the glyph from the alley entrance?"

"Yeah," said Hamilton. "I had to. MacDonald was snooping around too much. He was getting some seriously conflicting input."

"But this means that the alley will no longer be safe for our visitors. Anyone might see them enter the door to the new clinic."

"Can't really be helped," Hamilton said. "They'll just have to check the alley before disabling the door glyph. At least, even if they're seen by accident, nobody will be able to find the door they used afterwards. Additionally, we can't open the door from the inside safely, since we won't know who all is out there." Hamilton chewed on a thumbnail. "We need a viewport on the door for sure. Like a hotel door. And I need to pull down the glyph at the other end of the alley. I should have known better. Someone would miss an entire alley, eventually."

Interview with a Golem

"Isn't Naga the same guy who does contract work for Backside, now?" I asked.

"Indeed he does. He seems to spend more time here than necessary to fulfill the legal requirements of Backside," said the golem.

"So I assume that Naga convinced the administrator to separate the two clinics into two legal entities and hire Hamilton to run Backside, thus filling the requirements of the contract?"

"Correct. It took some doing, since Backside doesn't actually exist on paper in the human world."

"But Hamilton was still hanging around both clinics, wasn't he? Didn't MacDonald get involved?"

"Of course. He knew Hamilton had been terminated from Pembrook, so there was no logical reason for him to be appearing there, talking to Chopra and the others in Pembrook. He didn't appear often, spending almost all his time behind the hidden doors of Backside, but sometimes he needed supplies or help. Finally, MacDonald called the police, insisting that Hamilton was using the clinic to do drug deals on the side, which

unfortunately invoked some of the harshest retribution
from the enforcement curse."

"The contract voided him?"

"Quite." The golem coughed into a paper fist, a few
loose pages fluttering out, as though he was getting rid of a
bad taste. "MacDonald's various fluids and excrement
decorated the administrator's office from which he made
the call to the police. Cleaning up after him took days. It
was a week before MacDonald recovered from the event.
Administrator Gordon couldn't really fire him for being
sick in his office, but he did request that he leave Pembrook
with a small severance package. Naga talked to MacDonald
afterward, and reminded him of the consequences of
breaking the contract in the future. Naga related the
conversation to me much later, when he told MacDonald,
'You're fortunate that you didn't try to kill him. Your body
can void out your ears, too, you know.' He said he never
saw a man look so pale."

I nodded while scribbling some notes down.
"Alright, then. Let's get back to Hamilton. He shot the
Hunter at Clare's apartment..."

"This latest altercation with yet another Hunter
finally drew in Kraken, their leader, to deal directly with
Hamilton," said the golem. "And here is that story."

Chapter 19 - Kraken Flies Apart

Ever since Flying Charlie had been shot and Masterson stuck in jail for shooting him, Gutierrez had been out-of-favor with the boss. Except for the name 'Dave' that he overheard at Cord's Cafe, he hadn't found out who the guy was that saved the vampire bitch, the asshole who cracked his arm with a baseball bat. The guy might have been a cop, since he wore a bulletproof vest. But he didn't act like a cop. He'd explained the whole encounter to Kraken, including the fact that the waitress seemed to know both of them, and Kraken told him to do what he should have known to do on his own; go interrogate the waitress. Find out where the vampire disappeared to. *Fear muddles the mind. Good way to score points with the boss,* Gutierrez thought.

He stood in the shadows across the street from the restaurant and watched the activity through the windows. It was 3AM. The same waitress from the other night was working the counter. What was her name? *Maggie.* The bar crowd had already finished up, so the restaurant was mostly vacant. She'd probably know what went down at the vampire's apartment, if she was really friends with the mystery guy and the vamp. He rubbed the cast on his arm absently, then scowled, forcing himself to cross the street to the front door of Cord's Cafe.

He entered and sat at the counter, staring hard at the waitress. She smiled ingenuously at him. "Coffee?" she said.

"Sure." He glanced up and down the counter and at the tables. Nobody was taking any notice of him.

The waitress put down a decorative thin cork coaster with some strange abstract design on it. It looked like it was drawn by hand. He only got a glance at it before a coffee cup was put down on top of it. "Cream and sugar?"

"Just some of that stuff in the blue packets," he said. She brought him the sweetener and he stirred it in. Weird, she wasn't acting like she recognized him at all. Maybe the cast was throwing her off. His usual leather jacket wouldn't fit over it.

"Hey," he said to the waitress, pretending to look at a menu. "You remember a guy and a girl in here the other night, she had this long, straight black hair? The two of them left together." He took a sip of his coffee. If she gave him any crap, he could finish up the interrogation after she got off work.

"Ooo...I think I do remember her. That hair, what color was it again?"

He tried to remember. "It was long hair. The guy she was with, do you know what his name was?"

"What was that name? You mean the girl?"

"The...girl." He took another sip, eyes wandering, brow furrowed in concentration. "No a guy, wasn't there a guy?"

"Not sure I remember. Hard to remember. Things are so easy to forget. Do you want to order something?" She pulled out her order pad and twiddled a pencil.

"Uh." He frowned, struggling to hang on to fading memories. He stared down at the menu, feeling numb.

"Or just coffee?"

"Coffee. Just coffee, I guess." He lifted the cup and stared at the strange pattern on the paper coaster underneath. So detailed. What the hell had he come in here for? Just coffee? He stared at the blue sweetener packet, wondering if he'd already used one yet.

Gutierrez took another sip, stood up, and left, forgetting to pay or tip. Maggie didn't mind at all. She dumped the rest of his coffee and pocketed the coaster.

***

Gutierrez reported back to Kraken at his lab office. He stood in front of Kraken's desk looking bewildered.

"Well?" Kraken asked. "What did you find out?"

Gutierrez wiped a palm across his forehead, his eyes darting around the office. "What was it you sent me for? It's weird, but I can remember anything, except you sending me out."

Kraken simmered, glaring at Gutierrez, and started to wonder if he needed to be removed from the team. "You don't remember going to the restaurant?"

Gutierrez squinted nervously and shook his head. "Restaurant?"

"To find out information about this Dave person who killed Flying Charlie and stole his bracelet, and who put Masterson in jail. *And* fractured your arm. Is it coming back yet?" Kraken growled.

Gutierrez unconsciously rubbed the light cast on his forearm and stared blankly at the ceiling tiles, as if stoned. "No. Nothing. Man, I've got a headache."

Kraken sighed. More magic, or maybe drugs. Someone had messed with Gutierrez's head. Between the mysterious sorcerer-doctor and this killer Dave who'd teamed up with the vampire, he was having a rough time collecting bodies to absorb.

***

Kraken sent Joey Grice next and told him to watch from a distance. From Gutierrez's previous encounter, they had a good description of the guy to look for. Joey staked out the restaurant all day with specific instructions not to go inside, parking a block away and watching the place through a pair of Bushnell's. Joey knew something had happened to Gutierrez, but he didn't know what he was up against.

Finally, mid-day, Joey saw killer Dave enter the restaurant, talk briefly with the waitress, and leave. Dave got into his car, started it up, and drove off. Joey started his own car and pulled away from the curb, never taking his eyes off Dave's car. He wasn't going to lose the slippery bastard.

Dave turned a corner, out of sight for no more than five seconds. When Joey came around the corner, the car was nowhere to be seen. There were plenty of cars, but damn, they all looked the same. Joey slammed the steering wheel. *Magic!* This was why he took so much pleasure killing off the supernaturals; they just didn't fit, they didn't belong. He pulled over and thought about the problem. If he went back to Kraken without a lead, especially after Gutierrez had botched the job, Kraken would kill him. Or worse.

What did he know? The guy's name was Dave. Gutierrez gleaned that much info when the vampire bitch talked to him in the restaurant. More info than Joey had acquired; he hadn't even read the license plate. And why didn't he? That should have been automatic. Probably the same shit screwing with his head that made the car disappear. Was this guy a sorcerer, too? Like the dude at the clinic?

He drummed his fingers on the steering wheel, finally pulling into a regular parking space and shutting off the engine. He got out, walked back to Cord's Cafe, and ignoring his orders, went in and sat down at the counter. He didn't try to engage in conversation or ask questions, just ordered a burger and fries and coffee, taking his time to eat, and listened to the waitresses chatter with the customers. Maggie didn't say a word about killer Dave, but she also didn't recognize Joey and turn him into a blithering idiot like Gutierrez. No leads, though, and he couldn't sit there all day. At least the burger was good. He paid his bill and left an average tip, not big enough or small enough to be remembered.

He went back to his car, sat in it, and stared at nothing. It had been over a month since Pamela got whacked in the alley when they were tracking one of those freaks with the invisible skins. But what if these jobs were related? Geographically, they were almost next door to each other. What if this asshole sorcerer took her out? What if he was the guy in the alley? Joey saw the guy wave his arm at her and then BAM, down she went. He wasn't about to go back there. What if the killer Dave and that sorcerer-doctor…the one the bokor went after last week…Dr. Hamilton, wasn't it? What if they were working together?

Still. There was Kraken to worry about, too. A known serial killer who paid him well, and he didn't want to piss him off. He had to deliver something more than wild guesses.

He headed for the alley where he'd dropped off Pamela that night. It was only a few blocks away.

He stopped the car at the end of the alley and looked at the row of buildings on his right. Which door had the sorcerer come out of that one night? The guy who took down Pamela? He wasn't sure.

He drove down the alley, then cruised around the whole block. There were less than ten businesses in all, but no way he could watch all of them. So. Say it was Dr. Hamilton who was the sorcerer-doctor; Kraken thought so; after all, he sent the bokor after him. Say it was the clinic that the bullet-proof killer Dave went to. All he had to do was walk into the clinic, find out if "Dave" or maybe "David" worked there, along with Matt Hamilton, and all the pieces would come together.

His hands were shaking when he pulled up in front of the curio store next to the clinic. He checked his 9mm Luger in its holster, for what little good it would do, and climbed out of his car. He stood at the curio shop window, staring at a set of old wicker chairs and a cheap table, then glanced over at the clinic. There was a sign on the wall with Dr. Matthew Hamilton's placard at the bottom of a short list of doctors, right where he could see it.

Joey wondered if Hamilton was a zombie slave yet, and then a disturbing thought occurred to him. He picked up his iPhone and performed a web-search on Dr. Matthew Hamilton. There was one web page, Doctors Without Borders, where they interviewed him once. He opened it and found himself staring down at killer Dave.

Crap on a stick. Killer Dave and sorcerer Hamilton were the same guy.

Joey got back into his car. Kraken wouldn't eat him today. But he wouldn't be happy. If Hamilton was still alive, what did that mean for the zombie master?

***

Kraken remembered the ocean, hundreds of years ago. His father was master of the ocean depths. Nothing could defeat him. When he finally chose another smaller tentacled mate, he allowed her to live until she gave birth to two hundred small kraken, and then he ate her. The smaller kraken, like their father, were voracious and set upon one another, until only a handful of the strongest were left. It didn't take them long to realize that their father was more than he seemed, more than a king of the darkness. When they attacked and killed an opponent, they could, if they wished to do so, assume that opponent's shape, but remained locked in that new shape. Painful lessons for some of the kraken, where a moment's experimentation in shapechanging left them stuck in the body of a halibut or lobster, but good lessons to learn for a cautious kraken, watching his kin become easy meals for the rest of them.

The wise ones, the ones who wanted to leave the deeps to their hungry father, found larger and larger predators, working their way slowly and carefully up the food chain, daring the fates with each stronger, faster predator that they took on, shapechanging to the next level of viciousness. Few of them chose anything less than a shark. None of them knew, then, that the most terrifying predator didn't live in the water at all. The loss of brethren in the nets taught them that lesson. The taste of swimmers on the beaches brought them into their own, however, and they soon walked out of the waters, naked, on their own legs, the taste of shredded swimmers still in their mouths. And they walked into a new world of shapechangers, magic, gods, humans, and even stranger things. For a creature that knew nothing but the fight for supremacy, being one among many was not adequate.

But being limited to changing into one new shape, and being frozen there until your next meal, well, thought Kraken, that was completely unacceptable.

Kraken hired on at a small biotech firm in Manhattan Beach to learn more about the cells with which he was made, bullying, threatening, and killing his way to the top of the firm, now one of his many properties scattered around the South Bay area. Extensive research on stem cells from a variety of 'volunteer' shapechangers gave him a formula that allowed him to retain multiple shapes but required additional distillates from living shapechangers. It was, he thought, worth the sacrifice they made for him to sustain his abilities. Eventually it became an addiction, a distillate drug he could no longer live without.

"Another werewolf," he grumbled, his voice a deep base that rattled steel shelves. He held up a tube of brick-red fluid. "They taste like wet dog."

"They seem to breed quickly. And they're fairly easy for your Hunters to catch," said Vincent.

"It doesn't give me much variety. I need as many

different species of unnatural creatures as we can capture."
Kraken was a giant of a man, over four-hundred pounds.
None of it fat. A crown of thick black hair flowed over his
head like a mane. "I've had enough of wild dogs."

"The shapechangers are also easiest to distill.
Godlings and demons have proved problematic. Whatever
they're made of doesn't work with our current process. And
they are much more difficult to catch."

"We need a new process then." He looked out the
high window of the laboratory at the night sky. "I need
those abilities."

"This distillate will at least allow you to…"

"Survive. Yes, Dr. Vincent. I am well aware of that.
As long as my Hunters bring me a fresh supply of
shapechangers, I can be what I wish to be."

"One of the Hunters also brought in a new
shapechanger for you tonight. Not to be wasted on a
distillation."

Kraken looked at Vincent with a mixture of
anticipation and irritation. "You should have started with
that information. Where is this new changer?"

Vincent led him to an adjacent room. Gray, worn
cinderblock walls were dimly illuminated by hanging
fluorescent bulbs. In the middle of the room, an
unconscious man was strapped to a steel table. A mask
covered his face, connected to a canister of gas. "Aaron
brought him in. Caught him with a drugged dart. Strapping
him down is a bit useless, really. If he came to, he would
just fall apart and run away. Thus, the gas mask."

"Fall apart, you say?" Kraken rumbled. "How
interesting. You leave me in suspense." He put a hand the

size of a cow's head on Vincent's shoulder and squeezed it
lightly.

"Beetles!" Vincent squeaked, "He shape-changes
into beetles. Even if a few are lost, he retains himself."

"A beetle shape changer? Ah, that *is* excellent.
Delectable!" He let go of his shoulder. Vincent massaged
the half-crushed joint.

Kraken approached the table and placed his huge
hands on the shapechanger's chest. He closed his eyes and
started to knead the flesh of the body, crushing and
squeezing until his hands became one with the flesh, one
shaping the other, melded together. The man's extremities
lost form, becoming a single large, shapeless mass. Kraken
moaned, his arms now part of the body. Slowly, parts of the
semi-fluid mass dropped from the table to puddle on the
floor. In minutes, Kraken lifted his reformed hands from
the table. The remains of the shapechanger swirled around
his feet as he laughed. He stepped away from the table.
"See that the remains are incinerated, doctor."

He turned to the door just as Joey Grice entered the
lab. Joey glanced at the mess on the dripping lab table and
then at Kraken, who seemed bigger than before. He
swallowed.

"Mr. Grice," Kraken said. "Have you discovered
something, or has your mind been turned to sludge like
Gutierrez's?"

Joey nodded. "I'm fairly sure that your killer Dave
and Dr. Matt Hamilton are the same guy. And Hamilton
doesn't look like a zombie. Have you talked to your zombie
guy recently?"

The same man? The sorcerer who took down the

Hunter Pamela also killed Flying Charlie while taking out the other two Hunters, too, and now, maybe the bokor? Who was this guy?

Kraken pulled out his cell phone and called the bokor. The phone range twice, then a male voice answered, "Hello?"

Kraken stared at the phone. It wasn't the bokor's voice. He hit the disconnect, frowning at Joey and turning red.

"The bokor was using the 7th Street warehouse as a staging area. Someone will have to check on him," Kraken said.

Joey nodded. "I'll swing by."

Kraken ground his teeth and closed a fist as though crushing a head. "This Dr. Hamilton who keeps eliminating my Hunters, very soon, I will need to see who he is for myself. He is becoming an irritant. It will have to wait, however, until I sample my new form. It might be very useful against him."

He changed. His body segmented into ten thousand large cockroaches which scuttled into every crack and opening leading to the night air outside of the old building. His empty clothes fell like a collapsing tent on the floor. Dr. Vincent and Joey Grice stood perfectly still as the roaches crawled over their shoes and away.

***

A quivering mass of goo broke free from the rest of the liquefied corpse under the table, scared and confused, a formless shape. A few thoughts left over from the host body still lingered, driving the blob to hide fearfully in a gap between the cinderblock wall and the cement floor, squeezing into a narrow dark space. A spider living there found itself stuck in the plasm and was slowly absorbed into its mass as it struggled to escape.

The small blob waited until the last cockroach was gone, sensing at some primitive level that they were dangerous to itself, then slowly moved around the lab, cautiously searching for more food.

Interview with a Golem

Whenever the golem finished one of his little stories and his voice fell silent, I found myself leaning forward, unsure if this was the end of a story or the hanging sentence leading into the next paragraph. There was always a period of tense silence, that dead-air moment between the end of the song and the applause, just in case the song incorporated a long pause in its structure. This wasn't helped by the inscrutable expression on the golem's paper face.

I finally spoke after taking a slow breath. "I am curious as to how you found out about the origins of Kraken. Did you interview him at some point?"

The golem cleared his throat, an action that resulted in a puff of dust and a half-dozen spiders scurrying from his lips. "During the difficulties we had with him, we discovered that he had surviving siblings. We located one who had attained a somewhat neutral coexistence with the supernatural community and spoke with him. He filled in much of the story."

"We?" I asked.

"In my time as a book golem," he said, "I have

always had a desire to collect information, and eventually, I started my own library, adding to my own 'body' of knowledge."

"And size," I added.

"Indeed," said the golem. "I keep a smaller portable library just for the times I need to be transported from place to place, since I am in constant contact with a larger group of historians within the community and often need to travel. Thus, I use the collective 'we'."

"Excuse me for saying so, but as different as you look from humans, I would think it would be problematic for you to go anywhere."

"It used to be very difficult. There are now paths available to us that were not available before. But we will get to that point later in the story. First, I must introduce two other members who joined our company of actors, and who played important parts in the events that followed."

Chapter 20 – The Sprite's Story

The Backside Clinic had been open less than two months, but Hamilton thought he'd seen everything. He was, of course, wrong.

He was talking to a werebear patient who was regularly constipated; he'd figured out that the problem was being caused by hairballs that didn't disappear when the werebear shapechanged.

"You have a couple of options here," Hamilton said. "We can give you laxative while you're human, or we can induce vomiting while you're a bear. Either way, I highly recommend you start bathing while you're human, rather than giving yourself a tongue-bath as a bear."

Before the werebear could answer, the room lit up brightly with a floating spark of light, like a disembodied light-emitting diode.

Hamilton, unfazed, gave it a quick glance and said, "I'm busy with a patient. Give me ten minutes and I'll be with you." *Something new*, he thought.

The air vibrated with a low frequency, then the light disappeared in an eye blink and a pop.

He sent the werebear home with some off-the-shelf

recommendations, then sat waiting in the exam room, staring at the clock. Exactly ten minutes after its first appearance, the floating light reappeared. "Dr. Hamilton?" the air around him buzzed. It was a high voice, but softly pleasant. The light flickered slightly in time with the voice.

"That's me. How can I help you?"

"Do you do house calls?"

"To fairyland?" he guessed.

The thing was silent for a moment, then said, "Is this what a fairy looks like?"

"I'm not sure. I haven't met one before." Hamilton shrugged. "What are you, then? It would be good to establish that to see if I can actually do you any good."

"I'm a remote extension of a larger organism." The sparkling mote floated down to hover a foot in front of Hamilton. He could smell ozone. "The larger organism is located up around the place you call Griffith Park. It isn't mobile. I was hoping you could come see me. I seem to have lost part of my brain, and some of my abilities."

Hamilton glanced at a wall clock. "I've got no appointments the rest of the day. Let me grab my bag and I'll drive on up this afternoon. We'll see what we can do for you."

***

Hamilton arrived at the Griffith Observatory parking lot an hour and a half later. A bobbing mote of light, dimmed so only he could make it out, hovered next to his car. He squinted his eyes and shaded his eyes to see it better.

"Do you have a name?" Hamilton asked.

"Not that I know of," it buzzed softly. "What do I

seem like to you?"

"Some sort of fairy or sprite."

"I like the name Sprite. When you see the rest of me, you might change your mind, however."

"Let's stick with Sprite."

Sprite had warned him that he would be hiking for twenty minutes, so in addition to his regular medical bag, which he suspected would do him no good at all, he also brought a flashlight, hiking boots and a couple of liters of water. The sprite dimmed down to firefly brightness, a ploy mostly ineffective since fireflies didn't exist in California and would only attract attention. Most of the time it just stayed out of sight, leading Hamilton down a path by appearing momentarily far ahead of him. When they were alone, it flew alongside him.

"In essence," it explained to him, "I'm a dense electromagnetic field. My primary body can generate these fields in remote locations. The field is also my eyes and ears. I can detect sound, light, and other electromagnetic waves. I have humans to thank for that. If my body had never detected their communications, I never would have thought to experiment with it myself, and I never would have learned to make this sprite. Or meet others of my kind."

"If I remember my history, radio was first developed around 1900, plus or minus. You've only been around since then?" Hamilton asked.

"Oh, much longer, perhaps hundreds of years, but I had only myself to communicate with. It was a very small world indeed. I imagine that I would have gone insane in human terms, but at that time my body was isolated and fragmented into many small parts and each part communicated with the others. So, in a way, I was never actually alone, but in your terms, it would be like have someone with a multiple personality disorder chatting with their other selves to stay sane. Their insanity would preserve their sanity. A conundrum. When my parts merged and became one, we lost that ability, but gained the larger community of entities of which humans are a part."

Hamilton nodded. He would have to add another "cell type" to those he had already recorded. He was curious what sort of body could maintain something like the sprite.

The path to the sprite's body was mostly downhill through a forest of dead pines, their cracked and broken skeletons turning the hillsides into a gray wasteland. Hamilton found it depressing. The California drought was going into its fifth year, with promises of El Nino and torrential downpours always just around the corner, but never delivering. Could trees be generating the sprites? Would he have to tell the sprite that it would be nothing but firewood next year?

"I think we are near my body," the sprite said. "Did you bring a compass, as I suggested?"

"It's an app on my iPhone." He pulled out his phone and activated the compass app. "Seems to be working okay."

"I'm going to generate a field at my body's location. You should be able to see the needle deflect if you are near me."

Hamilton watched the needle display jerk to the left and stabilize.

"You may walk around and figure out where my

body is from the compass display," the sprite continued.

"Triangulation," Hamilton said. The sprite bobbed up and down. "You seem to have a lot of human mannerisms down pat."

"This is Griffith Park," it said. "There are plenty of humans to observe."

Hamilton kept his eye on the compass and ventured off the path. Thirty feet from the path, the display started spinning lazily. Some side-to-side movement narrowed down the location to within five to ten feet. Hamilton looked around. There was nothing but bare rock. "I don't see anything."

"I believe my main body may be underground."

Hamilton scanned the hard rock around him. It appeared to be made up of dense layers of mica patterned with other dark minerals. He reached down to touch it. The mica flaked away, sticking to his fingertips. He tasted it, then spat it out. "Salty. How deep do you think you are?" he asked.

"Shallow, I think. I have never had cause to measure it."

Hamilton pulled out a bottle of water and took a drink. "I would think you'd want to know that first."

"I didn't even speculate that I had a body at all until I lost part of my brain. I thought I was some sort of free-floating electromagnetic entity. Pure thought and energy. Losing myself was terrifying to me. That was why I contacted you."

Hamilton thought. Something buried that was alive? Something that makes electric fields? A computer? A naturally occurring self-aware computer? He looked down at the mica, then up at some patchy looking clouds. When was the last time it rained? It couldn't be that simple, could it?

"Tell me if this hurts," he said, and then poured the entire liter of bottle of water over a wide area of the exposed mica. It quickly disappeared into the cracks.

The sprite quivered and sparkled. "What did you just do? What was that? I felt it! You touched me."

He put the cap on and stuck the empty bottle back in his backpack. "Just water. I think I have a good idea what's going on. How far away is the missing part of your mind?"

"I am not completely sure."

"Can you send your sprite underground and detect electrical activity? Can you send it into your own mind?"

"That is quite painful. But I can do that, yes."

"Then send the sprite to scan the inside of the mountain near you. Start near your brain and—"

The sprite disappeared for a fraction of a second, then suddenly appeared right in front of him. "I found something!" it shouted. Hamilton stumbled backward.

"Okay—that was fast," Hamilton muttered.

"Speed of light! I materialized every meter in a cubic grid. No problem. I detected a weak electromagnetic field ten meters away, two meters down. The volume is over two cubic meters in size. What is it?"

"I think it's the missing part of your brain. If I'm not mistaken, the lack of water in the soil here from the drought has created an insulator between the two parts of your brain. I think your brain is made out of rock. Mica is a type of silicon, salt and water can make an electrolyte to carry electricity. You just lost the electrical umbilical between two of your masses."

The little light vibrated in the air. "How can that be? Brains are organic structures."

"But you knew you were buried here. What did you think you were?"

"I did not know. Perhaps some ground burrowing creature, like the giant worms on Arrakis in that documentary." It bobbed lower, as though somehow depressed. "You are saying I am made of the same things as a computer. Nothing but a thing of silicon and electrons, an accident of nature."

"We are all accidents of nature. And computers aren't self-aware. You're something different. You said there are others like you?"

"Yes. They will not take this news, this revelation, well. Although others have had the same problem as myself; parts of their brains disappearing and occasionally returning much later. None of my kind had correlated these events with the lack of rainfall."

Hamilton sat on the hillside and watched the first stars begin to come out. "You can wait for the next big rain, or you can have someone start watering you regularly."

"You have a liter left," it said, "And you can still urinate."

Hamilton chuckled. "It won't be enough to make a difference. It could take a year for water to percolate that deep, and the surface water could evaporate by tomorrow." Hamilton thought briefly of sneaking in a sign that said, 'Please Pee Here'. He shook his head to dislodge the idea. "And there are other issues you have to deal with. Based on the first bottle of water, I think your brain is exposed. It's going to start eroding. Rainfall and wind will wear away at your substrate. It might take hundreds of years to have any significant effect, but you might want to think about that problem. Maybe figure out a way to get a cement cover."

"Like a skull," the sprite said.

Hamilton laughed. "Just like that."

They sat and hovered quietly together for a minute as night deepened. Finally, the sprite said, "Did you instruct someone to follow you tonight?"

Hamilton sat up, suddenly watchful and glad he was off the path. "No, I didn't, why?"

"There is a man up the path waiting for you. He just made a phone call to someone called Kraken to ask if he wanted you eliminated or brought in. The man on the other end of the call said to eliminate you. That would be most inconvenient for me."

Hamilton stared into the darkness, wondering what sort of weapon the guy had. With his pendant on, it may not be an issue. But he still didn't know its limits. And it could still come off. "I can move along this hillside and go around him."

"The hillside steepens quickly. You will not be able to traverse the slope to circumvent him."

"Maybe he'll walk past."

"He is sitting in wait. He apparently expects you to come back up the path."

"Would you like to help?"

"I would be delighted to do so. You have already helped me considerably, and I have thought of a number of options to provide myself with the liquids required to reconnect my brain. We still need to discuss payment. I do not own any of the gold coins that exist in the rest of the supernatural community."

"Let's not worry about that quite yet. I want to ask this guy a few questions." Hamilton bared his teeth and stood. "When I get close, can you flash him in the eyes? Just to blind him before he gets a shot off?"

"Easily."

Hamilton marched up the path like he owned it. He clutched the pendant beneath his shirt, simultaneously doubting and trusting its effect. As he neared the turn where the man waited, a flashbulb light popped right in front of the man's face, illuminating the whole area. Hamilton saw a gun with a silencer pointed in his direction. It made a 'pfft' sound a couple of times as the shooter made wildly blind shots. The flash appeared again, brighter this time, and the gun flew out of the man's suddenly burned hand. "Son of a bitch!" the man shouted.

Hamilton walked right up to him. The man rubbed his eyes, saw Hamilton, then lunged at him with both hands extended. Hamilton sidestepped and pushed the man forward, tripping him as he went by. He slid along on his belly on the gravel path for a few feet, but jumped up neatly and pulled a knife from his belt. He was panting.

"Sprite," Hamilton whispered, "follow my lead, but don't speak. Appear between us."

A bright light popped into existence between the two men. The floating pinpoint of arc-lamp intensity dumbfounded the thug. Hamilton said, "You've already seen what I can do to your hand. I can put this inside your head before you can move. What do you think will happen to your brain? I can turn up the heat," the sprite brightened, "if needed to make the cooking go a little faster. Or you can drop the knife and answer a few questions." The sprite drifted toward the man's head. Hamilton thought it was nice improv by the sprite. He waved his own hands around to amplify the effect.

The man turned and ran.

"Aw hell. Get in front of him. Block him if you can."

The man fell over as the arc-light hit him in the chest, threads of lacey lightning bolts crawling across him. Hamilton walked down and stared at the prone man. The man stared at him with wide eyes. "But—you—you're human," he said.

Hamilton smiled tightly. "Am I? Let's try this again. Who do you work for?"

The man's mouth worked silently, his eyes darting side to side like a trapped animal. "He just goes by the name 'Boss'. I never seen him."

"The right answer was 'Kraken'." He pointed at the man's chest and the sprite obligingly zapped him again. The man cried out. Hamilton smiled grimly. "Next question. Why is he so intent on killing me and my friends?"

"I don't know." Hamilton lifted his finger and the sprite rose with it, ready to punish the thug again. "Wait! Wait!" he said, hands futilely up in the air to block the sprite. "He's got a standing bounty on all you freaks, but he pays a lot more for the living ones. He talks about you like…he calls you monsters, unfit to live with humans."

"So he called in the Hunters." The man looked like he was trapped again, his death moments away. "How many of these 'monsters' have you captured?"

The man said nothing, his eyes darting quickly around the hillside, looking for a way out.

"Being a doctor, I'm not in the habit of killing people," Hamilton said. His mind flashed back to the fight in Clare's apartment, and he winced. Nothing like this was supposed to have followed him to the clinic. It was supposed to be a low-key, cush job. Not a combat situation. "But you are going to have to come with me," he continued. "I have friends who want to talk to you."

"Okay, okay! I give up." Too easily. His eyes shifted left and right. Hamilton tensed. The thug slowly stood up. "Just ask your friends to take…" then he whipped out another concealed knife and lunged at Hamilton, driving the blade into his neck, where the blade skittered off some invisible boundary. Hamilton fell backwards and the world went dark.

Hamilton lay still in the darkness, then realized the thug was lying on top of him. He took a breath to check if he was gurgling blood, sighed, and rolled the man over. The man's eyes stared blankly. The sprite suddenly reappeared. Hamilton looked sadly up at it. "You went inside his head, didn't you?"

"Did I do wrong? Did you not threaten him with such an action?"

"I did. You did okay. He was trying to kill me." He couldn't, however, not with the knife. Probably not with the gun. The sprite didn't need to know that. He clutched at the pendant and discovered it was no longer there. Frantically, he looked around on the ground for it and found it near his feet. The thin chain had been cut by the knife on its first pass. His hands shook. Just one stab away… "You did really good. But he's dead now."

"His brain no longer functions?"

"That's right. He has ceased to be." Hamilton checked for a pulse just to make sure. There was nothing.

The sprite hovered and crackled. "I am sorry this came to pass."

"Me too. I had hoped our little act would convince him I had superpowers that he could report back to his boss. The Kraken fellow." He looked up the path, dimly illuminated by the light of L.A. reflecting off of cloud cover. There was no way to move the guy back to the car without looking like he was carrying a dead man. Time for a little practicality.

He removed the man's cell phone to do a little data mining, if possible, then pushed him off the path, down the hill, listening to his tumbling corpse crash through the underbrush. Since he was killed by having his brain fried, the cops, if and when they found the body, would find no obvious signs of foul play. Just some unlucky fellow who had a massive brain hemorrhage while hiking. It might be worth calling in an anonymous tip just to save some random hiker from the horror of stumbling upon a maggot-ridden rotting corpse a week from now, though. Sighing, he started back up the path.

"There is still the issue of payment," said the sprite.

"I think we're even on this one," Hamilton said.

"The community does not work that way. You would not have been in this predicament if I had not led you here."

"This Kraken guy would have found me somewhere

else."

"Still. I do have a resource of gold nearby."

Hamilton thought about the clinic's bills. It wasn't going to be easy or cheap to keep a secret clinic in operation. "Okay, Sprite. Where is this gold of yours? The clinic could use another coin or two."

"It is about one mile on the far side of this park. It is also underground, about three feet under the surface."

"Buried treasure?" Hamilton recollected no pirate stories from this area, and with all the books he'd read on California mythology and history in the last few weeks, he would have come across it.

"It is a melted mass, what humans refer to as a nugget. Approximately five kilograms. Technically, it is not mine to offer. But if I understand humans, it belongs to no one until it is actually removed from the Earth."

Hamilton caught his breath, then stopped and stared at the sprite. "Five…kilograms? How long have you known about this nugget?"

"Nearly thirty minutes. When I did the scan for electrical signatures, I found these unusual deposits and performed conductivity tests on them. I am fairly certain it is gold."

Hamilton whistled. "I hope it's not private property. Once we dig it up, I'll need to get you some change. Make some new coins. It wouldn't hurt for you to have access to coins. You could even pay someone to water you."

"That is an excellent idea. A decent long-term solution, since I have just discovered over two hundred other nuggets in this area. But most are much less accessible, deeper in the ground. Still, it would be convenient to have coins, as you suggest. Fifty-fifty?"

Hamilton shook his head and laughed softly. "It's best if you keep the other nuggets your personal secret until you need them," he said, "along with your ability to find them. No reason to destroy the gold market."

"Gold market?"

Hamilton headed for his car with Sprite drifting nearby. "There's this thing called economics…" he began.

Interview with a Golem

The battery was running low on my phone, so I stopped the recording, dug out a charging cord, and searched for an outlet. The golem sat still and politely remained quiet as I finished this process and turned on the recording app again. "So they dug up a five kilogram nugget..." I said.

"They considered trying to make a legal mining claim, but the property was part of Griffith Park. A little stealth was required to secretly dig out the giant nugget, for which Sprite hired one of the wolf-people, someone he'd known for quite a while. The nugget fit easily in a backpack, so was removed from the park with a minimum of subterfuge. Then the fairies processed the nugget and minted the coins, as usual, and payments were made as needed. As it turned out, the community's general knowledge of the existence of numerous other nuggets in the area had little to no effect on the gold market. The majority of them were inaccessible without digging a deep mine, something that couldn't be achieved under the watchful eyes of the Griffith Observatory Security."

"The Sprite was one of Hamilton's first allies,

wasn't it?" I asked.

"Everyone he helped was, in a sense, an ally. In his struggles against the dark elements of the community, however, some were more active than others. Another patient is worth mentioning before we continue, although his participation was, in a way, accidental."

"And he was…?"

"It was a demon from Hell," the golem said. "In a manner of speaking."

Chapter 21 – Coming Out of the Closet

Hamilton was happy when he found out that the old brick building had a walk-in closet near the back. It was an odd little room with the original wood paneling, wainscoting, high shelves for hats, and bars and hooks for coats. He wondered what the building had been before it was an army surplus store. Did they have speakeasies in Redondo Beach? The room was left relatively intact, except that florally decorated vases for umbrellas were added, resting gaudily on pressed tin plates for drainage. At the end of the small room was a bench so you could sit and remove muddy boots, if necessary.

Hamilton was removing his light jacket and knit beanie when Corwin materialized next to him. "Good morning, Dr. Hamilton."

Hamilton looked around for a coat hanger, finally found a couple on the floor, and hung up his jacket. He glanced at the ghost. Corwin was wearing a lavender shirt and black tie today. Hamilton tried to remember if he'd ever seen him wearing the same clothes twice. "Morning, Corwin." He tossed his beanie on the upper shelf, then tried to muss his hat-hair back into normality. "Hey, I've been meaning to ask you. You keep showing up in different clothes. Do you just think them into existence, or do you have a wardrobe in limbo?"

The ghost thought about it. "I guess you could call it a wardrobe. More like a miniature universe, from your perspective. A little bubble of nothing that I can store ethereal things in."

"Okay, but where did you get them to begin with?"

"I *trade* for them!"

"But…"

"It's not like there are shopping centers in the afterworld, you know."

"Hmm." Hamilton said. Bartering in the ghost world? There was much to learn from Corwin. "You going to hang out here for awhile?"

The ghost shrugged with his whole body. "Maybe. People here are getting so hard to surprise."

Hamilton smiled. "You need a new venue." He closed the closet door on his way out. He didn't get two steps before he heard something crash in the closet and loud voices shouting. Spinning around, he flung the door open.

"Demon thief!" called Corwin.

"Lecherous specter!" shouted the small coal-black figure. The two were wrestling with each other, grabbing, jabbing, and punching, though with little effect. The ghost spun around and caught the impish figure by the back of its neck. "Doctor, this creature tried to steal your coat!"

"Falsehoods! Never listen to a ghost." The imp suddenly set eyes on Hamilton and it stopped struggling. "Dr. Hamilton?" it said. "This is your closet?" It had something in its hand, which it suddenly whipped up behind its back.

Hamilton frowned at the imp and crossed his arms. "It's the clinic's closet. But I use it. Who are you, why do you know me, and what do you have hidden behind your back?"

He bowed slightly to Hamilton and said, "Among the demons, I am called Mbuzi. I know of you because I've been asking around for this…little problem I have, and your name came up in the Circles." He looked a little embarrassed as he showed Hamilton what he was hiding. It was a coat hanger.

"You're taking a coat hanger?" Hamilton asked.

Mbuzi looked sadly at it. "I was actually dropping it off. It's been my assignment for over a hundred human years. Adding damned coat hangers to closets. It's my punishment, I think."

Hamilton stared at the wire coat hanger in the imp's hand. "You wrestled with the ghost, and yet you can handle normal matter. That's curious…I need my notebook. But first," he sat down on the little bench in the room, "punishment for what?"

The imp looked embarrassed. "Will you look at my problem if I tell you?" it asked.

"Fair exchange. No guarantee I can cure it." The imp held out its hand to shake. Hamilton took it.

"No!" shouted the ghost, a moment too late. "Agh! You made a deal with a *demon*!"

They both glared at Corwin. Hamilton turned back to the imp. "Go on."

"Do you remember about a hundred years ago, all

these cows they found, butchered in the fields, and they didn't know how it happened? Blamed on aliens." The imp snorted disdainfully. "*Aliens*! Humans are so stupid sometimes. Anyway, my boss, he was really angry with some local sheriff who broke up some cult of his, and this sheriff was also a rancher who owned a lot of cattle and goats. So my boss told this one demon to kill a bunch of cattle and leave them lying slaughtered in his fields. But I was in charge of the sheriff's goats. I was supposed to leave them hanging from trees. I was supposed to be the goat hanger. But my hearing isn't that good. It didn't make any sense to me at the time, why my boss would want me to leave coat hangers in the trees, but I did it anyway. He was pissed off at me when he found out, so he punished me with my own little piece of Hell. And now, here I am, a hundred million coat hangars later. Plus or minus a million." He looked up at Hamilton with a tired, resigned expression. "You don't mind if I leave this one here when we're done here, do you?"

"Be my guest. Where do they come from?" asked Hamilton. "Is there a storage warehouse in Hell?"

Mbuzi chuckled dryly. "Naw. It's like I heard your perv ghost say when you two were talking. It's a pocket universe. It's got nothing but billions of wire coat hangers in it. Like a bonus punishment, being confined to a universe made of tangled wire. Nothing but closets and coat hangers for me. And the rare chance to scare the crap out of some kid at night."

"Lucky bastard," Corwin said.

"I'd rather have the run of a house, where I might peek in at anything anytime, degenerate phantom," said the imp.

Corwin whistled something tuneless, then disappeared into a wall.

"Pocket universes," Hamilton said thoughtfully, "could explain how ethereals can just materialize objects from nowhere."

Mbuzi nodded. "You got the hang of it. Some shapechangers even store surplus body mass there when they shape-change, so, like a small basilisk could turn into a giant dragon."

Hamilton raised his eyebrows. "Those exist?"

Mbuzi smiled knowingly. "Do people believe they exist?"

Hamilton grinned. "Point taken." He made a mental note to explore the relationship between the number of believers of certain things and frequency of sightings. If thought created mass, then there should be a mathematical correlation. He leaned closer to Mbuzi and quickly scanned his small body with his medically trained eyes. "So, what seems to be the problem you're having?"

"Besides the bad hearing, I've got this toe fungus that's driving me crazy." He held out a big toe covered in green moss. Something was growing out of the middle of it. "It itches like Hell."

"Is that a mushroom?" Hamilton asked.

"I prefer to think of it as a toed-stool. Get it? Anyway, I don't mind those so much, they taste okay. Sort of a nutty flavor. It's that moss that seems to get bigger each year."

Hamilton sat back on the small bench and drummed his fingers on his knee, thinking. "Let me get some things, and I'll be back in a minute." He left the closet and came back with his doctor's bag a few minutes later, along with some medical samples. He pulled out a sample tube of toenail fungicide. "This is a fungicide made for human use, so it may not be useful here. I don't think your species is made out of the same sort of matter as humans, and likewise for the parasitic fungus growing on you. But we can give it a try. This could require an herbicide, instead, for all we know. I'll take a sample of the growth to examine and test. It might reveal something useful." He retrieved a disposable scraper and vial from his bag, leaned over, and took the sample, dropping the small scraper inside the vial with it, then sealed it and wrote a label for it.

Mbuzi looked at the tube of fungicide. "So there aren't really any standard meds for angels and demons, then, huh?"

Hamilton was struck by the thought that the other species didn't have their own cadre of medical professionals and treatments. Maybe they were spread too thin, only a few in each city, not enough to warrant a species specialist. It was another puzzle to investigate when he had time. As if he had any spare time. "Not that I know of," he replied. He placed the vial carefully into his bag. "And I don't think human cures will be very effective. Your species appears to be made of thought-particles, where thought has parallels to human energy and mass. Belief in you is required for your existence."

"I guess I can try it. No other ideas if it doesn't work, huh?"

"Maybe. Just maybe. If your existence is based on belief by humans, then maybe a fungicide that only works based on belief will be more effective."

Mbuzi stared at him, brows furrowed. "How would that work?"

"Well," said Hamilton, starting to warm up, "there are a lot of quack medicines available on the internet. People propose really outrageous cures for things, like crystal power and such. So if one of these appears to work, and there's really no logical explanation for it, then it might be functioning off of belief. We sometimes call it the placebo effect."

"So by giving me a medicine that works only because people *believe* it works…"

"Could cure you since your whole metabolism is based on a type of matter created by belief."

The imp pursed its lips dubiously and raised a black eyebrow. "You'd research that for me?"

"It would be fascinating for me. If you don't mind being an experimental subject."

The imp shrugged. "Sure, why not? What could possibly go wrong? Now, about my hearing." His large ears were like bat wings hanging on the side of his head. Hamilton dug out an otoscope and peered inside one of Mbuzi's ears. Inside, he could see what looked like dozens of insects crawling around. He retreated hastily and checked the end of the instrument to make sure nothing was crawling on it.

"Do your ears itch?"

"Not particularly. Why?"

"There appears to be a colony of insects living inside your ear canal."

"Ah." The imp didn't seem surprised. "Wax beetles.

No wonder I have so much trouble hearing anything. Wax beetles for a hundred years." It shook its head slowly. "They prefer beeswax, but I haven't been near a candle since I was—given this task. Do you think you could get me a chunk of beeswax? I can lure them out."

"And capture them?"

"Seriously? Smash the hell out of the little bastards, that's what I'll do." Mbuzi smacked his palm down on the bench. He stood up and grinned at the doctor. "Things are looking up. If you find anything out, or get that beeswax, just step into any closet and call out for Mbuzi." He bowed once again and backed into the wood paneling at the rear of the closet, disappearing in a slow fade.

Hamilton sat staring at the blank wooden paneling for a minute, then grabbed his bag, and ran to his office. A set of black notebooks greeted him. His hand twitched above them as he read the Sharpie-inscribed spines; Laws of Ethereals, Thought-Mass, Laws of Objects, Ailments and Rules of Shapechangers, and more. A dozen labeled notebooks and a dozen more that were waiting for titles. He plucked out the Laws of Objects, created a new heading called "Pocket Universes" and started writing.

Interview with a Golem

I sharpened a pencil with a penknife as the golem ended the story, dumping the shavings into a small plastic wastebasket next to Dr. Hamilton's cluttered wooden desk. I often kept paper notes to supplement the digital recording and have always preferred pencils to pens. Questions would pop up in my head as the subject of the interview was talking, so I'd write them down rather than interrupt their train of thought. Putting away the penknife, I picked up my writing pad and glanced at my phone to make sure it was still recording. "Sprite is fairly well known to those who have dealt with Hamilton before," I commented. "This is the first I've heard of Mbuzi."

"And perhaps the last. I would venture to guess that Mbuzi will change his name if people reading this interview start calling on him for extra coat hangers. Although, perhaps, he might enjoy the attention."

"I'm starting to get the feeling that Dr. Hamilton is some sort of supernatural magnet. Isn't it a bit of a coincidence that a demon should be in his closet? And that he started working in a town that seems to be overrun with supernatural creatures?"

The golem shook its large head, spine and leather

creaking. "Humans are very good at disbelieving or ignoring what they do not understand. These creatures have always been here. Dr. Hamilton is just being introduced to them, so hiding or obscuring their existence is no longer necessary. Their apparent proliferation is due to his heightened awareness."

"And his usefulness to their community," I suggested.

"That is so."

"But you also played a fairly important part in the development of events surrounding Hamilton, didn't you?"

"Indeed. Not as directly as many others, but I played my part."

Chapter 22 – The Name of Things

A few days after Kraken sent one of his Hunters to tail Hamilton to Griffith Observatory, the news reported a dead man found by the police through an anonymous tip, and it didn't take long for Kraken to find out that it was his man. The last he had heard from the Hunter was his call to verify that Hamilton was to be executed. The Hunter was good; it should have been easy.

Clearly, Hamilton was a very dangerous man, and Kraken needed to find out whom, or what, he was dealing with. And why did he go to the Observatory anyway? Just to hike? It was another mystery surrounding the doctor.

Kraken planned his visit to Hamilton's office. Through some unfortunate explorations with his new body type, Kraken found out the hard way that cockroaches were a favorite food for rats and cats, a "meal on the run", and if he took to the air, an in-flight meal for birds and bats. While his mind was distributed through ten thousand bodies, all somehow linked together, he felt the terror of giant creatures jabbing, chewing, pouncing, and stabbing the collective mass of his distributed body. Each tiny death weighed on him. He kept most of the roaches back in the lab where Vincent worked, but sent a small squadron of flying units together, headed toward the clinic. Predators weren't quite so aggressive when there was a larger mass to deal with.

He had no idea there were so many damned crows in the city. Or that they liked cockroaches so damned much.

Most of his squadron reached Backside Clinic twenty minutes after he'd left the lab. The roof had an access door, a surprising number of potted plants with creepers hanging over the edge of the roof, and a wide skylight made of glass and lead, with no gaps large enough for a roach to enter. The door, however, was rusted at the bottom. Where weather-stripping should have lined the based of the door, there was a gap large enough for an army. Eight of his bodies entered the clinic.

He found himself on a cement landing. Stairs led down into the main area of the clinic. The buzz of voices came softly from one of the rooms below.

Aware of the rapid attrition to which this form was subject, he sent only half of his bodies scuttling down the stairs toward the generous gap below the door. The whisper of their tiny legs across the linoleum sounded like a waterfall through vibrations in his leg joints. He suddenly realized he had no ears to speak of. But he could still detect vibrations. He cautiously stuck one of his heads under the door to look inside.

***

"It is really just a matter of seeing what's inside their minds," an old woman was saying to a doctor in a white coat. Was this Hamilton? He didn't look like a threat. The old woman continued, "While others of my type read physical tells, for me, it's just a matter of knowing everything that they're thinking about. A little nudge this way or that, a suggestion that the girl they're too shy to approach might really be interested. It usually works out. I get referrals."

"I'm a little surprised you haven't spent time at the blackjack tables," Hamilton said.

The old lady shrugged. "I did. But I got greedy. Couldn't make myself lose the right number of hands, so I've been banned from the casinos. Took the money I had saved up and set up shop.

But now I've lost the touch, my ability to read minds. I figure, hey, it's got to be chemical or biological, I don't believe in all that supernatural garbage, so I think, hey, I should see a doctor. But what doctor is going to see me about mind-reading? Who's going to believe that bunk? So a Tarot reader, a friend of mine, she says, go see this Dr. Hamilton. He'll believe anything you tell him."

Hamilton smiled. "Succinctly put. I try to err on the side of skeptical analysis, however. It's difficult to put everything I've seen under the purview of science, but I'm getting there. Based on other cases I've had, I'm guessing that you can synchronize the electromagnetic patterns of your brain with someone else nearby, literally reading their thoughts. Running a simulator, sort of."

She nodded thoughtfully. "I could see that."

"Another possibility is based on a theory of belief-based creatures, like gods, spirits, Santa Claus, and so on, who have a physical presence based on the strength of people's thoughts. I think there's a separate class of matter made of thought waves, so perhaps you are actually intercepting and understanding thoughts just like a radio can intercept radio waves."

"Sort of the same thing."

"Sort of. Except we know how to measure electromagnetic waves, and we don't have any way of measuring thought waves. Regardless, it looks like whatever gave you either ability has changed."

"Yes. And I'd like it back. It's hard to run a business this way."

"Have there been any physical changes for you lately?"

She shrugged. "My diet hasn't changed. No toxic chemical plants have moved in next door."

"Are you still having your periods?"

She flushed red, frowning a little, and looked at the floor.

"This is nothing to be embarrassed about, Mrs. Hamey. Every woman goes through menopause."

"It's not something I want to talk about."

"Let me put it this way, then. There's a point in your life where your body stops producing as much estrogen and progesterone. These hormones are known to have some effect on brain activity. It'd be worth a try to put you on light hormone therapy to see if this helps you. They make patches for delivery nowadays. Or pills if you prefer. Did the loss of your ability seem to correspond with the end of your menstrual cycles?"

"Well, now that you mention it. They did seem to taper off about the same time." She looked hopeful. "You really think that's what's causing the problem?"

"There are other things that could affect your

brain's activity. But considering the timing of the loss of
your ability, this is a fairly safe and easy test. If it doesn't
help, come back in a week and we can run some other tests.
Since we don't have any sort of a baseline on how your
ability works, most of this is educated guesswork."

"But if this is permanent, what can I do? At this
age, I can't go changing occupations."

"I don't know what to tell you, Mrs. Hamey. Let's
hope this works and then address other options in a week
or so if it doesn't."

"Other options!" She sighed. "Like Alzheimer's?
May as well just put me down."

"Let's hope it doesn't come to that."

"I can still detect minds, even if I can't read them,
you know." She lifted her chin. "Yours is a bright light to
me." She extended her arms, like she was casting a net.
"Even in a closed room, I could find…what's that?" She
peered at the door. She stood suddenly and walked
purposefully toward it.

Four cockroaches scattered.

She yanked the door open and stared into the
empty hallway, looking both directions, but saw nothing.
She took off her glasses, wiped the lenses with the hem of
her blouse, and put them back on. "I could swear someone
was there. Eavesdropping. Gone now. Or out of range."

Hamilton leaned out and looked for himself. There
was only silence and stillness. Invisible people? Someone in
a skin, maybe? Or Corwin? She'd still be able to sense their
minds. He stepped back into the exam room. "I'll write that
prescription and we'll see if that helps. Hopefully you'll be
back up to speed fairly soon."

***

Kraken's roaches waited at the top of the stair until the old lady left. The doctor went into a different room, probably his office, based on the quick glimpse he got with his sixteen eyes. A few minutes later, a young woman entered the side-door of the building and headed straight for the doctor's office. She was carrying—no, *flaunting*—a bag of warm onion bagels and two cups of coffee. The scent of the bagels made all sixteen of his antennae twitch, but he repressed the base urge. It could have just as well been a rotten apple core, and his bodies would have reacted the same way. Kraken forced four of his bodies to stay on the stairs, and the other four quietly skittered forward to spy on the doctor and the woman.

The young woman and the doctor were inside, talking. Was this Hamilton? Yes—she said his name. Books were stacked on a table next to the coffee and bagels—god they smelled so good—and there was the book, The Name of Things, that the bookseller had told him was stolen from his store. Had Hamilton stolen it? Or were there two copies? No, he couldn't believe it. But regardless of how it arrived here, everything was in one place; Hamilton and The Name of Things. And a girlfriend: leverage he could use against him.

***

"Those bagels smell great," Hamilton said.

"Cream cheese in the bag. I picked them up at Cord's this morning," Maggie said.

"Just can't get away from work, can you?" Hamilton rummaged in the bag for the cream cheese. "You are awesome. What do I owe you?"

"I got them *for* you, dummy."

He blushed. "Oh, right, thanks."

She smiled and lightly ran her fingers over the books he had scattered on his desk. There were a couple of his notebooks, one open with his tight scribblings and sketches in it. She picked up a small volume, puzzled with the thin book's binding. "The Name of Things? What's this?"

"Ah, that accidentally slipped in with a couple of other books I got at that supernatural bookstore. I keep meaning to take it back, but the guy who works there gives me the creeps. I'll get to it. It isn't in English anyway. No use to me."

"There's a glyph for that," she quipped. "Odd that the spine would be in English and not the contents. She flipped it open and thumbed through it, then gasped. "These are name glyphs! This is a book for witches and sorcerers. How on Earth did it end up at that store?"

"The bookstore guy, he said he had a buyer lined up for it."

"I'll bet he did. This is…very powerful stuff. Like, if you needed to summon a creature to you, this is what you would need to command it. Natural or supernatural. I don't think you should take it back. There's another language in here, too, not glyphs. I don't recognize it. They could be instructions. Do you have a blank piece of paper?"

He raised an eyebrow. "For what? Weren't you just telling me this book is dangerous?"

"Powerful, but not necessarily dangerous. Like a baseball bat," she said. Hamilton winced at the memory. "I want to draw a translation glyph to translate the language characters."

He pulled a blank sheet of paper out of his printer and handed to her, reluctantly letting it go when she took it from him. "I'd argue that anything powerful is automatically dangerous. Like a car."

"One just has to follow the instructions in the operator's manual," she retorted, carefully drawing out a translation glyph that she knew.

"Heaven save us from drivers whose experience is limited to the operator's manual."

Maggie laughed. "You worry too much." She held up the finished translation glyph, smiling, then picked the book up off his desk. "Let's see what this puppy has to say." The book naturally fell open to the center, and she carefully placed the translation glyph on the page, her hand lying over the top of the name glyph below it. "Rangsaranoth, I summon…oh, crap."

The name glyph under her hand pulsed a sudden bright gold and the book dropped from her hand onto the floor. The book spun in a circle on the back of its spine, creating a whirlwind of dust and loose sheets of paper from Hamilton's desk. In seconds, his log books were whisked off the desk and were caught in the whirlwind. Maggie grabbed Hamilton's arm and lunged for the door, but they were both slammed into a corner by the force of the swelling tempest, where they clutched one another and tried to stay away from the center of the storm. A hundred other books and notebooks were sucked off the shelves, flapping and fluttering wildly as they joined in the blasting vortex building in the middle of the room. "What did you summon?" shouted Hamilton.

"I think…I think I summoned a golem!" she shouted back. The last word sounded too loud, as a sudden silence settled onto the office. They stared, transfixed, at the form sitting in the middle of the room. It stared back at them with white paper eyes, black pupils like letters on a page. It had leather limbs and a chest made of book covers and fingers like delicate thin book spines. Its lips were like pages fluttering in a wind.

"Yes and no." It rumbled. "You summoned a trap. And a golem." It scanned the room slowly, then stood up, no more than four feet tall. Embedded in the middle of its chest, Hamilton could see the embossed cover of The Name of Things, the letters glowing with a soft golden light. It spread its book-like hands apart and considered itself. "You have a disappointingly small library. But the content is appealing."

***

"Do you have control over it?" Hamilton whispered to Maggie.

"No, she does not," the golem said. "It wouldn't be much of a trap, otherwise, would it? A separate glyph is required for control of the summoned. I imagine she knew that, but curiosity is a hard beast to tame." It looked at its hands again. "The trap is more aligned toward the person springing the trap. I become what I absorb. If I absorb a library of ten thousand books, the primary subject of that library being torture, well, you might imagine what death by paper cuts is like for the unprepared summoner. But if I manifest in a library of handwritten notes on potential cures for supernatural entities, and informational texts on their care, habits, and feeding…" It sat down on the edge of

Hamilton's desk, making a soft rustling sound as pages slid against each other. "I'm afraid you'll have to wait awhile for me to get my dander up."

Hamilton reluctantly released Maggie and stood, offering his hand to help her up. He glanced over at his wall shelves, now devoid of books, and his cleaned-off desk, empty of notes or any sort of paper. "What just happened to my notebooks?"

"They will return when I go away." The golem cleared its throat. "They might be a little bit wrinkled. And disorganized."

"If I remember right, golems are a Jewish construct," Maggie said, while brushing dust off her clothes.

The golem nodded. "You are correct. The Rabbi Shem created some early golems, but their mindless nature led them to be tools used by the most ruthless men. He sought out a way to create a golem that had some intelligence and self-awareness. Something that could choose right over wrong. He was half-successful. He added information to the golem to make it placid and kind, but the process allowed for any information to become part of the golem. Once again, the demeanor of the golem was dependent upon the disposition and intent of its creator. He later turned this into a trap of sorts, allowed the intent of the priest creating the golem to become his own doom or redemption, removing the glyphs from the process that would allow any sort of control."

Maggie considered this. There was more to the story, she was certain. "But the book somehow ended up here. Why?"

"The book is sought by many and seeks a few. It is

a constant battle between good and evil. The book is not without its own will."

"And the other glyphs in the book? What are they?"

The golem rolled its cardboard shoulders. "Other creatures, the true names of real and mythological beasts, useful to summon them from other places. I have never seen their names. How could I without tearing out my own heart?" It put its hand to its chest where the book was imbedded. "Rabbi Shem wanted to protect all the work he had done during his life and put it in one place. I am the book's protection."

***

The eavesdropping cockroaches dodged the sudden maelstrom in Hamilton's office by climbing onto the backside of the hardwood door, hanging on desperately as the door rattled on its hinges. When the storm subsided, they listened carefully to the new voice.

This is better than I ever could have hoped for, Kraken thought. The girl, with her training in witchcraft and glyphs could teach him skills he never had and open the path to an entire book of unimaginable creatures he could summon and absorb. If he could capture the doctor, he could use his life as leverage to force the girl to do his bidding. But the doctor was a wildcard and had somehow been complicit in the deaths of three of his Hunters and the bokor. He didn't look like much of an opponent. And yet somehow he repelled bullets through skill, magic or armor, eliminated an invisible adversary, killed a flying assassin, shredded a powerful bokor through unknown means while stealing his slaves, and murdered the Hunter at the Griffith Observatory without leaving a mark on him. A powerful adversary that needed to be handled with care.

His little emissary bodies were becoming agitated by the smell of food. They had flown far and eaten nothing since then. He was having trouble controlling their base instincts. While Kraken wanted to leave them here to observe, he could not risk their little bodies being captured by the witch. She would certainly be suspicious.

He stuck around long enough to do some basic recon of the building. There were no protection symbols on the outside and no guards that he could see. One receptionist sat at a desk. She reeked of death, a smell not entirely unappealing to his cockroach bodies. Only the strength of his own will kept him from stopping by her workstation for a nibble. But there was nothing to keep anyone from just walking in the back door. This would be easy. He finally gathered his cockroach bodies together and crawled back up the roof-access stairway, wriggling out from the bottom of the rusted door with his eight small bodies.

Two dozen black crows were waiting for them, plucking and stabbing at them as they took to the air. Only one of his bodies got away, flying desperately to get back to his main body, though the rest of Kraken already knew what they had learned. He looked above him and saw two crows carefully and silently tracking him as he headed back to home. Tracking him. Following him back to the source. The bloody damned crows were supernatural!

Kraken sacrificed this last body near a restaurant, landing on the sidewalk and scooting under the foot of a passing pedestrian, suffering the small pain it caused him, just to keep the crows from finding his lab. His main body fused back into the man it used to be, but over fifty pounds lighter. A little less imposing. He fumed. Clearly, this ability had to be limited to doing short-distance work. The loss of body-mass was staggering.

Damned crows. Who did *they* work for?

One of the lab workers had paused nearby when Kraken reconstituted himself and was staring at him wide-eyed. "You!" Kraken roared, scowling at the man.

The man cowered and said, "Yes, sir?"

"Get me some onion bagels now! With cream cheese!"

***

Drawing a translation glyph for a cat was trickier than for a foreign human language, but easier than for a crow. The old woman drew it carefully, then directed the cat to sit on the glyph. The cat took its time to let the old woman know who was really in charge here.

"Canesaph, what do you have to report to me?" she asked. She'd been curious at first about this new doctor the community had adopted, sending Canesaph to look him over, never realizing that her daughter lived in the same apartment building. It complicated things.

"The human Hamilton continues to call me Old Man. I find it a little irritating, and a little amusing at the same time." The cat licked one of its paws, then stroked its gray whiskers on its chin, cleaning them. "If only he knew."

"Well, I don't expect you'll be telling him anytime soon unless Maggie draws the translation glyph for him. How is my granddaughter doing?"

"Your fears of heartbreak and molestation are unfounded. The human Hamilton is a gentleman to a fault.

If it were me, we would have sired a litter by now."

"I guess it's fortunate you can't change into a human, then. So she likes him?" She leaned forward.

"She has let him know she is a witch."

The woman sucked in her breath suddenly. "No, no!"

The cat grinned in the Cheshire manner his kind had mastered. "Yes, yes! It happened shortly after I brought a crawling finger to him from under his pillow."

"You what?"

"The finger belonged to a slave of a zombie master, what you would call a bokor."

"What!" She was pulling her white hair now.

"The doctor and Maggie located him, but we had already found him and eliminated him. He was certainly a threat to the two of them."

"Augh!"

"But then the bokor's master turned into a swarm of cockroaches and went to Hamilton's clinic, and our crow-form attacked…"

"Stop talking! Stop talking!" Her eyes were as wide as twin moons and her hands were over her ears, her lips pulled back like a feral cat.

Canesaph took to licking his other paw, the model of smug poise and relaxation.

"All I asked you to do was look out for my granddaughter!"

The cat stopped to stare at her, eyelids at half-mast, and said nothing.

"Not start a bloody war with voodoo killers and shapechangers."

The cat lay down, still relaxed. "Your granddaughter has some interest in Hamilton, which is obviously reciprocated. His body language is clear. Our protection of her would naturally extend to a love interest."

"By the spirits and the winds. Cats and crows!" She said it like a mild curse, then stomped over to a window looking out over her yard. Another dozen cats lolled in her yard. "I suppose the rest of you are in on this, too!" she shouted out the window. The cats ignored her. A confused mailman hesitantly waved at her as he walked by her picket fence. She slammed the window shut.

She walked back to her couch and sat down, her small form sinking into the cushions.

"Tell me everything you know," she said sourly.

The cat grinned again, clearly enjoying this far too much. "Let me tell you about the clinic..." he started.

Interview with a Golem

I found myself chewing anxiously on the end of my pencil when the golem paused, but still had a mundane question to ask. "I noticed you referred to yourself as 'it' in the story, but everyone I've talked to in the clinic refers to you as 'he'."

The golem nodded. "That's true. I do not think of myself as possessing a sex, and certainly have no need for one. But perhaps because of my voice or stature, others have come to speak of me with male pronouns. I do not understand why this is so."

"So," I said. "Kraken, Maggie's grandmother, the cat-crows, and you. Events seem to be coming to a point."

"Indeed," the golem said. "And others. The rest of my story details how that conflict unfolds."

Chapter 23 – Hamilton Goes for a Swim

The backdoor of the clinic had a small sign on it now that said "Backside". It opened into a small lobby area where Medjine sat on most days acting as a receptionist.

It was easy for Walters to find out what the glyph password was on the back door. Anyone in the supernatural community could learn it just by asking around. Walters strolled through the back door like he belonged there. He nodded to Medjine. "Hello there."

"Hi. Can I help you?"

"I certainly hope so. I've got a sick friend back at my house and I was told that this is the place to come for this sort of ailment."

"Did you bring your friend?"

"I can't. The nature of his species makes it very awkward to move him. I was hoping that Dr. Hamilton could come out and see him."

"He does do house visits on occasion for those patients who can't be moved. Please fill out this form."

Walters frowned a little but took the entry form from her. It was a fairly standard, except for a few questions like, "What species is the patient?" and "Are you allergic to silver, garlic, peanuts, or any other common item or religious symbol?" and "Have you ever eaten a human or part of a human? If so, under what circumstances?"

He looked at the form with feigned dismay. "Do I have to fill this out? I was hoping I could get him to come out right away. Collin is in a lot of pain."

"Is it an emergency?"

"I think it is. Collin was screaming at me to get Dr. Hamilton. Can a merman get appendicitis?"

"Uh...let me see if Dr. Hamilton is free."

She pushed an intercom button and spoke on her headset. One minute later, Hamilton came through the side door. "Hi, Mister...?"

"Walters." He shook the doctor's hand. "My friend, Collin..."

"...you said you suspected appendicitis?"

"He's a merman. So I'm not completely sure he has an appendix. Could be gas or food poisoning, I just don't know. He's currently visiting in my pool at home and I have no reasonable way to bring him here."

"Really? How'd he get into your pool to begin with?"

Walters hesitated just a moment. It wasn't a question he'd anticipated. Foolish. He shook his head and said, "Pardon? I'm afraid I didn't get that," covering for his delay.

"I said, how did he get into your pool?"

"Ah. Magic transport. And the mage is not available again for another week. Please, can you hurry?"

Hamilton stared at him, then touched his chest curiously. *What was that about?* Walters wondered. "Sure. But

I'll need to get my bag. And I'll need your address. Give it to Medjine, I'll grab it on my way out. How far away is it?"

"About fifteen minutes from here."

"Alright. I'll meet you there in thirty minutes, out front." Hamilton disappeared down a corridor.

Walters was smugly satisfied, but he couldn't let a hint of it reach his face while Medjine eyed him. He gave her the address and left. Was Hamilton suspicious? It wouldn't matter in thirty minutes. By then, he'd be in Kraken's lair.

***

Hamilton packed his medical bag when Agatha approached him and asked, "Did the man leave?". She fidgeted nervously with her purse.

"The man? That's a little ambiguous, isn't it?"

"I had a vision when you were talking to him. I saw octopi…octopuses…whatever, raining from the sky, and you were feeling around for an umbrella but didn't have one. I'm worried about this."

He stopped packing his bag and eyed her warily. "And then?"

"That's all I got."

"So…"

"Be prepared."

"For raining octopuses." He shook his head and went back to packing his doctor's bag up. "The guy made me a little suspicious, too. A little too relaxed about his friend's ailment. A little too evasive about how the guy gets around. Still…" he sighed. "With these supernatural elements, it's hard to tell whether there's something going on that I just don't understand yet. If this merman needs surgery, I'm not sure what I'm going to do about it. I'm not a surgeon. And I can't send a mermaid to the hospital."

"I think you're in danger. I don't usually get visions unless something bad is about to happen." She sniffed. "Seems like I never get a happy vision."

"Don't worry about me. I'll have insurance." He hoisted the bag and made certain the pendant was secure under his shirt.

***

Hamilton gripped his steering wheel and fretted. If this were really a case of appendicitis, and his patient was a merman, he was screwed. There was no way he could treat that at the clinic. He just had to hope it was something else, and that his preparations would be suitable to the task. If, in fact, this was really a sick patient.

The house was less than five miles from the clinic, on the border between Manhattan and Redondo Beach. Hamilton pulled into the driveway at the given address, shut off the engine, and stepped out of the car, grabbing his medical bag off the car seat. He stood with the car door open, staring suspiciously at the house. It was well kept, with a lush lawn and no fence in the front, and mature weeping willows centered in the two halves of the yard. A brick walkway led to a small slab porch with an oak rail. Walters waited on the porch.

Hamilton shut the door and approached. Walters held out his hand. "Thank you for coming so quickly, doctor. I can't tell you how much I appreciate this."

"No problem. Where is your friend?"

"In the pool out back. This way, we can go around the side of the house."

Hamilton could hear splashing from the pool and see the rippling reflections of pool lights off the sides of the fences. At least that was real. He glanced over his shoulder at Walters. The man was smoothing his jacket. Was that a bulge under there? He faced forward and gritted his teeth, hoping that his friend had received his message.

He stepped aside to let Walters open the gate, then followed him in toward the pool. A second truth; there was a half-man, half-fish in the pool, hanging on the edge, moaning in pain. "Doctor?" the merman said, "Oh, thank goodness you're here. My stomach is just killing me."

Hamilton walked up to the edge of the pool and knelt to be at eye level with the merman. The thing was larger than human; he guessed 300 pounds, the lower body more sea lion than fish. He didn't let go of his bag. "I'm Dr. Hamilton," and held out his right hand.

Kraken leaned over the edge of the pool and took his hand, holding it firmly. "My name is Kraken. You know doctor, you don't really look as tough as I thought you would."

***

The merman's arm shapeshifted into a tentacle and others slithered quickly around his legs. Hamilton dropped his bag as his feet were pulled out from underneath him and he was forcefully dragged into the swimming pool. A tentacle squeezed around his neck. He took in a mouthful of water, trying to breath, then jammed the hypodermic he had palmed in his left hand into the hide of the monster.

Kraken flung Hamilton onto the cement slab next to the pool and screamed, a subsonic rumble that shook the tiles. He stared at the spot where he thought he'd been stabbed, then started flailing his limbs wildly as the syringe of tarantula hawk venom started to course through his veins seconds later. He lunged for the side of the pool and pulled himself out, switching quickly back to human shape, then stumbled to his knees. "What have you done to me?" he screamed, hard eyes piercing Hamilton. He transformed into a Roc, then flew into the side of the house, landing in a flowerbed, then transformed back into a human. "Shoot him! Shoot him!" he howled. "Too dangerous to take…"

Walters pulled out a gun and didn't hesitate, shooting Hamilton in the head twice. Hamilton felt a soft pressure thump against his entire body as kinetic energy of the two slugs was distributed over his frame. Walters stared in disbelief. Hamilton walked towards him. Walters unloaded the whole magazine; kneecaps, forehead, body, it didn't make any difference. Hamilton threw a punch that Walters easily dodged. He dropped his gun and grappled with Hamilton, yanking his arm behind his back while wrapping his own arm around Hamilton's neck. Hamilton struggled for air.

"Bit of a novice, are we? Bullet proof but not hand-proof. Interesting, but not enough to leave you alive, is it?" He started squeezing just before a weight smacked into his head from behind and dropped him to the ground.

Hamilton rubbed his neck. "Nice timing, Raoul."

A voice came out of thin air. "What do you want to do with these two?"

Hamilton reached into his bag and pulled out another hypodermic syringe, glancing over at the large writhing man in the flowerbed who was struggling to stand up. "This one should knock him out, then we can decide."

Tapping the syringe, he approached Kraken. The man's eyes widened and he disintegrated into thousands of cockroaches that scattered to the corners of the yard, though somewhat sluggishly and haphazardly. "Ah." Hamilton said, eyes widening, backing away. He stared at the bumbling rushing creatures, then stomped on one of them. He picked up a few gooey pieces of the crushed body, dug a sample vial out of his bad and placed them inside.

He considered Walters' unconscious form. "Can you help me drag him inside the house?"

Together, they hauled Walters to the back door of the house. At it opened, the front door of the house slammed shut, followed by the sound of footsteps as someone ran away down the sidewalk. Hamilton shook his head. "One out of three, anyway. And a link to Kraken."

"A shame he bugged out on us," Raoul said.

Hamilton winced. "Any more of that, and I won't ask you to save my life next time," he said.

They dragged the body inside the house. Hamilton searched for a closet and found one next to the front door. He stepped inside and called out "Mbuzi!" The imp appeared within seconds. "Dr. Hamilton! The beeswax worked great. Not sure about that fungicide yet."

"I need your help."

"We're even, you know. We agreed."

"I have coin."

The imp's eyes nearly glowed. "Coin? I haven't seen coin in a very long time. But it's hard to earn or spend in closets, as you might imagine."

"I'd like to pay you to store this man in your

universe of coat hangers." Hamilton said. "And feed him when he regains consciousness."

"Is he dangerous?"

"That depends. How good are you at twisting coat hangers together?"

The imp chuckled unpleasantly. "As it turns out, I am highly skilled in exactly that art form."

"Then he probably won't be dangerous."

"If he is there for an extended duration, then feeding him will cost, I don't know, maybe a coin a week?"

"If I'm supplying the food? One per month. Until I ask for his release."

"Every two weeks."

"Done." They shook hands again and Hamilton gave him a gold coin in advance. Raoul and Hamilton slid the body into the closet. Walters disappeared into a universe made of wire.

Hamilton solemnly handed Raoul another coin, and said, "Thanks for the help, Raoul. The Oracle will be happy that I paid attention to her."

"Oracles always are," he said.

Chapter 24 – The Barometer Drops

Kraken sulked. He was a few pounds lighter from the cockroaches that had wandered into the swimming pool and drowned. He knew that Hamilton had dragged Walters into the house but couldn't find the body. And Gutierrez had run off shortly after Walters mysteriously collapsed. Of course, Kraken had heard the disembodied voice, while Gutierrez had not. He knew that the glass people had been involved.

That meant that they could no longer lure Hamilton or the book into their clutches. If he was always so prepared, it was far too dangerous. Somehow, he guessed that Kraken would attack him and was ready for him. Somehow, he knew he'd need help subduing Walters, and recruited help. Somehow, he made Walters disappear without a trace. Kraken kept underestimating the abilities of the young man and the level of danger he represented.

He paced the warehouse room angrily. There was little reason to chastise Gutierrez for bailing out, even as annoyed as he was at the little weasel. The man could smell which way the wind was blowing and made the best move available. But Kraken's options were shrinking. He wanted

The Name of Things. He'd seen Hamilton's notebooks in his office, and coveted the information within them. He knew that the witch could teach him things if he just had leverage against her. Or captured her.

So what were the options? Attack Hamilton at the clinic, when he had no time to prepare hidden syringes and secret backup? Attack him at his apartment, which might be better protected than the clinic? With a witch as a friend, the place could be a death-trap of protective glyphs. Did he actually *want* Hamilton, or was he just a dangerous inconvenience he needed to avoid or eliminate? Should he allow his ire at the man to force him into making bad choices?

The Name of Things would give him vast powers if he knew how to use it. He could steal that book, along with Hamilton's notebooks. Bloody vengeance would be satisfying, but potentially costly, and he was beginning to run out of human assets. The remaining Hunters in his employ could still bring him new bodies to absorb, and Hamilton was just too well protected. And apparently bulletproof. Kraken stopped pacing and stared at the floor, thinking. Could that ability be absorbed? Only if Hamilton were some sort of shapechanger himself, though there was no evidence of that. Not worth the risk, unless Hamilton was laid out unconscious in front of him.

The clinic, though, was seemingly defenseless, a fact he had already verified with his last visit. And it was closed at night. That would be the place to begin.

***

Kraken waited until 2AM, then parked near the front of the clinic. He got out of his car and scanned the dark street for any observers but saw none. Under the stairwell next to the clinic buildings, he changed into cockroaches, his empty clothing falling to the ground. He scurried up the brick wall and onto the roof, between the potted plants and under the rusted door. His multitudinous bodies stayed perfectly still as he sensed the environment for vibrations and odors. Nothing stirred in the darkness of the corridor below. He scurried down the stairway, a small river of beetles, then skittered under Hamilton's office door and reassembled into his normal body. And there were the books. He smiled. How easy was that? He took The Name of Things and flipped through it, shaking his head at the illegible arcane characters, then closed it and tucked it under one arm, wondering if any witch at all could translate it for him. He might not need Hamilton's witch at all. Next, he gathered the dozen small notebooks that were filled with Hamilton's tightly scribed notes.

"Thief!" he heard behind him. "Alarm! Thief!"

He spun around and tensed, every muscle ready to attack or dissolve into a torrent of scurrying beetles. The hovering ghost loomed over him. Kraken laughed and relaxed. "Ghost. Go away. You cannot hurt me and the building is empty. The worst you can do is tell Hamilton that I was here, and he will already have figured that out." He flicked his fingers at the ghost dismissively. "Begone."

***

Corwin was flustered for a moment, then disappeared. He reappeared in the clinic's closet. "Mbuzi!"

Mbuzi appeared seconds later. "Do you know what time it is here, spawn of a used bedsheet?"

"Do you sleep, ill-conceived imp?"

"No, I don't. What is it you want, lowly spirit?"

"There's a thief in Hamilton's office, stealing all his books."

Mbuzi shrugged. "I'm sorry, but I can't leave my closets to apprehend the villain. It's against the rules I am bound to follow."

"Do you know where Hamilton's closet is? The one in his apartment?"

Mbuzi snapped his fingers. "Of course! I'm a fool. I will notify him forthwith." Mbuzi turned and faded into the closet.

***

Hamilton woke to the sound of banging. "Hamilton! Get up! Someone is stealing your books at the clinic!"

He jumped out of bed, rubbing his eyes, and cautiously opened his closet door. "Mbuzi. What's going on?"

"Corwin told me that someone is stealing all your books at the clinic. He didn't know who it was. Just said it was a very large man."

"Kraken. That son of a bitch." He threw on some dirty clothes and ran down to his car. The clinic was only eight blocks away, less than a mile. He started the engine, then thought about what he would do when he arrived He had no weapons. And Kraken was a large shapechanger who could easily subdue him. He could stop at Cord's Cafe and retrieve Maggie off the third shift, but she would likely lose her job if she suddenly left.

He drove to the clinic and sat in his car, parking down the street and watching the front of the clinic after verifying that there were no cars in the alley. Kraken had the audacity to walk out the front door of the clinic in his human form, leaving it unlocked for anyone passing by. Hamilton had already written down all the license numbers of the few cars parked along the street this time of night, for all the good it would do. He thought about following him, but realized it was a waste of time. If Kraken figured out he was being tailed, which was likely on a nearly empty street at 2:30AM, then he might decide to come after Hamilton. And even if he didn't find out where Kraken was going, well, Maggie could track him down tomorrow using the remains of the cockroach body he'd retrieved from the swimming pool encounter.

Once Kraken was gone, he went into the clinic and Corwin told him again what he already knew. The books were missing. He stared blankly at the shelf for five minutes while trying to recall everything he'd written there over the last couple of months, then slammed his palm down on his desk, growling at nothing and everything.

He suddenly remembered the vial containing the remains of a cockroach body, worried that Kraken had also taken that key piece of evidence, but when he opened the clinic's refrigerator, he found the vial just where he left it. Kraken must have been too distracted by the pain from the venom to realize that he was being sampled. Hamilton grabbed the vial, locked the clinic and left.

Cord's Cafe was only a few blocks away. He parked on the street nearby and could see Maggie inside working the counter. He walked in and sat on one of the padded red stools, nodding at Maggie.

She automatically poured him coffee while frowning

at his beard stubble and wrinkled clothing. "You look…disheveled. I always wanted to use that word."

"Kraken stole my notebooks. And the Book Golem."

Maggie was stunned for a moment, gaping at him. "How do you know it was…"

"I saw him. Just now, leaving the clinic. I've got to find him." He pulled out the vial from his pocket. "This is some of Kraken. I need your help to track him down."

Her eyes swept the restaurant. There were plenty of customers from the bar crowd, and only two other waitresses on shift. "You know I can't just leave," she said softly. "I need this job."

"Do you?"

Her lips tightened. "So your job is important, but mine isn't?"

"That's not what I mean, Maggie." He put his hand over hers, on the counter. "If Kraken reads my books, he'll know everything I know about him. He'll know about the pendant. He'll know about Mbuzi's universe. He'll know all my theories about the different species. He'll know about witches and your glyphs. He's already dangerous. What will he become when he learns all this? What will become of us?"

She pulled her hand out from under his. "You write too much stuff in your notebooks. I get off work at six. We can track him down then. He has to sleep, too, so I doubt he'll learn much between now and then. And we need to plan what we'll do when we find him. Go get some rest."

He felt defeated and miserable. He took a sip of coffee, realized how counterproductive that would be, tossed a few dollars on the counter, and left.

Chapter 25 – Not Dead Yet

Someone banged on his apartment door at 6:30 AM. *Maggie*, Hamilton thought. He answered with a toothbrush hanging out of his mouth, barefoot, but in clean clothes. He felt groggy. Maggie smiled at him, but not in a pleasant way. "Let's get this over with. Do you have the sample?" She held her hand out.

"Just a minute," he groaned. "Come on in. Let me make some coffee."

"Time's a wastin'" She said. "You were in such a big hurry a few hours ago."

'Look, I'm really sorry about what I said. I know you like your job."

"I didn't say I liked it. I said I need it. You know what a pain it is to deal with those drunks every night? And their tips suck. They can tip the bartenders a buck to hand them a beer, but leave twenty percent for the waitress who pampers them for an hour? Forget it."

Hamilton put on a kettle and dropped a coffee-bag in a dirty mug. "Well, sorry anyway." He leaned on the counter, his head hanging down.

She put a hand on his back. "It's okay. I was only a

little pissed off." He turned towards her and found her face far too close to his, where they both hesitated. He could feel her warm breath on his chin, their lips separated by inches. Hamilton thought about the episode with Clare. He hesitated.

Maggie pushed away from him, but her fingers somehow ended up laced lightly with his own.

The teakettle squealed and he let go of her, grateful for the interruption but a little disappointed that the awkward moment was over. "Let me have just one cup, then we can make the tracker for Kraken's sample. Do you want a cup?"

She shook her head. "I need to sleep after this."

He poured hot water over the coffee bag, added some sweetener, and followed Maggie over to her apartment, mug in hand.

In her apartment, she repeated the process she used to track the crawling finger, powdering the cockroach bits with a dash of iron fillings. When she finished, the arrow hung from a thin string, pointing south. "We won't know how far away he is until we triangulate the direction," she said. "Do you have any idea what we should expect when we get there?"

"Kraken, for one. He's a really large guy who can morph into multiple shapes. The forms I've seen are human, a giant bird of some sort with a nasty-looking beak, a merman, a giant squid, and a zillion cockroaches. There are probably others I didn't see. He has a variety of Hunters working for him, but I think they're all human. Not incompetent, though, just unlucky. Figure on a few of those guys. The bokor was taken out of the picture, but who knows what other allies he has tucked away."

"And on our side?"

"Beside us? The vampires aren't going to be able to help during the day. Wolfman and his friends might help. The glass people helped me deal with Kraken and one of his guys yesterday, they might help again. They really, really hate the skin hunters, so that's a bonus. And I have the pendant. That'll help."

"Pendant?"

He opened his mouth in surprise, realizing he hadn't mentioned it to her. "The pendant. This pendant." He pulled it out of his shirt. "It makes bullets bounce off. Or redistributes the kinetic energy over my whole body, if that makes more sense. Doesn't work so good on slow stuff. I almost…"

"Where did it come from?" She frowned. Hamilton suddenly realized he liked Maggie more than a bit, and the whole story about Clare may not play out well if he wanted the relationship to last longer than the next ten seconds.

"Um, Clare loaned it to me after the attack at her apartment. She was worried that I might still be in danger." *And then I brought her unconscious body home to my bed. Totally innocent, trust me.* "After the attack, she went to a safe house somewhere. I haven't heard from her since." He heard Old Man interject a meow that sounded suspiciously like *liar* to his ears. He gave it a *shut up, cat* glare. If cats could talk…

Maggie stepped toward him, took the pendant to examine it, handed it back, then stared in his eyes like she was trying to pry secrets out of his head. "Hmpf. Just like superman, now, are you?"

Sometimes I can dodge bullets, he thought.

"You go in first, then," she said. "The invisibles can trail you in. I can bring up the rear with some glyph magic that I prepped last week. Explodey stuff, if we need it."

"I need a new chain. This one was cut."

"I have spares." She rummaged in her trinket jar and pulled out a cheap chain. "Use this. It's more solid than your old one. How did it get cut?"

"My neck was the target. The pendant stopped the knife."

Maggie opened her mouth to ask him for more details but was startled by a dim red light that appeared suddenly next to Hamilton. A weak, raspy voice came from the pinpoint; "Dr. Hamilton. You are not easy to locate, sometimes. I think I am dying. I need your help."

Hamilton stared at the small red mote, concern darkening his face. "Sprite?" The light faded and disappeared. "Aw, crap," he said, and rushed back to his own apartment to get supplies. "You stay here and get some sleep. I have to take care of this."

"Like hell," Maggie said, rubbing her eyes. She grabbed his coffee cup from her countertop, took a long drink from it, and followed behind him. "Who or what is Sprite?"

***

Maggie and Hamilton had eight gallons of drinking water in the trunk of the car and two empty backpacks, which was all they thought they could carry. Sprite had insisted that he'd been receiving plenty of water and had tenuously reconnected to the other part of its brain. An odd reunion, since the other half thought that it was its own entity. It took days to merge the two together, and the data transfer rate was still slow between the halves. He was having trouble getting enough energy to do anything, though. It was like he was running out of juice.

Hamilton tossed the puzzle pieces around in his head as he drove. Of course Sprite needed some sort of power; he couldn't be broadcasting light-points and plasma balls miles away without a power source of some kind. Why didn't he realize that before?

Maggie slept in the car on the way up to Griffith Observatory. She'd be wiped out by the time her shift came up. When he finally arrived at the parking lot, he shut off the engine and looked at her sleeping figure. Her head was tilted back and she was snoring lightly, which made him smile. He let her sleep. In the event she woke up while he was gone, he scribbled a little note for her with the name of the trail he'd be taking.

As he stepped out of the car, he observed a small man sporting a backpack surveying the parking lot. Hamilton habitually patted his chest to make sure the pendant was still there, and positioned himself between the stranger and Maggie. The stranger saw Hamilton, gave him a friendly wave and approached. "Are you Dr. Hamilton?" he asked.

"I am."

"Hi, my name's Roger Kinnick. I've been working for Sprite for the last few weeks on the water run. I'm, uh, part of the wolf community." He glanced up at the sky as though looking for something. "Anyway, Sprite told us you'd be coming by. If you need help, we're your guys."

Hamilton looked back in the car at the sleeping form of Maggie. She looked so peaceful with her mouth hanging open, snoring. "I have eight jugs of water in the trunk. Can you help me carry that?"

He stared past her at Maggie. "Is she okay?"

"She's just tired. The car is glyphed, so chances are good no one will notice it here while we're gone. I'll let her sleep. She'll be safe."

They gathered the jugs and arranged them in the backpacks, then headed down the trail. When they arrived at Sprite's rocky body, Hamilton could see a narrow ribbon of water between the two rock-masses containing its brain. It still hadn't rained since he'd last visited, and more pine trees had fallen or lost limbs. He examined the area.

"Any ideas?" Roger asked.

He put down his backpack full of water jugs and walked around the area, taking in the details. "Sprite is essentially a naturally occurring silicon computer. It's a lucky break that my guess about salt water acting as a conductor between its two brain sections actually worked. It means my model isn't too far off. But if it's correct, then its brain needs a power source. A battery, or radio waves, chemicals, or something."

"So it's been getting power from somewhere all these years?"

"Hundreds of years, by Sprite's accounting. Before computers or electricity were even discovered by humans. So its source of power existed even before the Griffith Observatory was built, before power poles existed. It's some natural power source."

Roger scanned the hillside. "Well, if the Sprite-ster is getting runoff from up above during normal rains, maybe it's picking up some chemicals out of the ground, or organics from the trees. That could act as a flow battery for him."

"A flow battery?"

"Yeah. The dissolved active elements flow through a fuel cell, basically, and it's converted directly to electricity. Although in this case, it'd be acting as a one-shot power source. Once the source chemicals are gone, so is the flow battery."

"I take it you're an engineer."

Roger smiled with his canines. "Yup. When I'm not chasing small animals through the forest. Anyway, we can pour some water into the ground uphill from his brain and see if it helps. Can't hurt, anyway. Another possibility is that his brain is running off piezoelectricity generated when the mountainside expands and contracts from daily solar heating. Certain crystals, like this mica here, can generate electricity based on pressure changes. That'd be more of a surface effect, since the sun doesn't really penetrate that deep. Go down a few inches, the temperature is pretty constant. Still, his brain cap is exposed, so that might be a good possibility. On the downside, the day-night cycle is a little slow to generate much energy from that."

"Any other ideas? Neither of those sounds promising."

Roger shrugged. "Peltier devices depend on thermal gradients to create electricity. But they use a chemistry different from silicon devices. If Sprite's brain is silicon based, it'd be a bit of a stretch to think that these other chemicals would exist in the soil, too. Especially since he's mentioned that there are others of his kind here and there. What are the odds?"

Hamilton was sure there was something they were missing. "What else?"

Roger held up his hands, out of ideas. "It just gets weirder from there. Maybe magic?"

"Magic is just science we don't understand yet." Hamilton quoted.

"Or it's just magic."

Hamilton snorted. "Anyway, if magic was providing the power, it'd imply that magic was used to provide power to all of Sprite's species."

"True. But you're dealing with supernatural creatures here. Where do any of them get their abilities? Such traits might have evolved, if there are magical laws of evolution."

"I'm working on that," Hamilton said. "The one thing we have as a data point is that the ground is much drier than normal. If there's some chemistry that's acting as a...a..."

"Flow battery?"

"Yeah, then we just add water and hope for the best. If there's a relatively large chemical deposit uphill from Sprite, then he's not getting the chemicals he needs. Let's try that first. I can't do magic."

"Whatever the doctor prescribes," said Roger. They both walked uphill from the Sprite's brain, checking the flow channels downhill. "You know, if this is correct, it implies that there are a hell of a lot of inactive mountain brains out there that just haven't been juiced with the right chemicals. Maybe millions to one. Unborn minds."

The two of them stopped thirty feed uphill from the brain cap. Hamilton removed the cap on a water jug and started pouring, watching the water get sucked into the hillside, the runoff barely traveling downhill. "What if," he said, "there was a time when the world was so wet that all the brains were connected together in one vast intellect?"

Roger poured another gallon into the channel leading down. The water traveled a bit further. "I'd say it'd be damned lonely with no one to talk to but yourself."

Farther up the trail, Maggie approached. "You let me sleep," she accused.

"You needed it," he replied.

Maggie didn't argue the point. She slowly climbed the side of the hill to where the two men were. "Did you come up with an idea?" She rubbed the moist dirt with her hand and smelled it. "Is this Sprite?"

"Maggie, this is Roger; Roger, Maggie." They nodded politely and warily to one another. "Roger here thinks the water and chemicals in the ground might act as a battery for Sprite's brain, which is mostly down there," he pointed to the mica deposit. "Those shiny bits down there. It might be the water runoff that provides the chemicals that power the brain."

She twisted her lips and scratched her head through her thick blond hair. "So, Sprite needs a lot of energy, like lightning."

The two men stopped pouring water and looked at each other, then stared at her.

"I think Griffith gets a lot of lightning. At least, when it rains," Maggie said.

"Capacitance," Roger said. "Of course. The brain is storing energy using natural capacitance. Not as good as a battery, but the field generated by a lightning strike is huge.

And it wouldn't run out once the chemicals are leached out of the soil. Lightning every year. But with the drought…"

"No lightning," said Maggie.

"Fine. Where are we going to get lightning?" Hamilton pointed at the cloudless sky.

Maggie pulled a handful of carefully drawn glyphs out of her pocket. "You know that preparation I was talking about? If we have to fight Kraken?" She held up one of the glyphs. "Lightning!"

Hamilton jerked his chin at the piece of paper. "Can I see that?"

"It's safe," Maggie said as she handed it to him, "It takes a secret key word to trigger it."

"What, like 'zap'?" Hamilton said.

Maggie cringed and her eyes widened. "Don't experiment, please!"

Hamilton examined the curlicues of the pattern and couldn't make any sense of it. "Magic. I don't have any good theories at all yet how this glyph magic works. I'll need to start a new notebook."

"Once you figure out how to hide your notebooks better, maybe?"

He looked wounded. "Right." He handed the paper glyph back to her and pointed to all the dead trees and dry brush surrounding them. "Let's move to a clearing first. We might upset the locals if we set Griffith Observatory on fire. And if the lightning is too close, it might fry a circuit in Sprite's brain."

"He's been here hundreds of years," Roger reminded him. "Certainly lightning struck close to him before."

"Maybe. Or it just went after the high points. Trees might have offered some protection from direct strikes."

The three of them hiked along the path a few hundred yards to a barren patch of rock, checked to make sure they were alone, then placed the glyph on the ground. They backed up to a comfortable distance. Maggie said, "Everyone close their eyes. Ready?"

She shouted "Bazorch!" Hamilton felt the hair on the back of his neck suddenly stand up and smelled ozone saturate the air. It only took a second. A white bolt of lightning flashed through the clear blue sky, struck the glyph, and burned it into carbon dust as it crackled into the dry mountainside. The blast of charged air knocked all three of them off their feet.

"Oh, yeah," Maggie shouted, "cover your ears, too!" She laughed. "That was a good one!"

Hamilton belatedly put his hands over his ears, blinking away the spots in his eyes that appeared despite having his eyes shut. "You liked to play with firecrackers as a kid, didn't you?"

"You bet!" she shouted. She looked back and forth between them. "Am I shouting?"

A glowing sphere of plasma the size of a baseball appeared out of the rock and slowly approached them. "Crap," said Roger, "Side effects. St. Elmo's fire." He started to back up.

The ball spoke, "Hamilton? Kinnick? And a new visitor!" Its voice buzzed with energy.

"Sprite?" Hamilton said. He put his hand in front of his eyes. "Can you tone it down? You're sucking up energy like crazy right now."

"What? Oh…" The ball of plasma oscillated in and out, then shrank to a bright point. "Sorry…it's been awhile since I've felt like this." The voice tinkled like small bells.

"I think we have your power source nailed down." He glanced over at Maggie. "Which is good, because I think we're going to need your help."

Chapter 26 – The Clouds Gather

Kraken felt vast relief the night that he stole Hamilton's notebooks. With the notebooks and The Name of Things in hand, he just had to find another more cooperative witch to decipher the cryptic text of the golem's book. Money might be more effective than threats in that case. Having eavesdropped through the whole conversation with the golem, he knew what precautions were needed to unlock its secrets. As enjoyable as it might be to destroy Hamilton and Maggie, it would be smarter to avoid them for now. He could rebuild his power base and acquire more abilities before encountering them again. Then toy with them before he absorbed their flesh along with whatever unique abilities they had.

He put the books down on the counter in his warehouse and realized how tired he was. But the allure of sleep could not overwhelm the desire to see what Hamilton had written about him. The volume labeled "Ailments and Rules of Shapechangers" caught his eye. He sat down in a massive leather armchair and flipped the notebook open to the last few entries and read.

"Kraken lured me to his house, or maybe one of his

many houses, today. He's a polyform shapechanger, unlike any of the others I've worked on, apparently able to change into a variety of shapes. It seems that this ability does not exist in most shapechangers. Perhaps there is a subclass that can do this. He assumed the figures of merman, a giant bird, a giant squid, and then broke himself up into thousands of cockroaches, and, of course, he was also a large and brutish human. The cockroach form is most interesting, as it implies a distributed intelligence where all the entities are still communicating, otherwise they would be too stupid to ever reform into the original creature. Could trauma to the head ever damage Kraken, or would he just move his brain into another part of his body, or perhaps distribute it to multiple locations?"

Kraken stopped there and considered that possibility. It wasn't a bad idea. Although, if his brain were in his gut and eyes in his head, there might be a delayed response time. Something to keep in mind, though. It could be a useful defense. He read on.

"This is the best proof that shapechangers are descended from colonial cell forms, where the cells can reconfigure themselves into new shapes, and haven't been restricted by the differentiation of forms that humans have, like the liver and heart and muscles cells that exist as common programming in the embryo prior to differentiation in the blastocyst.

"It's fortunate that I gathered some bits of his body after the last encounter; the cells will be an invaluable source of information to me."

Kraken's eyes widened as he read this. Hamilton had a way to track him down, if his witch was not a complete fool. There was no longer any choice. He had to kill them both, and quickly.

***

"Kraken. So unusual to see you." Sharmal stared at him through the laptop's Skype window.

"Sharmal. You are still the same size, and human."

Sharmal gave him a twisted smile. "This form is the top of the food chain, Kraken. I just chose to take advantage of their skill at manipulating each other, rather than run around absorbing monsters and turning myself into a shapechanging freak."

"We are all freaks among men, brother."

"Those who renounce their past are more able to change their own future."

"You quote dead humans?"

"I quote myself, Kraken. You've chosen your path and I mine. What is it you called about, anyway?"

"A human doctor has taken a sample of my cells and seeks to understand what I am. I need to eliminate him. I seek help in this endeavor."

"Hmm. Well, good luck with that, Kraken. I have no interest in risking the small empire I've built."

"But brother…" Kraken started. Sharmal disconnected without another word.

Kraken stared angrily at the blank screen, grinding his teeth. Once he finished with Hamilton and Maggie, perhaps he would try to absorb Sharmal's form. It wasn't so long ago that they rose out of the ocean together, forming a temporary alliance against the other spawn of their father. But an alliance with such a creature could never really hold, could it?

***

Maggie slept again on the way to recon Kraken's latest lair. She left the tracking arrow hanging from Hamilton's rear-view mirror. They headed south on the 405, passing Long Beach before the arrow started to twitch. It was late afternoon.

"We're close," Hamilton said softly. Maggie stretched, sat up, and rubbed at her eyes.

"Where are we?" She stared out the window.

"Near Long Beach."

He took the 710 exit to Shoreline, watching the arrow, following it to an old industrial warehouse on 4th Street. "This is it. Kraken is in there right now."

They drove around the block taking notes. The building was made mostly of grey cinderblocks. There was a roll-up delivery door on the back of the building accessible from an alley, next to a personnel door, but a fence topped with barbed wire enclosed the area. A rolling gate in the middle of the fence appeared to be radio-controlled. There were no gaps big enough to squeeze through. There was also a ladder to access the roof of the building, but the bottom section was retracted out of reach. A van and two cars were parked in the rear lot.

The sides of the building were shared with the two adjacent buildings. The front offered the only easy street access with a double-door and an uninviting, dark lobby. There were windows front and back on both stories, but the bottom ones were blacked out, and no one was visible in the upper windows. Contrasting the dismal industrial view of the rest of the building, there was a well-kept lawn bordering a brick walkway leading up to the steps in front of the lobby. Mature California pepper trees grew next to the sidewalk.

"One obvious entrance," Hamilton said. "Probably locked."

"Have you thought about what we're going to do to him even if we catch him?" Maggie asked.

"Is there some sort of law enforcement in the supernatural community?"

She shrugged, unsure. "There are people you can call."

Hamilton remembered the night with the invisible guy, Raoul, when Clare came to take care of the Hunter woman that attacked him. "Yeah. I might have access to a little pocket-universe prison we could store them in instead, assuming we come out of this okay."

"A prison?"

"Made out of coat hangers."

She raised her eyebrows but didn't ask him to expand on it. "That sounds…unpleasant."

"I hope so." He pulled away from the warehouse and headed back to his apartment. "But if Kraken pulls his cockroach trick, he might be hard to catch. We have some planning to do."

***

Late afternoon sun lit the inside of the warehouse through the upper western windows. Two men and a woman stood before Kraken's desk. Gutierrez was the only one of the three who had met Hamilton. Kraken leaned on the front edge of the desk, facing them. "Hunters," Kraken began. "As you know by now, Dr. Hamilton and his associates have eliminated many of your members from our ranks. He has developed means to track us and deal with us and is working with a witch to help him do so. The two of them must be eliminated. We know where his apartment is, thanks to our late bokor, but I don't know how fortified his apartment might be, or what sort of allies he might have at the clinic, which could include invisibles, so I believe our best opportunity to eliminate him will be when he leaves for work in the morning. We can grab him as he enters his carport."

"Can't we just shoot him?" one of the Hunters asked. Gutierrez snorted. The other Hunter glared at him.

"He has protection of some sort against bullets. But he seems to be somewhat susceptible to hand-to-hand combat. As for the witch, I don't expect her to be with him, but if she is, shoot her. In the head, just to be sure. If we take Hamilton alive, he can probably lead us to her. Or her to him if the need arises. The three of you take the van. You have the address. We'll meet at his apartment at 6AM."

***

At Sprite's insistence, Hamilton paid Maggie five coins out of its stash from the nugget they processed, which she placed in a glyph-protected box in her apartment with a few other gold coins she'd acquired over the years; it gave the appearance of being full of old buttons. Maggie caught a few more hours of sleep early evening, then left for work at Cord's Cafe.

Hamilton sat in his own apartment, wondering how the cat got back in, or if it had ever left. One of the windows was generally left open while the weather was mild, but he was also on the second story and the nearest tree branch was a good eight feet from the window, a crazy jump for a housecat. After grabbing a quick bite for himself and opening some tuna for Old Man, he made calls to Raoul, the invisible guy, and Roger Kinnick, the werewolf, explaining the situation and the need to attack Kraken at his current location. They arranged to meet at his apartment the next morning to discuss the details, along with Maggie and Sprite.

Maggie had given him an exploding glyph on a sticky note to put on the inside of his locked front door and then wrote down the keyword for him to activate and deactivate it, holding her hand over his mouth to keep him from vocalizing it. "It won't blow up unless someone comes through the door uninvited," she'd said. He put it on his door and stared at it, remembering the lightning blast, then considered who might walk through the door uninvited. Paramedics? Fire department? The apartment manager? Kraken's men? There was already an "ignore me" glyph on the outside of the door, so the odds were pretty low that anyone was going to accidentally walk in, or kick in the door. Still. He pulled the glyph back off the door and left it on his counter, unwilling to take the risk. Exhausted, he retired to his bed, not expecting to sleep, but asleep in a matter of seconds anyway.

Old Man sat watching him for a minute, then jumped up on the counter, picked up the glyph in its mouth, carried it over to the front door, and stuck it back up. It read the words to control the glyph but didn't activate it. It would hear any threats before Hamilton and be able to respond in time if necessary.

Then it went into the bedroom, curled up next to Hamilton, and fell into a light sleep.

***

At midnight, a crow landed on Hamilton's windowsill and turned into a cat. Old Man immediately woke up and quietly padded out to the living room.

"Cacaresh," said Old Man.

"Canesaph," the other cat nodded. "Do you have anything to relay to the old woman?"

"Yes. Hamilton intends to attack Kraken's warehouse in Long Beach tomorrow. He is having a meeting with the wolves and glass people tomorrow. Maggie and a creature he calls Sprite are expected to assist."

"Maggie?" The other cat seemed surprised. "This will upset the old woman quite a bit."

"All one's offspring, and their offspring, must see battle before they are truly adults," quoted Old Man.

"You know that humans don't think that way."

Old Man shrugged, indifferent.

"I will deliver the message. I do not doubt she will ask us to help."

"Nor do I." Old Man stretched long across the floor, claws extended to the fullest. "I look forward to the conflict."

Cacaresh jumped up on the windowsill and transformed, then disappeared into the night.

***

Maggie was dead on her feet at work; her intermittent naps throughout the day weren't enough to carry her all the way through a shift. She fell asleep in the little office at the back of the restaurant during her fifteen-minute break. The other servers could see how sluggishly she moved. When she finally woke up, the manager said to her, "Go on home. I can cover for you. Not so many drunks tonight."

"I'm so sorry. I didn't get much sleep today."

"S'okay. I can use the extra tips. More for me and Jimmy. Well, me anyway. Nobody wants to tip a face like his."

"I heard that!" he called back.

"Thanks, guys. I can really use it. I'll pay you back."

Tips, she thought, driving back to her apartment. *I just got paid five grand in gold coins for feeding a lightning bolt to a rock. Do I need tips? Or just a different job?*

The idea of becoming a full time witch appealed to her, but it helped to show some income on taxes, and the feds tended to get curious when you were jobless and still made monthly rent payments. Still, there had to be an easier 'cover job'.

She got in by 3:30AM, deactivated and reactivated her door glyph, got undressed and collapsed onto her bed.

Chapter 27 – The Storm

Joey Grice and the other Hunters rode together in a nondescript white van, and Kraken left a few minutes later in his Escalade. They arrived outside of Hamilton's apartment shortly after sunrise. Gutierrez positioned the van with a clear line-of-sight to Hamilton's apartment, tilted the dash-cam to view it, then retired to the back of the van with the others, out of sight.

Kraken parked a half-block away, opened a newspaper, and acted like he was waiting for a carpool buddy.

Within fifteen minutes, another car pulled up near Hamilton's apartment building and disgorged three men. They went to Hamilton's apartment and entered when Hamilton answered the door.

Kraken lowered his opera binoculars and keyed his walkie-talkie. "Who the hell are they? Do you recognize them?"

"Don't recognize any of them," said Gutierrez. "Nobody here knows who they are."

"Hell."

"We got some photos. We can hunt 'em down later for you."

Within the next couple of minutes, another car pulled up with a single man inside. He also entered Hamilton's apartment.

"If I'd known he was having a party," Gutierrez said, "I would have crashed it and saved us all this trouble."

"A war party." Kraken said. "We wait and see what happens."

Overhead, crows gathered. One split off to deliver news.

***

At 7AM, Maggie woke up, stretched, had a quick shower, nuked a cup of yesterday's coffee and grabbed a granola bar for breakfast. She headed over to Hamilton's, activating the glyph on her door as she left.

In the white van, Gutierrez keyed his mike and said, "Hey, I recognize her. She's the girl from the…uh…the restaurant." He knew there was something else important about her, but the memory was as slippery as an eel, evading his attempt to quite grasp it.

Through his binoculars, Kraken watched her go from apartment to apartment. "It's Maggie, the witch from the clinic. They are the same person. And she lives in the same building." He shook his head. "Why did I not know this already?"

"Because she's a god damned witch," said Joey. "And by now she undoubtedly knows that you're after Hamilton. There are probably spells protecting both of them."

"Hmm. Let's continue to observe. They can't be in

there forever. He has to go to work eventually..." Kraken thought about that for a moment, then looked up the phone number for the clinic on his phone. He called the clinic, but only got a recording with their hours. No way to find out if he was actually supposed to be working today. Not until they opened at eight.

Frustrated and angry, he waited.

***

Maggie, Sprite, the three werewolves and two glass people, one the driver and the other completely invisible, surrounded Hamilton in his apartment. One of the werewolves handed Hamilton an M1911 semi-automatic along with two loaded magazines and a belt holster. "Here's the gun you asked for. You know how to handle it?"

"Yeah, I'm pretty familiar with it." He glanced at Maggie, who frowned at him. He shrugged. "Is it registered to anyone you know?"

"No, it's not, but I'd like it back. Guns like that ain't cheap."

"Okay." He put the holster on his belt at the small of his back, slipped a magazine into the gun, and put the gun in the holster. He turned to the group.

"The plan is fairly basic," he said. "When we get to the warehouse, I want Sprite to electrocute any Hunters it finds inside. If we can avoid killing anyone, I'd prefer that. If Sprite is successful, then Kraken should be the only target. While that's going on, Maggie can blow the front doors off the building with a glyph..."

"Or use an unlocking glyph." She pulled a sticky-note out of her pocket and twiddled it in the air.

"Uh, yeah, or that. I go in first since I'm immune to

bullets and explosions to verify that there's no trap, followed by the glass people, then the wolves."

Roger raised a hand for attention. "Isn't this, like, daytime? Are you sure you don't want to use the back door to break into a building if you're going in with a bunch of wolves?"

"Um, probably. There is a radio controlled gate there…" He glanced over at Maggie.

"Got it. Same glyph. It opens stuff. Mayo jars, safes, conversations, whatever."

"Okay then. Once we're in, we ad-lib with Kraken. He's around three-hundred pounds and can change into a large human, a merman, lots of cockroaches, a giant squid, or a giant bird."

"That was a Roc we saw," said a disembodied voice. "They can be nasty. Raptors, you know."

"Thanks, Raoul. Anyway, there are bound to be other shapes he can become that we haven't seen yet. If we can disable him, I can drug him. Sprite, if you can zap him before he goes all cockroach on us, we should have a chance at bringing him down. If he does break up, then the rest of you stomp as many of him as you can. If you get a clear shot at him, take it, because I'm not really sure what he else he can do."

"And if everything turns to shit, what then?" asked one of the werewolves. "Do you have a backup plan? Escape route?"

Hamilton shook his head. "Nope. This is strictly voluntary. I won't hold it against anyone if they want to back out, but you guys know what Kraken is responsible for. He's been using Hunters to gather supernaturals for some scheme of his."

One of the other werewolves nodded. "Hunting for Hunters. What's more rewarding than that?"

"Great. Let's meet at the Long Beach warehouse at 9AM. At the north end of the alley."

***

"They're leaving," said Gutierrez.

"I see. All but Hamilton and his pet witch. Keep waiting."

Three men loaded into one car and the fourth into the other. They drove off. Kraken kept waiting. Ten minutes later, Hamilton and Maggie left the apartment. He was carrying a medical bag. Kraken could see the witch put her palm to the door and say something; more damned magic. He'd been wise not to attack Hamilton in his apartment. He keyed his walkie-talkie. "Showtime!"

The Hunters waited until Hamilton and Maggie were close to their car, then popped open the back door of the van and poured out in a group, guns out. Hamilton and Maggie spun around to face them, and then two dozen crows smacked into the Hunters' gun arms and faces. The shots went wild as Hamilton jumped in front of Maggie.

"God damn crows!" Kraken shouted, then sprang from his car and ran toward the melee. The Hunters struggled to close the gap with Hamilton so they could grab him, but as Kraken ran, he saw a crackling glow of electricity like blue lacework wrap around Gutierrez's head, dropping the man in his tracks. Magic? But not from the witch; she was fumbling to get something out of her pocket. She was occupied. More sorcery from Hamilton?

As he ran, he transformed into a fire drake and took

to the air, blasting short bursts of flame at the tormenting crows. The crows scattered with singed tail feathers, regrouping at a distance. After their decimation of his other body, Kraken wanted to show them who was really king of the skies, but first he had to deal with Hamilton.

An old man with a dachshund out on his morning walk stood a hundred feet away and stared, gaping. The dog cowered behind him, the leash wrapped around his legs. A jogger on the other side of the street hid behind a car when the gunfire started, but peeked out when the fire drake appeared, gliding toward the two victims. Bent half over, he started running the opposite direction.

Of the two remaining Hunters, Joey Grice dropped to the ground with a halo of electricity wrapped around his head. The last one dodged Hamilton, lifted her gun, and shot at Maggie from three feet away. As her finger squeezed the trigger, Maggie finished a word, and disappeared. The shot took out a no-parking sign instead.

Another cloud of crackling electricity formed around the Hunter, but never quite touched her, as though a dampening field surrounded her. She smiled smugly. Wasting no time, she redirected her gun at Hamilton and got off a shot to his head. He flinched as the sound rang in his ears and the punch of the bullet dissipated across his body.

She seized his left arm just as his right hand pulled his own .45 out of the holster and brought it around. Expertly, she twisted his left arm up before he could bring his gun to bear and slammed him down on the pavement. His gun skittered down the sidewalk as his hand smacked into the cement.

She put her gun against his temple and fired. The gun recoiled hard into her hand and flew away onto the lawn nearby. The flattened bullet fell to the ground next to Hamilton's head.

"Shit," she said, shaking her hand in pain. She jerked a cord from her belt and quickly slipped it around Hamilton's neck.

In the same few seconds, Maggie materialized behind Kraken's fire drake form and slapped a yellow sticky note on his scaly metallic hide. Kraken's momentum carried him away from her as he turned to see exactly what had just hit him. Maggie shouted out "Krack-a-boom!" just as Sprite appeared around the fire drake's head. A loud explosion set off car alarms for the whole block and shattered car windows. A huge hole appeared in the side of the fire drake, oozing some amorphous protoplasmic goo, while the head tried to shake off the electrical bolts bombarding it.

The blast knocked the Hunter off Hamilton's back, where she lay stunned for half a second, then struggled to crawl toward her gun, forgetting momentarily that Hamilton was immune to it. Her choke cord was still wrapped around Hamilton's neck. Hamilton rose to his hands and knees, jerked the cord away and flung it into the street, then scrambled for his own .45. She reached her gun first, pointed it at Hamilton, realized her mistake, and fired at his gun instead where it lay on the sidewalk. Hamilton's gun skittered away down the sidewalk another ten feet. Hamilton glanced over at her and she smiled wickedly at him.

Next to Maggie, Kraken fell to the ground, stunned, then the cells morphed and he slowly hoisted himself up

again, half the size he was before, and blasted fire at
Maggie. She ran, barely out of range of his attack, thumbing
through a small stack of glyph drawings.

Kraken glared at Maggie and then Hamilton, trying
to decide whom to kill first. The remaining Hunter seemed
to be holding her own, and the witch was definitely pissing
him off. He felt...small. He flapped his wings and headed
for her. The halo of electricity around him was irritating,
but with his brain distributed through his whole body, it
wasn't incapacitating.

The electric halo changed, condensing into a hot
point of plasma, and entered his head. The cells there
immediately boiled, and his vision disappeared. His hearing
was gone. Kraken stumbled and tried to spit fire, but
nothing came. He moved more healthy cells into his
damaged area, but the damned furnace of energy still
hovered there, cooking his reformed head. Charcoal cells
shed from his skin like black snow. What the hell was this
thing? Kraken struggled, feeling his body shrink by the
second.

Kraken shook violently and managed to dislodge
the plasma-ball momentarily. It appeared to be dimming;
redder and smaller.

Maggie continued to thumb through her stack of
glyphs, but Kraken, now less than a hundred pounds of
fire-spitting anger, went after her, knocking her down to the
pavement, her glyph-notes flying everywhere. One of his
talons gripped her right leg, puncturing it. She screamed.
Kraken sucked in a breath to boil her face off, but the
aggravating little plasma ball entered him again. He paused
to move his body mass around, but the little ball of light did

little more than warm him up. It was depleted. The dim red light disappeared out of his head and flew toward Hamilton. Kraken laughed, a barking screech from the fire-drake's throat, and leered down at Maggie as she flailed around for one of her sticky notes.

Hamilton, in the meantime, leaped for his gun and grabbed it before the Hunter landed on him again. He spun around and pulled the trigger, but nothing happened. A quick glance told him that the gun was damaged from the hit it took. She laughed and pounced on him, easily overpowering him again, then pulled a short fighting knife from her belt. She put it to his neck and saw a thin line of red appear as the blade slowly sawed into him. She leaned close to him and said, "I'll bet you can't stop *this*."

And then a hundred crows hit her.

She screamed and fell backward, swinging her knife wildly at the crows, but only for a second. Their merciless attack on her demanded the attention of both of her hands as she batted them away. Some of the crows shape-shifted mid-flight into cat-shape, biting and tearing away at the woman's skin. Hamilton snatched the loose gun from the ground and trained it on her as the cats and crows continued their assault.

Sprite appeared hovering next to him. "My power is depleted. Shoot the dragon."

Hamilton turned to see Kraken looming over Maggie, pinning her down, ready to let loose with another flaming blast, head rearing back, chest expanding. He took quick aim and fired. Kraken's head exploded and a bloom of flame erupted from his neck into the sky. Kraken quickly reformed his head and twisted around to glare at Hamilton.

Hamilton walked steadily toward Kraken and shot him in the head again. Then again. And again.

Each time, Kraken lost mass. He reformed his head close to Maggie, too close for Hamilton to shoot, then opened his toothed beak, and went for her throat. She threw up an arm to block it but he clamped down on her arm. She screamed as his teeth sank into flesh.

Hamilton closed with Kraken and blew most of his head off point-blank from the side, grabbing his body and yanking it off Maggie. The shredded jaw of the fire-drake, separated from the head, was still gripping her arm. He slammed Kraken onto the ground next to Maggie and fired four more rounds into his torso as Kraken's momentarily blind body raked Hamilton's arms and chest. Hamilton started hammering what was left of Kraken with the butt of the empty pistol.

Kraken struggled to reform into any shape; his original tentacled shape was too small and too weak to handle Hamilton's ferocious attack. His drake form wasn't much more dangerous than a fire-breathing chicken now, and Hamilton had his free hand clamped firmly on his throat anyway.

Kraken knew he couldn't take any more damage. His body dissolved into the thousand cockroaches that its mass could still create, which scattered across the lawn and street in a thousand different directions. More crows descended on the skittering monsters, grabbing and pecking their little carapaces efficiently, snipping off their tiny heads, then dashing off to the next. The beheaded cockroaches reshaped new heads from their hypermobile cells and renewed their journey toward safety. A hundred crows became cats, hunting down and tearing apart every roach they could find.

***

Hamilton surveyed the area. The crows and cats were still tormenting the one conscious Hunter. She'd curled into a fetal ball on the lawn with her hands over her face, her body a red lacework of scratches and punctures. *She won't be going anywhere soon.*

He attended to Maggie, examining her arm and leg where they'd been bitten and taloned. Though both were bleeding and the skin torn, there was no arterial bleeding. He looked down at himself, thinking that he could be the hero by tearing his shirt into strips and binding her wounds, but his clothing was shredded and saturated with his own blood from where the drake had attacked him with its talons. "I have some bandages in my medical bag," he said. "Can you stand?"

Maggie nodded slowly, came up on one knee and stood carefully as Hamilton supported her. They stumbled together to where the remaining Hunter lay. Crows and cats danced around her, still pecking and scratching, a dangerous game of tag. Hamilton surveyed the carnage around them. The entire fight had lasted less than two minutes. It seemed like an hour. He retrieved his bag, pulled out a syringe, and injected the Hunter. She relaxed and lay still, unconscious.

A car pulled up and a small old woman jumped out of the car. "Dammit, Maggie, you were supposed to be in Long Beach!" she ranted. Her eyes took in her bleeding wounds, and her voice changed. "Are you alright?"

"Grandma?"

The old woman glared at Hamilton and ran her eyes

up and down him appraisingly. "You must be Dr. Hamilton. You look like you've been in a fight."

He slid the Hunter's gun into his belt holster and smiled at the small woman. "I am. I have. You missed the party." Sprite, now a dim red glow, hovered at his left side.

Business-like, she approached Maggie. "Hold still," she said, gripping her wounded arm. She muttered a few words under her breath and the bleeding stopped. The wound closed, leaving a thin white scar across her skin. She handled her leg wound with the same quick efficiency. She glanced up at Hamilton. "You can take care of yourself, I trust?"

"I think so," Hamilton said.

"Good. That magic is exhausting." She surveyed the aftermath of the fight. "At least my companions were here to help. Did any come to harm?"

The three of them looked around. One crow had a cut wing, some bore singed feathers, one howling cat had a broken leg and another had been sliced across the chest by the Hunter's knife. She picked up the three that were wounded the worst, whispered a few words to them and released them, healthy again. She wobbled a little on her legs, clearly weakened further by her effort. Maggie leaned into Hamilton and whispered, "I want to learn that."

"If you do, we could use you at the clinic."

"She depends on those damned glyphs too much," the old woman said. "She needs to learn how to control the power herself, not trap it on paper."

"Old Man is one of hers, isn't he?" he said quietly to Maggie.

She nodded. "Or grandma is one of theirs. I'm not

totally sure which way it goes." She shook her head. "I should have realized that much earlier. Like when Old Man caught a zombie finger."

Hamilton could hear sirens in the distance. "We need to load the Hunters in the van and scram." Across the street, the old guy with the dachshund was still standing on the sidewalk, watching. "Hey, buddy, can you help us out here?" Hamilton shouted.

The man stared at him in disbelief, shook his head, turned, and quickly walked away.

"Why don't we just let the cops take care of it? Your gun's not even registered. Wipe your prints and leave it with the Hunters. Three thugs attacked us, raving about abortion clinics, and we overpowered them."

It would be a hard story to sell. Bits of cockroach too small to form new bodies were scattered all over the lawn. Three unconscious bodies armed with guns and knives, one bleeding from a thousand small cuts. There were probably dozens of witnesses who saw a small fire-breathing dragon and some scenes straight out of Hitchcock's Birds. It was also possible that someone saw him injecting the Hunter to put her out, but he could admit to that if necessary. Likely that detail would be lost in the larger tableau.

"Man, that story has a lot of holes," Hamilton said. "Overpowered three armed thugs? Seriously?"

"I think they'll like it better than the stories they're going to hear from witnesses. And these guys were loaded for bear, and we're helpless. And the community has a clean-up crew for stuff like this. In case it was videoed."

"Okay. Okay. What a mess." He shook his head.

"Oh, man." He pulled out the Hunter's gun, furtively wiped the grip, and tossed it on the ground near the woman. "Better call them, I guess." He retrieved his borrowed gun and holstered it.

The old woman surveyed the carnage and said, "They already know, I'm sure. Some of the beast's little bodies probably got away. We will need to track them down."

"I've got a tracking arrow for Kraken, grandma. We can chase down the little buggers."

"Kraken? Was that the beast's name?"

The air buzzed. "Dr. Hamilton, if you think my help is no longer necessary, then I feel quite drained and would like to quit the battlefield. Maggie, I will need to contract your services again shortly to recharge."

"I'd be happy to help, Sprite."

"I owe you, Sprite," said Hamilton.

The Sprite bobbed up and down. "Indeed," it said, and disappeared.

"Matt, give me your gun and holster," Maggie said. "I'll put them in your trunk. Your car still has my 'ignore me' glyph on it, so it should be safe there."

"Good idea."

The police showed up at roughly the same time that a car full of strangers arrived; the cleanup crew. They nodded curtly at Hamilton, Maggie, and her grandmother and the few dozen crows still monitoring the area. They talked to the police and the police looked more dumbfounded by the minute, but eventually they took the cuffed criminals into custody, loaded their unconscious bodies onto stretchers and took them away in two ambulances under heavy guard.

Hamilton went back to his apartment and patched himself up from his own medical supplies while the cleanup crew worked. He butterflied a few spots that he knew would need stitches. Once all the bleeding was stopped or covered, he tossed his bloody, torn clothes in the trash and put on fresh ones. Maggie, two doors down, was also changing out of her shredded clothes while her grandmother berated her for getting attacked. They met back out on the front lawn of the complex.

"What does the cleanup crew do when someone posts a video on the net?" Hamilton asked.

"Usually they claim that it was done by some Hollywood special effects group. Find the person who posted the video. Then make them forget the whole thing or remember it like a dream. They've got a lot of experience at this. Every time something happens that draws too much publicity, they're there. By the time they're done, it's just another fantasy feature trailer that never made it to the theater."

"This is going to cost us plenty of coin, isn't it?"

Maggie nodded. "You betcha. Minus the reward for the three Hunters. You'll do okay."

"Reward?" he asked. She laughed. He raised his eyebrows. "Maybe I should let them know about the one I've got stashed away in Mbuzi's closet universe," he said. "Though technically, that was Raoul's tag."

Chapter 28 - Cleanup

Ten minutes later, two of the cleanup crew stood behind Hamilton in his apartment, one with a Taser and the other with a small stick. Hamilton didn't ask what the small stick was, for fear that the man would tell him. Standing before his closet, he called out, "Mbuzi!" The imp appeared in moments. It gazed suspiciously at the two men standing behind Hamilton.

"Everything okay, Dr. Hamilton?"

"Yeah, Mbuzi. We just need the guy back that you were storing for us. You won't be needing to feed him after all."

"Yeah. About that. Feeding him wasn't really a problem." Mbuzi fidgeted nervously.

Hamilton calmly stared at the imp and waited for him to continue.

"Just forgot that you humans need oxygen. Coat hangers, you know, they don't create a lot of oxygen. And I don't need it, so y'know, I don't really think about it much."

Hamilton sighed and shook his head. He glanced back at the cleaners. They were putting their weapons away. "Can we get the body, anyway?"

"Sure, I'll be right back." Mbuzi was gone for a minute, then returned dragging Walter's corpse. "He's kept good. Well, no oxygen, so no surprise, right?"

The cleaners removed the body. Hamilton remained in his apartment with Mbuzi, thinking about Walter. "No air, huh?"

"Oh, there's air there. Just no oxygen."

"How'd you get his body here so fast? Kraken's house was miles from here when we stashed it in the closet."

"Only about twenty feet in my universe. Closet holes don't take up a lot of volume."

"No kidding." Hamilton thought about that for a moment. "So, let's say I wanted to walk from here to, I don't know, maybe New York, that would take…"

"Oh, that's a *long* way off. Ten, maybe fifteen minutes unless I move the closet entry closer, but that's kind of a pain. Nice to keep them in order so you know where you are. And, of course, you'd need air."

"Really?" Hamilton said. "Does your boss check in on your universe very often? Would he notice a significant increase in traffic through it?"

"Not at all. He said he'd check in when all the wire is gone. Then I can go home. That's going to be a really long time," Mbuzi said dejectedly.

Hamilton couldn't believe it. All these years, the imp had been sitting on a potential gold mine and had absolutely no clue. "How would you like to make a disgusting amount of coin in the travel business?" Hamilton asked.

***

Hamilton sat in Michael Gordon's office. On his right sat Lucy's mother, the estranged wife of Reverend Orley. She was a tall woman with long arms and thick, grey straight hair. Her jaw jutted slightly forward, but intense green eyes had an Asian tilt that added an alien beauty to her otherwise odd appearance. Looking at Gordon, he could see some family resemblance. His features were more hidden by weight, but he was a little taller with the same strange jawline. Hamilton wondered why he hadn't noticed it before.

"Well, Matt, as you know, the regents at Western Baptist cut off our funding thanks to your antics with Lucy." Gordon grinned when he said it. "But with the new funding rolling in, I don't think that's going to be a problem. We received thirty of those gold coins last week for that...outside work...you did."

Technically, *he* had received the coins from whatever group doled them out as a reward for the Hunters, minus cleaning fees, but he wasn't going to quibble over details. The gold he'd acquired from Sprite's nugget would last him a long time, so it wasn't like he needed it. And he still had a paying job.

"So thanks for that," Gordon continued. "I'd also like to introduce you to Marcie, Lucy's mother, who has recently acquired custody, thanks to you. Once she found out what you did, she came to me asking to work with you. She has a good amount of medical experience."

"Where did you work before?"

Marci glanced up at Gordon, who nodded curtly to her, then turned back to Hamilton. "I was an Earth Doctor in another dimension. What you'd call a witch doctor here,

I think."

Hamilton studied the two of them, frowning slightly, examining the physical details of each. "You're telling me neither of you is human, aren't you?"

"Part human," corrected Gordon, "I'm a quarter what you'd call ogre, and Aunt Marci is half. But fifty years ago, quite a few ogres came to Earth as refugees. This occurred during a temporary connection between the universes called the Breach during our war there. Amazingly, some found human mates. Or took them, we're really not too clear on that part of our family history."

"So, a witch doctor, working at the clinic?"

"Doctor," said Marci, "I understand that you're trying to define the supernatural world in terms of human science. This could give you direct access to a lot of unique information. Reproducible experiments. You could possibly even explore other dimensions and compare their physical characteristics. With our help."

He blinked his eyes, a little stunned by her words. "Dimensions, like pocket universes?"

"No. Dimensions like other entire universes with their own planets and stars. Entire worlds inhabited by other species, different magic and different physics. Different rules."

"I...see." Hamilton stood. "Excuse me, but this is a lot to digest in one sitting."

"Let me add one thing," Marci said. "I understand that you were concerned recently about a possible case of appendicitis and your inability to deal with the malady at the clinic."

Hamilton nodded. "Turned out it was a case of

attempted murder, but yeah, it's true. We can't handle surgery, and we can't send them off to the local hospital if they aren't human-shaped."

"I can help with cases like that. Non-invasive surgery."

"You mean magic."

Marci smiled. "Certainly you've been around long enough by now to start thinking of it as a different branch of science."

Hamilton thought of his notebooks, trying to create order out of the chaos of this new universe he was just beginning to discover. Magic as a science! But the notebooks were still missing, most likely still at Kraken's Long Beach warehouse, along with The Name of Things. "Yeah, I have been leaning that direction," he said finally. "Look, the last word is Gordon's, but I'm up for having you work here. I'd like to learn about some of your techniques, and I'd sure as hell like to learn about other universes. So," he brushed off imaginary lint from his white lab coat and straightened the narrow lapels, "do you have any experience with demonic toenail fungus?"

***

"We have a witch doctor working at the clinic now, just started," Hamilton said. "Lucy's mom, if you remember me talking about Lucy. Her name is Marci."

"Really?" Maggie said. "Another witch? Is she good at healing?"

"Not sure yet. We'll see. But she had some good suggestions for Mbuzi's problem, and it looks like she may have some experience with surgery. I'm beginning to see that magic and thought have similar characteristics, a duality, maybe like electricity and magnetism. Different aspects of the same thing, but with their own set of rules. Anyway, I want to see how she manages with something serious."

They were having dinner at Adrianna's Italian Food. He was thinking "first real date" but didn't dare to say it outloud. He played with some spaghetti marinara, forgetting how incredibly uncouth a person could appear while sucking down a strand of spaghetti while flipping red sauce all over. He cut it into finer and finer bits with the side of his fork.

"I was thinking a week or two back," he said, "that it's kind of strange that with all these supernatural beings, they don't have their own cadre of medical specialists already. Why is everyone coming to me?"

"But that's not really true. There are no other normal doctors dealing with the supernatural in the Los Angeles area, but there are healing angels, belief-based remedies, witch doctors, magical cures and glyphs, home remedies and so on. And frankly, you charge less than some of the other practitioners."

"You think there are other doctors like me in other cities?"

"I don't see why there wouldn't be. Supernaturals have been around a long time," she mumbled around a piece of lasagna.

"Hmm. I'd like to swap notes with them, if I ever run into one. You think your grandmother could teach you that healing she used on the cat and crow?"

She finished chewing, swallowed, and said, "So, like, I could help you out at the clinic? Work for you, you mean?"

The tone of her voice was flat and she wasn't smiling anymore. Hamilton cautiously said, "Well, um…"

She put down her fork and studied him. "You're thinking my waitress job isn't good enough?"

He sighed. There went any hope of this being a date.

***

Acquiring his own pocket universe took a little time. It was a week before a shaman came into the clinic and announced that he had a spare universe he could unload for twenty coins. Hamilton offered him ten and they settled at fifteen. The guy handed him an ornate brass key and showed him how to use it in conjunction with a word of his choice.

"The key has been reset, so the first time you use it, just say whatever word you want, and the key will remember it from then on. To create a new keyword, just say the old one three times, then the new one three times, and it will reset. This universe is only about twenty cubic feet. All it has in it right now is some stale air."

"These pocket universes are pretty common?"

"Like dirt. The cost comes from the skill of crafting the key." He bowed slightly and handed him the ornate key. "Please try it now. The current key word is 'password'."

Hamilton smiled, wondering if there was a supernatural IT department somewhere. He said 'password' three times to erase it, then said "Hamilton," three times and put the key into thin air, where the shaft disappeared. He rotated the key and an opening appeared. He removed his hand from the key and the opening remained, floating in front of him. He'd store his notebooks there from then on, once he retrieved them from Kraken's warehouse in Long Beach. Its secondary purpose would be to research how pocket universes worked. He nodded and closed the portal, removing the key. "Looks good to me."

"Be sure to change the keyword again when I leave."

"Of course." He tapped the key in palm of his hand. "Out of curiosity, will this work in a moving car?"

The shaman looked uncertain. "I…think so. If the car turned, perhaps not. I've never tried such a thing."

Another experiment to try, Hamilton thought. *Does a moving pocket universe obey momentum laws? And are they a natural resource, like lakes, or did someone make all of them?* "If you don't mind my asking, how does one end up in the business of selling pocket universes?" he asked.

"It's been a family business for thousands of years. The story passed down is that one of our ancient ancestors, a genius by all accounts, discovered pocket universes when he was trying to make something bigger on the inside than on the outside. Some giant machine created for a pharaoh in Egypt. We refer to him as The First Machinist."

"Fascinating. The machine is long gone by now, I imagine."

The shaman nodded. "I imagine so. Swallowed up like so many things in the desert."

Hamilton shook the shaman's hand and bid him farewell.

***

Hamilton enlisted the services of Sprite and Maggie to fetch his notebooks and The Name of Things from

Kraken's Long Beach warehouse. Kraken and his Hunters were probably all accounted for, but Hamilton didn't feel like taking any more chances this week. They pulled into the empty parking lot in front of the building, walked up to the front door, and let themselves in with one of Maggie's lock-glyphs. It took only a few minutes of searching through the silent warehouse to find Kraken's office and the missing books. As they readied to leave, they heard footsteps echoing near the entry of the building.

Three men approached them, all wearing suits. The lead man was smaller and more slender than the other two. They stopped ten feet away from Hamilton's group and the man in front nodded to them individually. "Dr. Hamilton. Miss Holman. Sprite. I'm pleased to meet you all."

Nobody had pulled out any weapons, so Hamilton was willing to entertain the scenario for a moment longer. "I'm afraid I didn't catch your name."

"It's not relevant. What *is* relevant is that I walk out of here with that small black volume you have tucked under your arm, The Name of Things. Kraken called me a few days ago to ask for my help in dealing with you. I refused. Certainly that has some value, hmm? It wasn't until this morning that I learned he was in possession of this particular volume. As far as your other books are concerned, they are of no consequence to me. My library of books on the dark arts is considerable. I seriously doubt if your personal notes will offer anything useful or any fresh insights. And I would like to see this as a friendly, amicable exchange."

"An exchange, huh? An exchange of what?"

Hamilton glanced back at Sprite, ready to send him

into action, but the stranger said, "The Sprite's ability will
have no effect on us. After Kraken called me, we started
observing him to see what lessons could be scavenged from
his misadventures, so as to expand our own operations. The
fight in front of your apartment was observed and recorded
by our own personnel. The female Hunter's immunity to
Sprite's unwanted attention was noted and her
countermeasures duplicated." He smiled threateningly. "But
as I said, we can settle this without any sort of violence at
all. Just give me the book. It will be at home in my library
of dark magic. Even though you technically stole the book
from the bookstore, in exchange for it, I will offer you ten
coins. And your lives, of course."

Maggie and Hamilton gave each other a knowing
look. "Sounds fair to me," Maggie said. "Give him the
book."

Hamilton nodded, slowly. He stepped forward,
slipped the little volume out from among his other
notebooks, and handed it to the man. One of the thugs, in
turn, poured ten clinking gold coins into Hamilton's open
palm. The leader's smile widened as he flipped through the
pages of the book. "Ah! The creatures within!" He snapped
the book shut and tucked it under his arm. "A word of
advice. You've met the Hunters and hurt them badly,
effectively chasing them out of town. But word of your
activities will certainly be reaching other groups, such as the
Collectors and the Dark Council. Be prepared. Neither of
these groups is weak." He nodded to the three of them. "A
pleasure doing business. May our paths never cross again."
He turned around sharply and walked out of the building,
his lackeys watchfully trailing behind.

Sprite, Maggie, and Hamilton all remained still in the warehouse as they heard the stranger's car start up in the parking lot and drive off.

"A library of the dark arts, eh?"

Maggie shuddered. "I wouldn't want to be within a mile of that library when he meets the Book Golem."

Hamilton nodded. "Maybe I can talk to one of the cleanup guys, see if they can't snag the book back after…whatever happens to that poor, stupid, evil bastard."

Maggie shook her head. "The book was never really yours, you know. You stole it by accident, Kraken stole it on purpose, and now this guy steals it from us. The book, I think, can take care of itself."

"But ah! The creatures within!"

Maggie laughed and put her hand on his shoulder. "Let's get out of here. This place gives me the creeps."

***

Beyond any reasonable odds, pursued by the sharp eyes of dozens of crows, eight of the cockroach bodies made it back to the biotech laboratory in Manhattan Beach, the place where they were originally spawned. A few of them were missing legs where the crows had nearly caught them, but they were otherwise intact. He hadn't bothered growing the legs back. Kraken knew most of his mind was gone—it was all he could do to concentrate on herding his remaining mass of bodies back to a single location.

The beetle-bodies merged together, and a three-inch tall man stood, fierce and angry. "I must *eat*," Kraken said, his tiny brain struggling to form the words. The road back to the massive, feared entity that he once was would be a long road, and full of the deaths of his many enemies.

Across the floor, not six feet from the tiny figure, was the blob of protoplasm that had escaped the carnage that Kraken had visited upon the original cockroach-man. With a free run of the lab at night, the mass of shapeless cells had located and absorbed enough insects to double its own mass. It was beginning to remember who and what it used to be. It extended cilia-like appendages that sampled the scents in the air. Something was close by. Something small, and warm.

And the blob was very hungry.

Interview with a Golem

The golem just stopped right there, I swear. He didn't say a word about the blob eating Kraken or becoming some spawn of a late night Steve McQueen horror film. Once again, I found myself leaning forward in my seat. "Well? Did Kraken get away? Did the blob grow in size until it ate Manhattan Beach?"

The golem chuckled. "I'm sure you would have heard that news report if such a thing had happened. Even the cleanup crew has limits. And Kraken is no more. We have no fear of him raising his various heads again. His chief scientist Vincent disappeared, perhaps finding another master to serve. The blob-creature did finally gain enough mass to reform a human simulation but could never again turn into beetles. Still, his new alternate form has its uses."

"As a blob," I said.

"Of course."

"And I'm guessing you dealt with the Sharmal fellow and somehow found your way back into Hamilton's library?"

The golem nodded. "Yes. But that is another story for another time. I think I have talked enough for one day.

I am very tired."

I looked at my phone; it was only 5:30. And I still had questions to ask! There were just too many things he left out. I needed to know the rest. "And what about Clare, the vampire? You kind of suggested that Hamilton and Clare hooked up. What about Maggie? Was she angry? Did she know? How did it happen?"

The golem yawned like a book left open too long; I could hear the spine crack. "Same story. It happened when he went to Hell."

My pencil actually flipped out of my hand as I involuntarily twitched. "Hell? He actually went to Hell and came back?"

"Hell is not the place you think it is." At this, the golem closed his glowing blue eyes, and his leather chin dropped to his chest.

"Wait," I pleaded, "I have time. Don't leave me hanging like this. Can you tell me about…"

The golem started snoring, a sound of pages flapping in a breeze, then dissolved slowly into piles of scattered books, sliding off one another until it was just a shapeless quiet mass of paper, leather, and cardboard. I looked down and saw The Name of Things at my feet and sighed.

"…Hell." I stood and stared at the books for a moment, unsure what to do. What was the protocol when the person you're interviewing falls asleep and dissolves? "Thanks for your time," I finally said, nodding at the small leather book, The Name of Things, satisfied that I had at least made some attempt. I stepped over the other scattered volumes, grabbed the doorknob and looked back, frustrated and elated at the same time.

Hamilton had been missing from the clinic for a month. The Book Golem never even got close to discussing that fact.

This was clearly going to take more than one interview.

THE END

Stories from the Case Files of
Dr. Matthew Hamilton

If you enjoyed this book, you can find a few more stories about Dr. Matt Hamilton in the short story collections "Shards" and "Fell Beasts and Fair," from Spring Song Press and available at Amazon. The second book in this series, "Unnatural Remedies," is due to come out late in 2020.

ABOUT THE AUTHOR

Tom Jolly is a retired astronautical/electrical engineer who now spends his time writing SF and fantasy, designing board games, and creating obnoxious puzzles. His stories have appeared in Analog SF, Daily Science Fiction, Compelling Science Fiction, New Myths, and a number of anthologies, including "As Told By Things" and "Five Minutes at Hotel Stormcove" from Atthis Arts. He lives in Santa Maria, California, with his wife Penny in a place where mountain lions and black bears still visit.

You can discover more of his stories at
www.silcom.com/~tomjolly/tomjolly2.htm.

Made in the USA
Monee, IL
06 September 2021